ADVAN...
MACHIN...

"A fun, fast-paced two-hander that switches between a creepily perfect English village and a dark vision of the cities of the near future. This imaginative tale deftly explores the dangerous results of combining technology and the punishment-for-profit industry."

—Kate Blair, author of *Tangled Planet* and *Transferral*

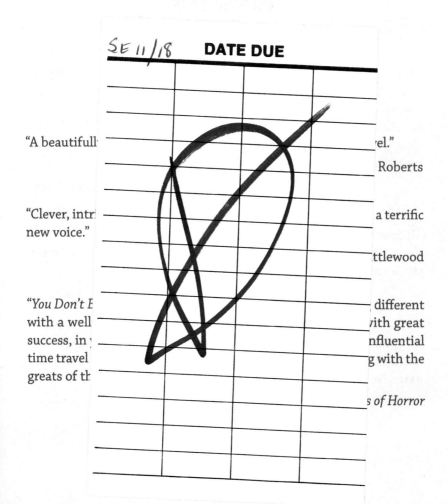

"A beautifull...   ...el."

...Roberts

"Clever, intr...   a terrific
new voice."

...ttlewood

"*You Don't E...   different
with a well   ...ith great
success, in ...   ...nfluential
time travel   ...g with the
greats of th...

...s of Horror

"*You Don't Belong Here* is that perfect blend of cautionary tale, psychological horror and introspective character study. Tim Major does a great job of picking apart his protagonist and also keeping the reader on their toes. This is the sort of suspenseful writing I always enjoy. This story feels like it should sit somewhere between an episode of *The Twilight Zone* and *Tales of the Unexpected*. Highly recommended."

—*The Eloquent Page*

PRAISE FOR
BLIGHTERS

"*Blighters* is an effortlessly readable book sprinkled with subtlety and insight, humour and honesty, and was a very pleasant surprise. It is everything that I was not expecting a book about giant space-slugs to be, and is so much better for it. Gorehounds and schlockfiends steer clear—this is strongly recommended for fans of original and uniquely weird fiction."

—*Ginger Nuts of Horror*

"This was a fun, meaty novella that was a creature feature, but *so* much more. Highly recommended—especially to fans of the old Sci-Fi/Fantasy stories and magazines!"

—*Horror After Dark*

". . . stand-out story, *Blighters* . . . which feels like *Starship Troopers* meets *Body Snatchers* for the Snapchat generation . . . with its fast-paced narrative building to a beautiful reveal."

—*Starburst*

PRAISE FOR
CARUS & MITCH

"*Carus & Mitch* is punchy and scary and tense and genuinely moving. The central portrait of the book's sibling relationship captures its mixture of friction and love spot on, with heartbreaking precision. Tim Major is an exceptional writer."

—Adam Roberts

"Tim Major takes now-familiar tropes—an apocalypse, a resourceful teenage girl heroine—and recasts them in a bleak miniature portrait of a world ending with a whimper rather than a bang. More *The Road* than *The Hunger Games*, blending a John Wyndham-esque melancholy with a dose of existential despair, *Carus & Mitch* is a compelling, unconventional page-turner. Once I started reading it, I couldn't put it down until I reached the end."

—Lynda Rucker

"*Carus & Mitch* has similarities to many previous horror classics: Matheson's *I Am Legend*, *The Sundial* by Shirley Jackson, Cortázar's short story 'House Taken Over.' But Tim Major has succeeded in creating something wholly original from his influences, an intimate, original, and character-driven take on the post-apocalyptic genre. Looked at in one light, *Carus & Mitch* is a plot-driven page-turner; in another it is a compelling puzzle to be pondered over. As such, it's a book which will no doubt find a loyal readership fascinated by its intricacies."

—*This Is Horror*

MACHINERIES OF
MERCY

FIRST EDITION
Machineries of Mercy © 2018 by Tim Major
Cover art © 2018 by Erik Mohr (Made By Emblem)
Interior & Cover design © 2018 by Jared Shapiro

Distributed in Canada by
Fitzhenry & Whiteside Limited
195 Allstate Parkway
Markham, Ontario L3R 4T8
Phone: (905) 477-9700
e-mail: bookinfo@fitzhenry.ca

Distributed in the U.S. by
Consortium Book Sales & Distribution
34 Thirteenth Avenue, NE, Suite 101
Minneapolis, MN 55413
Phone: (612) 746-2600
e-mail: sales.orders@cbsd.com

Library and Archives Canada Cataloguing in Publication

Major, Tim (Science fiction writer), author
        Machineries of mercy / Tim Major. -- First edition.

Issued in print and electronic formats.
ISBN 978-1-77148-469-5 (softcover).--ISBN 978-1-77148-470-1 (PDF)

        I. Title.

PR6113.A445M33 2018   823'.92   C2018-904668-6
                                                                   C2018-904669-4

CHIZINE PUBLICATIONS
Peterborough, Canada
www.chizinepub.com
info@chizinepub.com

Edited by Leigh Teetzel
Copyedited and proofread by Joel Giroux

Canada Council   Conseil des arts
for the Arts   du Canada

We acknowledge the support of the Canada Council for the Arts which last year invested
$20.1 million in writing and publishing throughout Canada.

ONTARIO ARTS COUNCIL
CONSEIL DES ARTS DE L'ONTARIO
an Ontario government agency
un organisme du gouvernement de l'Ontario

Published with the generous assistance of the Ontario Arts Council.

Printed in Canada

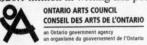

TIM MAJOR
MACHINERIES OF
MERCY

For my Guisborian friends

```
0011 01111001 00100000 01110111 01100001 01110011 00100000 01100001
0010 01101001 01110100 01110100 01100101 01101110 00100000
1001 00100000 01010100 01101001 01101101 00100000 01101101 01101101 01100
1010 01101111             00101110 00100000 01001100 01100001 01111
1111 01110101 01110100 01110100 00100000 01100001             01100100 00100
     01100010 01110011 01101001 01101001 01100111 01101110 00100000 01100
     01001010 01100001 01100001 01110010 01100101 01100101 01100100 00100
                         01110000 01101001 01110010 01110010 00100 0110
     01101001 01101101 01100001 00100000 01100001 01110100 01111001
```

```
01000011
0101
```

```
01000101 01010010 01000011
```

```
01101000                   00100000 01110111
                  00100000 01101000 01110101
         01100000 01101001 01101110 00100000
01100101 00100000 01100001 01101001
                  00100000 01110010 01101001
01110100 01100101 01100100 00100000
         01100000 01110100 01101000 01100101
01110010 01100011                   00100000
00100000 01110100 01101000 01100101
                                    01110010
         01100111 01101000 01110100
         01110010 01101111
```

```
01101111 01110101 00100000 01100010
                           01110101
                           01110100
```

CHAPTER ONE
The Break-In

MERCY. The word hung in the air, riveted to the arch of the wrought-iron gateway.

"You brought a mask or something, right?" Lex tugged down her headscarf so that it covered the upper part of her face, then arranged it so that she could see through the eyeholes cut into the blood-red fabric. She watched as Ethan pulled a balaclava from the pocket of his duffel coat. "Don't just stand there holding it."

The balaclava was bulky but too small for the kid. It looked itchy too. Lex imagined that Ethan's mum might have knitted it. Still, one good thing about the balaclava being so thick was that it would muffle the sound of shouting from the street. Ethan had actually been shaking as Lex had led him here through the alleys.

"And do you have something for me?" She held out a hand.

Ethan stared at her blankly.

"The card?"

Ethan patted each of his coat pockets in turn. Then, with a guilty expression—he must have known where it was all along—he produced the identity card from the breast pocket of his shirt. He cradled it protectively before passing it over. Lex glanced at the photo above the strip of patterned black blocks. Cecil Wright looked almost exactly like his son, only more plump. He had the same worried expression.

"It'll be all right," Lex said. "He'll never know." She swiped the card through the slot of a silver device attached to the gatepost. The gate swung open. She smiled. "Don't expect it all to be that easy."

Mercy's headquarters was a tall, wide building in the centre of the walled compound. Gleaming metal struts broke up the expanses of tinted glass.

"Won't our footprints give us away?" Ethan pointed back the way they had come. They had left deep tracks in the snow.

"We'll be long gone before anyone spots them. Anyway, we haven't broken in, so nobody will have been alerted. You don't have a criminal record, do you?"

Ethan gaped at her. It was clear that the idea horrified him.

Lex noticed flickers of movement against the dark walls of the building. CCTV cameras, adjusting their angle to observe them. They wouldn't have long, but Ethan didn't need to know that.

The muffled yells, thuds and splintering noises from the street increased in intensity. Bricks meeting glass. Ethan spun around in alarm.

Lex gripped his shoulder, making him flinch again. "Cool it. The only reason Mercy get away with having their HQ smack-bang in the city centre is because nobody with any sense would come anywhere near."

Nobody with any sense. She felt a sudden wave of sympathy for Ethan. How old was he? Fourteen? Fifteen? Only a few years younger than her—her nineteenth birthday had come and gone without her acknowledging it—but he'd lived a far more sheltered life than she had. She felt twice his age.

"I had no idea it was this bad," Ethan said, nodding towards the sounds of rioting.

"Yeah. I blame the government." Lex grinned. "I'm guessing it isn't like this behind the Gates."

As they approached the main entrance of the building Lex waved the ID card, hoping to distract Ethan from the cameras. In a smooth movement she swiped it through the reader, which bleeped twice before the door clunked open. If only all her investigations were this straightforward. Then again, it wasn't every day the ultimate key to an investigation—Ethan, rather than the ID card—waltzed up to her online. It had taken her only a few minutes to feel certain he was legit, and to discover his reasons for showing up in the RealWorld forum. He'd heard all the usual rumours about Mercy, but it wasn't that, exactly— he didn't have a political bone in his body. His dad had let slip that he worked for Mercy, but then had clammed up and refused to give the kid any details. So, Ethan wanted to know if his dad was rotten. It couldn't have been easy for him to betray his dad and start ferreting around for the truth. He might not look it right that moment, but the kid had guts.

Inside, the only light came from the street lamps, made bluish by the tinted windows. A wide, sterile lobby led to a corridor lined with thick glass walls. Each room was plainly furnished with large oval tables and wide, plush chairs. The corridor smelled of stale coffee. Lex couldn't help feeling a pang of disappointment.

"It's not what I was expecting," Ethan said, as if reading her thoughts.

She pulled two small torches from her pocket and passed one to him. "Did you expect to find an evil master plan written on the walls in blood?"

"I dunno. What now?"

"I know where I'm going." Then, in response to Ethan's look of scepticism, "I'm following my nose."

She shone her torch onto the stencilled signs on each door. "This is the public face of the company. Politicians and Mercy execs sitting around congratulating themselves. There'll be nothing interesting on this floor."

They reached a stairwell. Lex darted up, taking the steps two at a time. Ethan's tiptoed-footsteps followed her up.

The desks of the first-floor offices were stacked with piles of paperwork. Lex entered a room at random and began rifling through the papers. Public reports, PR. The same old stuff she had seen a thousand times. In each room she tutted in disgust at the contents of each successive in-tray.

"What about this one?" Ethan said when she emerged into the corridor. He was pointing at a sign reading, "Branch Managing Director."

"That's more like it!" She bounded inside, pulling open desk drawers and retrieving printouts.

"Lex?" Ethan whispered. "What are we even looking for?"

"Evidence."

"Of what?"

Lex rolled her eyes. She leaned into the Managing Director's chair and steepled her fingers as though she had all the time in the world. "Those riots out there. I bet you, your family, your friends, you all think of those people as being in the wrong, am I right?" She didn't wait for him to respond. "Feral teenagers, good-for-nothing unemployed. But Mercy caused all that—well, first the government failed, which started it, of course, but mostly it was Mercy. Beginning back when it was only a security firm hired to bolster the police. The organization didn't bother to deny being a gang of mercenaries for hire—it was even stated upfront in the labels they gave their teams: Merc A, Merc B and so on, all the way to Merc Y. When things turned really ugly—when people realized how much their government had screwed them over—the police force shrank while Mercy grew, but the extra troops only provoked more tension. The riots are *because* of Mercy."

"You make it sound as though it's deliberate."

"Don't be an idiot. And anyway, that's not what we're investigating. Bringing in cops wasn't the answer, so the prime minister made a song-and-dance announcement—the justice process would respond accordingly, yadda yadda yadda. They pledged to charge offenders immediately, overnight where possible. Harsh justice, long sentences. Lots of manpower involved, so it had to be outsourced. To Mercy. And then Mercy took over the courts too, because Her Majesty's Government was desperate. Courts, lawyers, prisons, everything."

Even in the low light she could see that Ethan's face had become pale. She could imagine his thought processes. From behind the Gates, this must all seem a world away. As far as well-off people were concerned, Mercy dealt with criminals, end of story.

She pushed her way past Ethan and out of the office. "I wonder who really cracks the whip around here?"

"If that's a reference to my dad—"

"Shut up."

"I'm serious, Lex. I'm not going to let you—"

"Shut *up!*" Lex crouched down and pulled Ethan to the ground. "Do you hear that?"

Ethan's eyes widened as he finally registered the sound. The voices were coming from further along the corridor, both male, a conversational tone.

"Security," she whispered. "Doesn't sound like they're particularly worried though. Just routine."

"You said there wouldn't be any security."

Lex shrugged. "How could I possibly know that? This might be the moment to let you know that I'm winging it, kid."

She was impressed at how much wider Ethan's eyes could go. Silently, she motioned towards the stairwell, then gestured with a thumb: *up*.

Ethan scurried ahead of her, then crouched in wait on the next landing. "You lied!" he hissed.

So naive. What had he expected? He was the idiot who gave all his personal details to a stranger on a conspiracy-theory website. He was the one who let himself be coerced into stealing his father's ID card and then breaking into a building, with only a balaclava between himself and a criminal record.

"You could explain," she said. "Those security guards probably have guns. But maybe they won't shoot immediately if you go down there with a sign saying, *I'm here against my will, it's her you want.* Your dad will come and get you, take you back to the Gates, and that'll be the end of it. But that isn't what you want, is it? You daren't see him again without evidence proving he's not a wrong'un." Manipulating the kid was almost too easy. She held up a small piece of paper covered in scribbled digits. "And I know how to get it."

"Is that it? Evidence?"

"Hardly. But our friend the Branch Managing Director can't even remember the door codes in this building. So he wrote them all down." She continued up the stairs. "If in doubt, head for the top floor."

They trudged in silence up the stairs to the fourth floor. Consulting the scrap of paper, Lex tapped at the security panel. It beeped twice and the lock clicked. She traced her fingers along the upper edge of the door frame, then paused. She winked at Ethan. With both hands raised, she bumped open the door with her hip, and in the same motion she slipped her right hand upward around the frame. A bell sounded above, then stopped immediately. Not enough to alert the guards two floors down.

"Pressure sensitive," Lex said. "The klaxon won't go off as long as it's pressed down." With her free hand she reached up, fumbled underneath her headscarf, and retrieved a hairpin. She pushed it into place above the door, jamming the button. "That should do it." She folded the Branch Managing Director's scrap of paper several times and squeezed it under the door, forcing it to remain open, then sauntered into the room. Sometimes it was nice to have a witness to her ingenuity.

A huge oblong table filled an open-plan central area and rows of smaller glass-walled offices lined the huge space around it.

The table was empty, so Lex shifted her attention to the surrounding offices. She raised a finger, pointing at each in turn, picking one at random. Inside, a desktop computer took up most of the small desk, but her attention was focused on a grey filing cabinet at the rear of the room.

"You're not going to use the computer?" Ethan said behind her.

"I've already tried to hack the system from outside. No dice. It'll be just as well protected from here. Concentrate on paperwork, anything that looks official and important. Go and get started somewhere else."

She glanced up to see Ethan dithering beside the long central table, and shot him a look to get him moving as she moved into the next office. Only the photographs on the pinboard calendar behind the desk distinguished this room from the first one.

Ethan's voice came from the adjoining room, through the thin wall. "So this is about the prisons for you?"

"Yeah."

"The trials?"

"The lack of them. Find anything yet?" Lex called without looking up.

"Still looking. But why do you care? Is someone in your family mixed up with Mercy too?"

"No!" she retorted indignantly. Then she made her voice sound calmer—there was no use in making Ethan feel any worse about his dad. "Not with Mercy. The other side."

"They're in prison?"

Lex rubbed at her eyes. She felt suddenly tired. She was glad that she and Ethan weren't in the same room—there was no way she wanted him to see her cry. "James. My brother. He was innocent, but that's not the point. The point is that he wasn't given the chance to *protest* his innocence. No lawyer, no trial."

"But that's illegal."

She felt like smacking her forehead on the desk in her annoyance. "You've not been paying attention at all, have you? Mercy *are* the law. Now keep looking. What we're looking for is some document that proves. . . I don't know. Anything."

"And what about my investigation?"

"What about it?" she said, sharply. "Look, I'm sorry if this setup isn't exactly what you imagined. I needed to get in here, and the only way was to use a Mercy ID."

"But you—" Ethan's voice stopped abruptly.

"I what?"

After a few seconds of silence, Ethan replied in a quieter voice. "Never mind."

Lex padded out of the office she was currently searching and into the room in which Ethan stood, facing the open-plan area. He blinked rapidly as he noticed her approach. What on earth was wrong with him?

As she entered the tiny room, she saw what he had been looking at. A piece of paper had been sellotaped to the window, facing inwards. She lifted the piece of paper on its taped hinge, exposing a drawing of two stick men, one tall and one short. The taller figure had ringed eyes, representing glasses. The shorter had a mop of wild hair. Beneath the drawing was a scrawled message in a child's handwriting, with each letter 'e' written backwards.

happy fathers ~~dad~~ day love ethan xxx

Poor kid. So Cecil Wright worked on the top floor. Ethan wasn't stupid; he'd worked out that his dad had to be pretty high-up within the ranks at Mercy. And that meant that his dad was partly responsible for locking up offenders without trial.

She hovered behind Ethan. Partly, it was due to her uncertainty about how to comfort him, but mainly she just wished she could rifle in the filing cabinet tucked behind the desk without the kid making a scene.

She didn't have to make the choice. They both spun around at a sharp sound from the direction of the stairwell.

"What was that?" Ethan said.

Lex didn't answer. They listened in silence.

"Probably just the door shutting," she said finally. While Ethan's attention was elsewhere, she pushed at the filing cabinet drawer with her foot to peer inside. "Go and take a look, will you? And make sure you don't set off the alarm."

"But—"

"It's fine, I promise. Go ahead."

The moment Ethan slipped out of the office, Lex knelt beside the filing cabinet. A dozen or more grey cardboard separators rattled in the empty space of each drawer. She pulled all of the separators out. Why would someone working on the top floor not have a single document to file? She tapped on the bottom of the drawer. Hollow. Scrabbling at the edges, she pulled away the base entirely. Tucked into the hidden area below was a single lilac-coloured cardboard folder.

It contained around twenty sheets of paper. The pages must once have been filled with dense text, but someone had carefully blanked out most of the words in each paragraph with a black marker. The text that was legible was a mix of dull phrases and legal language. As she leafed through, a few phrases stood out: "necessary streamlining," "proxy defence," "generalized offender profiles." She held a page up to the light. Maybe the blacked-out text would become visible if she ran it through imaging software.

A few sheets at the back of the pack had been stapled together. Written in a neat typeface on the first page was a title, *Project Q.* Beneath it, in smaller text, were the words, *Towards a swifter sentencing.* Text in stamped red ink announced, *SENSITIVE—eyes only.*

"Hey Ethan, I think I've got it!" she hissed. There was no answer. How long had he been gone? She closed the filing cabinet with her foot and left the office, pausing only to glance again at Ethan's drawing taped to the window.

The door to the stairwell was still propped open.

"Ethan?" she whispered. Was that a noise from downstairs? She froze. It sounded like muffled voices.

"—got someone else up there, have you?" a deep voice said.

She heard others, one almost as deep as the first, the third higher-pitched and wavering. Ethan.

"Let's go have a look, shall we?" the first voice said.

Footsteps echoed up the stairwell. There was no chance of Lex getting downstairs now. She dashed back into the central area. What now? The lilac folder lay on the desk in Cecil Wright's office where she had left it. She darted inside, placing both hands flat on the folder as if it might help her plan an escape.

The voices came from the stairwell again. "Hey, Grimmy? Do me a favour and hit the lock-down."

The response was only a grunt. Before Lex could react, the glass door to the office slid closed, as did the doors to all the other offices. She tugged at the handle. It was locked tight.

Heavy footsteps clanged on the metal steps of the stairwell.

With the door locked, Cecil Wright's office seemed tiny. Other than the desk, the filing cabinet and a single chair, the room was bare. The heavy desk was positioned up against the glass wall. There could be no hiding place beneath it.

Stupid, stupid. She flung her head back in disgust at herself and her lack of planning.

She blinked. Directly above the desk was a white plastic grille.

It was her only chance. She leapt up onto the desk and pulled at the grille with fumbling fingers. It gave way more easily than she had expected, and soon dropped down. A reflex sent her left hand shooting down to catch it before it clattered onto the desk. Not knowing what else to do with the grille, she held it between her knees. She looked up at the opening, wiping the perspiration that had broken out on her forehead.

She leapt upwards, scrabbling at the edges of the square hole. Her arms strained as she pulled herself into the narrow gap. The rough metal edge scraped at her skin.

"Grimshaw! He's only gone and monkeyed with the alarms. Top floor! Come up here, wouldya?"

The klaxon rang again. Lex's mind reeled with disorientation and the shrill sound.

With a final wrench she dragged herself fully into the vent. It was wide but low, so that she was unable to raise herself into a sitting position. She contorted her body to retrieve the white grille from between her knees, nearly dropping it again in the process. It fitted into place in the hole with a dull click.

"Bollocks. We'll have to do a full search then," the deeper voice said.

Lex lay motionless in the tiny space, trying to keep her breath under control.

"Make it easy on yourself, son," said the second voice, the man the other had called Grimshaw. "You got any accomplices? Speak up."

"No." Ethan's voice sounded desperately faint. The poor kid was terrified. This must all be beyond his worst nightmare. Lex tried not to dwell on the fact that she had been the one who had put him in danger. Feeling guilty wasn't going to help her get out of this mess.

She shuffled backwards so that her face hung directly over the grille. If she pressed her cheek flat she could see out into the central area. She could see Ethan. He was actually shivering with fear. And who could blame him? His arm was gripped by a burly, bearded man in a black uniform. A dark, vertical line of blood snaked along Ethan's right cheek, dripping freely. The wound looked pretty deep.

Grimshaw plodded towards Cecil Wright's office, peering all around the central area and into each office he passed. He held a torch in his left hand and a pistol in his right.

"All right. I'll open the doors again, you can do the search," Grimshaw said.

"Always me doing the legwork, innit?" said the first guard.

Lex couldn't take her eyes from the wound on Ethan's cheek. It wasn't her fault. He was to blame. He must have gone downstairs, or at least stuck his head out into the stairwell, when she'd only told him to check the door. He wasn't cut out for this sort of thing. As if to prove the point, she realized that he was staring at his dad's office—the room in which she was hiding. Didn't he realize that he was drawing attention towards her? She followed the direction of his gaze.

Her stomach lurched when she realized what he was looking at. On Cecil's desk, directly below her, was the lilac folder. The evidence. Project Q. Seeing the folder there, so close but unreachable, made her feel physically sick.

Grimshaw approached a wall panel. Lex craned her neck to watch as the glass door of Cecil's office opened again. Could she drop out of the vent, grab the folder and make a run for it? She knew the answer immediately. Grimshaw, holding Ethan captive, now stood at the top of the stairwell, blocking the only exit.

The other guard stepped into Cecil's office. His bald head reflected the neon strip light. He lifted the lilac folder from the desk, tapping it on the palm of his other hand.

Lex held her breath. Her heartbeat sounded so loud in her ears that she felt certain that the guard would hear it.

The bald head swayed from side to side. Then, as if in slow motion, it turned upwards. Out of the corner of her eye she saw Ethan glance up too, his eyes wide with horror. Lex scrabbled away from the grille. Too late.

"Bloody hell! There's one of them up there!" the guard roared.

Lex fought her panic and her sudden claustrophobia. Thumping sounds came from below. The guard was clambering up onto the desk. Still facing the grille, she pushed herself away from it, her neck jammed at forty-five degrees and scraping painfully against the cold metal. Light streamed into the enclosed space. The bald head thrust up from below. The guard was facing in the opposite direction and was close enough for Lex to see the deep folds of skin on his neck.

A thought struck her: this vent was a ridiculous place to spend her last moments of freedom.

The head turned. The guard's eyes narrowed as they adjusted to the dimness. "Got her! I've got her, Grim!"

She yelped when an arm as thick as a tree trunk appeared. Fat fingers scrabbled for purchase on the surface of the vent. Lex pushed against the sides of the vent with her feet and finally managed to double up, performing a graceless, agonizing somersault in the confined space, ending up facing the opposite direction. Her breaths were shallow with panic as she clawed her way forward.

The bellows of the guard became more muffled behind her. Her breathing calmed a little, but she muttered, "Stupid, stupid," like a mantra. Any sense of triumph about escaping was overwhelmed by the sting of her idiocy, the loss of the evidence. The wound on Ethan's cheek.

The vent widened a little. Now she was able to stand on her feet, so long as she kept her neck cricked. Loping like an ape, she made her way along the passageway as it curved gently upwards.

Bars of light shone at the end of the passage. Icy air screeched along the vent, nipping at her skin. She staggered to the dead end and pushed at the bars with both hands. The outer covering of the opening rocked and then gave way, falling noiselessly.

She peered over the edge to look at the tall exterior wall of the compound and, below her, the sheer wall of the HQ. This must be the rear of the building: it was windowless and lacked any features that she might use as handholds. Upwards was no different. Three floors below, the base of the wall was obscured by a deep snowdrift. What might be below the snow? Grass or concrete?

There was only one way to find out. She shuffled forwards until her feet hung over the edge. The snow made it impossible to judge the distance to the ground.

Just as well.

She wondered if she should say a prayer. Instead, she just mouthed the word, "Sorry," though she wasn't sure who it was aimed at.

Then she jumped.

She entered the snowdrift with a violent crunch. Displaced mounds of white burst up around her and her lower back flashed with pain as she hit the concrete.

Since the death of her parents she had taught herself not to cry, but now tears came to her eyes freely. She lay there, gasping for breath, wishing that somebody—anybody—might comfort her.

She had to stop wallowing in her misery. She nipped at the skin of one cheek to snap herself into alertness. How badly she had been injured? As she hefted herself to her feet she grimaced at a jabbing sensation along her spine.

She spun around, aimless and drunk from the pain.

She bobbed around the corner of the building, just for a second. Nothing. The guards were heavy and slow—but so was she, now, and she had spent longer in the vent than it would take them to get downstairs. They might show up at any moment.

She was no more free out here than she had been in the vent. The exterior wall of the compound was impossibly high and ringed with barbed wire.

For a lack of any other plan, she aimed for the front gate. She was limping badly.

Dimly, she recognized that her reflexes were slow. She barely registered that the gate was swinging open before it was too late. Pain surged through her thighs as she threw herself onto the ground to hide. Frantically, she pulled clods of snow up and onto her body. She pressed her face into the snow, which burned her skin as if it were hot rather than cold.

She heard the crunch of heavy footfalls of at least three people, tramping through the snow from the outer gate to the HQ. This must be the cavalry, summoned by the security guards. Her body tensed as she heard the unmistakable *snick* of the safety catch of a pistol being flicked.

The footsteps passed by. The door to the HQ slammed twice—once as it opened, once as it shut.

She waited a few moments before she dared look up.

She saw nobody.

And—

The gate to the compound was ajar.

She laughed out loud.

She heard the slap of a door being thrown open behind her. Without checking to see who might be emerging from the HQ, she darted through the gate, pulling it shut behind her with a clang.

Her pace was desperately slow. There was no way that she would outrun the guards—or the cavalry, who would be far less stupid and bulky—for long. The distant shouts from a few streets away seemed to be jeering at her.

The riot!

She wheeled around, aiming for the source of the noise. The street opened out. A line of Mercy police officers stood across the road from a gang of teens wearing dark hoods. While the police were barricaded behind thick plastic shields, it was clear it was the gang that was on the defensive. A Mercy cop darted forward, flanked by two others, trying to pick off one of the weaker kids. The rioters shouted, hurling rocks and bottles to ward them off.

Lex pulled her headscarf back to reveal her face. She held up both hands in a gesture of peace as she slid in among the crowd of hooded teens. Only a couple of them paid her any attention.

It wasn't a moment too soon. The two security guards appeared at the end of the street, and skidded to a halt as the angry crowd turned to face them. In their pristine uniforms, and without shields, they must have appeared perfect targets. Both guards ducked under a hail of projectiles from the crowd. They retreated with their hands held up.

Lex ducked from the rear of the crowd and slunk away in the opposite direction, further into the city, disappearing into the darkness.

But even in her relief, she thought of Ethan. What would they do with him?

She couldn't let herself dwell on it now. Ethan would be okay. It was just like she'd told him. *Your dad will come and get you, take you back to the Gates, and that'll be the end of it.*

00011
10010 01110100 01110100 01100101 01101110
11001 00100000 01010100 01101001 01101101 00100000 01001101
01010 01101111   00101110 00100000 01001100 01100001 011
01111 01110101 01110100 00100000 01100001 01101110 01100100 001
00100 01100101 01110011 01101001 01100111 01101110 00100000 011
11001   01001010 01100001 01110010 01100101   0010
010011 01101000 01100001 01110000 01101001 011
01111 00101110 01000010 01101001 01101110 01100001 01110010 0111100

01100110

C11APTEO

CHAPTER TWO

Welcome to My World

10001
)1101000

Ethan awoke gradually. Sunlight turned the inside of his eyelids a rich orange, making the veins appear like forked lightning. The right side of his face was warm. He reached up to feel the smooth skin of his cheek. He still felt surprise that he didn't have a scar.

His heartbeat matched the ticking of the clocks on the landing and in the downstairs hallway. They were slightly out of sync with each other, marking the passing of every half-second.

He opened his eyes. Light played on the ceiling, filtered through the patterned curtains. It made complex, shifting shapes that danced in time to the ticking of the clocks.

"Ethan! Breakfast!" a voice called, startling him. The walls in the house were thin.

He rolled over to face the wall and pulled the duvet up around his ears.

"Ethan! Breakfast!"

1 00101110
0 01010100
1 01110010
01100111
0 01101000
0 00101100
0 01100101
0 01101111
0 01100001
01100110
0 01110111
1 01110101
1 01101001
0 00100000
1 01100001
01101111
1 01101000

An old sixties song seeped through the house from the kitchen radio. "Welcome to My World" by Jim Reeves—his dad used to play it all the time, back at home.

It was Monday morning, not that it made much difference. On both weekend days Ethan had attended school for "club" sessions indistinguishable from normal lessons. He rolled off the bed, holding on to the duvet so that he now wore it like a thick cape. Could he skip having a shower? No, there would be repercussions if he changed the routine.

He washed as swiftly as possible and dressed in his school uniform. The trousers and shirt were rough inside, as if they had been designed to itch. At his old school he had been allowed to wear whatever he wanted.

Greg was waiting patiently outside the bathroom. His hair stuck up and his Spider-Man pyjamas were creased, but he didn't look at all sleepy. Ethan offered a thin smile and sidestepped around him. Greg continued watching the door of the bathroom, as if he were caught in a daydream.

The radio singer's voice grew louder as Ethan padded downstairs. The music stopped as he pushed open the door to the kitchen.

"Ethan! Breakfast!" his mother called.

"I'm right here," Ethan muttered.

His mother didn't respond and didn't turn from the kitchen counter. Her yellow apron was spotless and her blonde bob was as perfect as ever, as if she had just come from the salon. She was ladling hash browns and baked beans onto a plate.

Ethan was distracted by Greg, who had somehow made it downstairs already and was sitting at the pine kitchen table, shovelling food into his mouth.

He took his seat and nodded at the man who gazed at him from the end of the table. The man's beard was neatly clipped and he was dressed in the same tweed suit he wore every weekday, in contrast to the flannel shirt and blue trousers he preferred at the weekend. He hadn't yet touched the breakfast before him. "Morning, son," he said, as if he had only just noticed him.

"Good morning," Ethan replied.

Ethan's breakfast appeared before him. He began to eat. Several minutes passed in silence.

"I would appreciate you addressing me properly."

Ethan stopped chewing, weighing up his options. It was too early to start a fight.

"Good morning, Father," he said. The word stuck in his throat.

His father beamed suddenly. "What will the day bring for you both today, boys?"

"I'm going to build a fort in the garden today," Greg said.

"What a splendid idea." The reply seemed too quick. "And how about you, Ethan?"

"It's school today. The usual."

"Perhaps you could help by—" His father paused, as if racking his brains for an appropriate task. "Washing the car."

Ethan gulped his last few mouthfuls of food. "I have to go to school."

"It would be a big help to your mother and I."

"The car's spotless. It doesn't need washing. And I have to go to school."

His father didn't reply. He sat with both hands flat on the table.

His mother took her seat but only stared at her full plate as if unsure what to do with it. She looked blankly at Greg, then at Ethan.

His father appeared deep in thought, staring out of the window. Ethan realized that his sense of discomfort at being in the same room with the man had become worse recently. He actually hated him. Those piggy little eyes above that ugly tweed suit.

Abruptly, his father smiled broadly, but then a moment later he was frowning again. He twisted to look at the clock above the kitchen counter. Its second hand had stopped.

Then the second hand began moving again, out of sync with the ticking from the hallway.

"Perhaps you could help by paying the paperboy," his father said.

Ethan nodded, pushed away his plate and left the table.

00   01100101   01111000   01110100   00100000   01000010   01110010   01100101   01100001   0110101

Ilkley Grove was always deserted at this time of the morning. Later, when Ethan returned from school, five-year-old twins would be sitting on opposite curbs, bouncing a ball between them. A grey-and-black-striped cat would parade up and down and, every few minutes, would stop and curl up to doze in the sunshine. Neighbours would gather to remark on the blossom in the branches of the single tree in the grassy area at the end of the cul-de-sac. "We're so lucky that spring has come early," one would say. "I feel so lucky in so many ways," another would reply. The woman who insisted that Ethan call her "Mother" would be in the front garden of his house, collecting the washing. It was certainly warm enough for it, as it had been every day since he had arrived, two weeks ago. He squinted against the morning sun. The hill and trees that rose behind his house were vivid green, glowing beneath a too-bright sky.

"Morning, young Ethan!"

The postlady appeared from the junction to the Ledbury estate, pedalling furiously as she struggled up the hill. Ethan waved hello. The postlady whistled as she made her way along the cul-de-sac. It was the same melody he had heard earlier in his house; she must have been listening to the same radio station.

He passed the row of shops on Enfield Chase. The newsagent was closed, as was the video rental shop where a poster in the window declared, *All VHS rewound before hire.* In the third shop whole pigs hung on hooks behind the metal counter. The butcher leaned over the display in the front window, arranging hams on a bright carpet of plastic grass. As Ethan passed the butcher looked up and winked.

On Rectory Road a red saloon car passed him, then the school minibus and, thirty seconds later, a taxi with no passengers. The same cars, every day. He wished he owned a watch so that he could time them to the second. Further along the road, he passed the embossed map of the village, with its slogan written in a childish typeface: *Welcome to Touchstone . . . where only the best will do!*

In the village centre shopkeepers and a few early-bird customers had begun their daily routines. A young mother and a grocer paused their conversation to beam at the woman's child, who bent forward from his pram to pluck a pear from a crate. A woman wearing a purple suit walked her Labrador, both strutting along the street appearing equally satisfied. An elderly man stood before a cobbler's shop, gazing up at the sky. His folded arms pinned his long, grey beard against his chest. As Ethan approached he pointed up at the sun, beamed and gave a thumbs-up sign.

The first school pupils appeared from the directions of the other housing estates. Ethan stiffened. He still hadn't got used to his fellow pupils, even though they behaved in as pleasant a manner as everyone else in Touchstone. Soon the high street was filled with the bobbing heads of pupils walking in silence. Ethan came to a halt and watched them pass.

"Good morning, Ethan," a girl said. He'd noticed her before, at precisely this same spot on the way to school. Her hair was a dark chestnut colour, with a long fringe. He wondered if it tickled against her eyelashes.

He nodded politely and gave a tight smile.

The girl swept past him and merged into the cluster of pupils. Ethan followed. He kept his head down and walked at the same speed as the others. Ever since his arrival his instinct had been to avoid attracting unnecessary attention. The gaggle of children trooped in single file past the church with its tall clock tower, along the edge of the graveyard and onto the school sports fields.

The school building squatted at the far end of the fields. From here it was merely a dark silhouette on the horizon. Unlike every other part of the village Ethan had visited so far, the school appeared as though it had been designed to look as unappealing and unfriendly as possible. It was enormous too—far bigger than a village warranted—but then again there were more children in Touchstone than he might have expected. The grey bricks of the building were stained with rain Ethan had never seen fall, and the mottled walls gave the school an almost organic appearance, as if it had risen from the earth.

The plodding crowd of pupils passed the sagging nets and cracked tarmac of the tennis courts. Ethan passed into the shadow of the sports hall and shivered at the sudden cold. He passed the floor-to-ceiling windows of the assembly hall and the canteen, where white-coated women served glutinous dollops into silver trays. Finally, the line of pupils turned left and through the main entrance into the school.

00   01100101   01111000   01110100   00100000   01000010   01110010   01100101   01100001   0110101

"Once you've drawn both axes, don't forget that they must both be properly labelled."

Ethan fished into his pencil case for a ruler and drew two lines at right angles. The pencil lines strayed from the gridlines printed on the page. He felt terribly sleepy. The ticking of the classroom clock seemed to be getting slower with each second and the teacher's voice was almost soothing in its dullness. Ethan felt that he was barely here and that his body was on autopilot.

"And you must add the title, of course," Miss Earnshaw said. She sat perched on her tall stool in front of the grimy blackboard.

What title? Ethan glanced down at his exercise book, at the two straight lines he had drawn. Had he missed an instruction?

"Without a title," Miss Earnshaw continued, "anybody attempting to decipher your graph would have their work cut out!"

Laughter rippled across the classroom. Ethan turned to see the smiling, upturned faces of the other pupils. Their laughter stopped and they returned to their tasks. He realized that Miss Earnshaw was watching him, her forehead creased, her lips puckered. Was she suspicious because he hadn't laughed at her comment, or because his graph was untitled? At the top of the page he wrote *A graph to show the correlation between x and y*. Miss Earnshaw's expression softened.

The classroom was narrow and long. Anyone sitting at the back would struggle to hear the teacher's words, as she rarely left her stool beside the blackboard. A tall cupboard was crammed with beakers, clamps and Bunsen burners, though Ethan had never seen anybody use them during the fortnight he had been attending the school. A window spanned the length of the classroom, giving a view of the mottled wall of the sports hall and a tiny, dull green triangle of grass beyond.

The tatty posters that lined the opposite wall of the classroom must have been at least as old as Ethan himself. One was labelled *Healthy Eating* and featured illustrations of unappealing foodstuffs: a handful of beige potatoes, an anaemic roast chicken, a bowl of liquid that Ethan supposed was soup but might as easily have been soapy water. On another poster was a scratchy diagram of a flowering plant, but it didn't have any labels or any text at all. A print of the periodic table had faded so badly only the first handful of elements were legible, the rest a murky grey.

He was dimly aware that Miss Earnshaw had started speaking again. Her monotonous voice sounded far away and he could barely make out the words. He blinked, trying to wake himself up.

". . . and who was responsible for forcing King Charles the First from his rightful seat?"

In his befuddled state, Ethan thought at first that Miss Earnshaw was accusing the class. Anyway, wasn't this supposed to be a science lesson? He turned to see five hands raised in the air.

Miss Earnshaw appeared to be waiting for something. "Shall I repeat the question?"

The five hands were still raised. Ethan's classmates were all immaculately presented, with neat hairstyles, pristine uniforms, alert expressions. All had their eyes fixed on the teacher—apart from one pupil, a burly boy who sat three desks to Ethan's left. His shaven head was bowed in concentration as he stared at his desk. Neither he nor anybody else spoke.

Finally, Ethan raised his own hand. It broke the spell. Miss Earnshaw blinked and trained her gaze on him. "Ah, Ethan. Yes?"

"Oliver Cromwell, miss."

She blinked again. "Have you included a title above your graph?"

"Yes, miss."

She came closer, leaning to peer at his exercise book. There was something strange about her eyes, as if they were constantly in motion even when they were fixed on his.

Her mouth suddenly snapped open, wide enough for Ethan to see all the way into her throat. He pressed himself into his seat and gulped.

But she was smiling. She reached out and pressed her hand onto the top of his head. Her long fingernails dug into his scalp. He squirmed and almost wished he had angered her instead—anything but this awfulness.

Miss Earnshaw didn't loosen her grip. Ethan froze and willed the moment to end.

"Remember," the teacher said, finally retracting her slim hand, "the bell is a sign for me and not for you."

Ethan glanced at the red-painted bell above the doorway, then jumped as it began to ring.

"Very well," Miss Earnshaw said. "Class dismissed." She strode to her stool and perched upon it, watching the class with a neutral expression.

The other pupils packed up their belongings in silence. As Ethan passed the desk of the boy with the shaven head, he noticed something carved into the wooden desktop: a crude stick figure hanging from a gallows. The boy had been playing a game of Hangman. Underneath the drawing were nine horizontal lines, each with a letter scrawled above, spelling out *EARNSHORE*.

Ethan slipped into the queue to leave the classroom. In the corridor a group exiting another classroom merged seamlessly into the line and continued in the direction of the canteen. Ethan tried to stifle his frustration at their slow pace. He tried to pretend that he was like them.

He yelped as a hand clamped onto his shoulder.

"Don't turn around," a whispered voice said. Then his shoulder was released and instead a finger prodded at his lower back. "Here, take the next left."

When they reached the junction Ethan was tempted to stay within the crocodile line of pupils. As if reading his thoughts, the finger jabbed into his spine again. Trying not to think too closely about what he was doing, Ethan slipped away from the crowd, into the empty corridor. A short, fair-haired boy overtook him. He wore round-rimmed glasses that magnified his eyes. Ethan recognized him vaguely—hadn't he seen him in another of his classes that morning? Without turning, the boy gestured furtively with his hand at waist level. He paused at a row of metal lockers, rummaged in his pocket for a key and then opened one of the lockers at head height.

"Stay on that side," the boy said through the barrier of the locker door. "Keep facing forwards."

Ethan did as he was told. He felt a fool, staring at the lockers for no reason. "Who are you? What—"

"Not here," the boy said. "Later."

Perhaps it was a test of some sort. "How do I know I can trust you?"

"Shut up, would you? Come to the forest at the top of the hill. Dawn, tomorrow morning. Got it?"

Questions swirled in Ethan's mind. "How will I—"

"We've talked too long. Look, you go first, okay? I'll follow at a safe distance. We'll explain everything tomorrow."

01001010 01100001 01110010 01100101

010011 01101000 01100001 01110000 01101001 011
01111 00101110 01000010 01101001 01101110 01100001 01110010 0111100

01100110

C11APTE0

CHAPTER THREE
Lex Alone

A deep, bloody wound on a boy's cheek. A plain lilac folder on top of a desk. It was difficult to judge which mental image caused Lex more pain even now, a fortnight since the botched break-in.

She kept to the side streets of the Innards, her hood pulled up over her greasy blonde hair, hiding her face. The snow had become slush that seeped through the seams of her battered boots.

The rioters were at it again, near to the shops. Mercy cops versus gangs or, possibly, one gang pitted against another. There had been more and more territorial spats in the last month. It was more than likely political: the Fagins kicking up a fuss, making land-grabs. They had no qualms about playing their bloody game, sacrificing pawns as necessary.

Someone was banging on something hollow and metal: an oil drum perhaps, or a police car. The sound echoed along the narrow streets. Sometimes Lex wondered why

Mercy and the government needed actual prisons. Weren't they all trapped together anyway, here in the remnants of the city?

She wasn't following her usual route and was making her journey longer than it needed to be. At each junction she picked a direction almost at random, trying to lose herself in the narrow, dark streets. She crisscrossed the street often, avoiding the few cameras that were still operational. The blank windows of abandoned buildings watched her pass. These days, most Innard dwellers—at least, those that weren't already part of one gang or another—had no fixed address, moving from house to house before they were, inevitably, rounded up. The original residents of the inner city had cleared out well before the high-street shops had emptied, and they hadn't returned. Any hopes of safety hadn't lasted long, of course. The suburbs had held out for a while, but once the gangs had cleared out the streets of the Innards, they had shifted their attention outwards. Now these innermost buildings were little more than storehouses for loot raided from the suburbs.

Lex took a right turn, away from the faint sound of a siren. Most nights, Mercy cops would barrel in, pluck out a few gang members and then duck out before things became too ugly. It was all for show, a halfhearted demonstration to the government that everything was under control. The main confrontations between police and gangs were usually in the high streets. For publicity, and maybe for old times' sake.

Lex slipped into the alley alongside the abandoned shell of *Sweetheart's Dessert Parlour*, not pausing to check if anybody was watching. James would have been horrified. "The best place to hide is in plain sight," he had always said, but there were rules all the same. She fumbled with the padlocks on the steel door behind the dessert parlour, dropped one of the three keys, then input the wrong passcode in to the digital display and had to wait thirty seconds before she could try again. By the time she pushed her way into the flat she was flustered and sweating.

Lights flickered on, triggered by motion sensors. She never had gotten used to that.

A teetering pile of electrical equipment formed a tall central wall in the rubbish-strewn sitting room. It was the barricade between her side of the flat and the area her brother called his "lair." They'd argued constantly about the hum of the fans that cooled James's computers and the coiled snares of power cables that snaked across the floor.

But James wasn't here anymore. There were no more arguments. There wasn't much of anything.

Two months ago, when James had gone missing, Lex had been furious. He must have put himself at risk, sticking his nose into some bad business. That first night when he hadn't returned by nightfall, she'd taken out her anger on the barricade of computers and hard drives, toppling the whole lot. The next night, when he still hadn't shown up, she'd rebuilt the wall. It had remained there since, a humming shrine.

She had become lazy after that. Lazy and angry. She had almost got herself killed after stumbling blindly into one of the biggest riots in years, the Fagins that operated each gang watching her with beady eyes. She hadn't even had her camera with her, so she couldn't even pretend to herself that she was reporting for RealWorld. Afterwards, she'd shaken herself down and began digging for the truth.

Once all the public channels had been exhausted she set to work in earnest, James Raymond-style. She'd always insisted to James that she wasn't a hacker. She was the digger, the journalist, the blogger, and James did the grunt work at the screen. But she had picked up a thing or two, watching him at work.

She awoke her main terminal from standby. Above its screen was a sticker she had made herself, all that time ago when her ambitions were a search for a general truth, rather than a specific one. She had written the "X" and "RAY" in *LEX RAYMOND* thicker and bolder than the other letters. Below her name she had scrawled, *Journalist at large*. She had been proud of the "X-Ray" pun and annoyed when James insisted on calling her Alexandra.

The console screen clicked on. Lex flicked through windows rapidly, checking that each of the worm programs was working. Each window contained reams of text but none of the worms reported a success. Maybe James wouldn't have been proud of her new hacking skills after all.

Sighing, she slung her rucksack onto the sagging leather sofa. The remains of last night's meal lay on the kitchen counter: a sausage roll liberated from a freezer in an abandoned supermarket. She tore off and swallowed a chunk, hardly registering the taste. She slumped onto the sofa, kicking her legs up onto the armrest. The springs beneath her groaned their dismay.

She almost choked when a siren sounded nearby. She leapt to her feet. No. It wasn't a siren. And it was inside the flat, not outside.

She spat out the last mouthful of sausage roll and bounded over to the terminal. Nothing, nothing, nothing, *there*. One of the worms had pushed its way in. The lines of programming had disappeared, to be replaced by a crested logo.

She had finally done it. She had hacked into the Department of Conviction website.

Her heart pounded as she worked, skimming through menus to locate the correct search field.

Time passed, but Lex had no idea how much. Her stomach growled but she ignored it.

And then there it was. Stark green text on white, and a pixelated, years-out-of-date photo.

JAMES RAYMOND / d.o.b.: unknown / conviction: inciting violence and theft / sentence: 15 yrs redbrick 22.

She felt faint.

The only live button would take her back to the search box. This was it. This was all she was going to get.

Frantically, she scoured the desk for a notepad and pen, scribbling down the details in the sudden fear of a power cut and being unable to retrieve the information.

What did it mean? Now that her panic was beginning to subside, she found herself smiling at *d.o.b.: unknown*. When they'd first moved into the flat, when they were at their lowest ebb, James had wiped his details from government records: date of birth, academic career, family relationships. He was proud of that, though he hadn't managed the full house. They still knew his name.

She didn't believe the charge of *inciting violence and theft* for a second. James was the most calm, peaceful person she had ever known. But there was a horrific irony that he, of all people, could be accused of such a thing. He had worked tirelessly for years to research and understand the real reasons for the riots, looking beyond the gangs, scraping beneath for the underlying problems. It had been Lex Raymond the X-Ray and her brother James against the world, investigating wrongs and exposing injustice. They had always reassured each other that they would be the ones to bring Mercy down. It was all they had left. Their parents hadn't left them enough money to buy their way into the Gates, and instead of scurrying to the suburbs along with everyone else, she and James had gone against the tide. They had done what nobody else in their right mind had done: they moved to the Innards. It was a typically bloody-minded decision, but it was consistent with the way they'd always acted. Twins were like that, Lex had always supposed.

The phrase *15 yrs redbrick* didn't mean anything to her at all. She drew in a deep breath and set to work. This would take more than software; it would take honest journalistic graft.

.00   01100101   01111000   01110100   00100000   01000010   01110010   01100101   01100001   0110101

The monitor showing a feed from the outdoor camera had brightened with dawn by the time Lex pushed her chair away from the terminal. Her legs were shaking uncontrollably.

The word "redbrick" was more a nickname than an official term—she had found it used only in password-protected forums, posted by users who she deduced were low-level government aides. From what Lex had gathered, the redbricks were any buildings not designed as prisons, which had been converted in the early days of Mercy's new role as all-in-one provider of the justice system, when the sentencing rate had really begun to skyrocket. Traditional prisons had overflowed with Mercy's successes. In response, the government announced more and more institutions, dotted around the country, housed in the most secure buildings they could locate.

Redbrick 22, the building in which James was imprisoned, was situated on an island off the Northumberland coast. The single photo that Lex had unearthed showed a converted medieval castle on a rocky mount, reinforced with red-painted concrete and ringed by walls and turrets. A single guarded causeway led to the mainland.

The muffled noise of the riots outside sounded like swelling waves, which made her think of the tide lapping against the base of James's castle prison. Would he hear the waves? Or would the walls be too thick? Would his cell even have a window?

She flicked through windows to another bookmarked site. She had found the same photo of Redbrick 22 as a meme on a right-wing private forum. Overlaid on top of the image was a simple caption: *No escape.*

01101001

01101001

01000011

0101

01000101 01010010 01000011

01101000 00100000 01110111
00100000 01101000 01110101
01101001 01101110 00100000
01100101 00100000 01100001 01101001
00100000 01110010 01101001
01110100 01100101 01100100 00100000
01110100 01101000 01100101
01110010 01100011 00100000
00100000 01110100 01101000 01100101
01110010
01100111 01101000 01110100
01110010 01101111

01101111 01110101 00100000 01100010
01110101

CHAPTER FOUR

The Rendezvous

Ethan stood in the back garden, gazing upwards. The sun hadn't yet risen but the sky was already brightening. It flickered where it met the horizon. He squinted and the white pinpricks of stars appeared against the pink sky, without forming any patterns he recognized. Where was the Pole Star, even? He traced an imagined outline of Orion in the air with his finger. He felt a sudden wrench of homesickness.

Voices carried from inside the building. His "family" must be sitting around the kitchen table, waiting for him to return. He'd already been out here for more than fifteen minutes on the pretence of taking out the rubbish. He ought to be cold out here in only his T-shirt, but he didn't feel it.

With a sigh, he pushed open the door. The people who insisted that they were his mother and father spun to look at him.

"Ethan, you haven't finished your breakfast," his mother said. She looked down at his plate, her face a picture of sadness.

"That was half an hour ago. There's only a handful of baked beans left."

"You don't want them?"

"No. I don't want them."

She brightened. "In that case, I'll clear the dishes."

Ethan forced a smile.

"Wait," she said, her voice hardening. "Your father wants a word."

His father rose from his seat, smoothing the lapels of his tweed suit. "Where are you going? Do you have homework? Greg is in his bedroom, doing homework."

Ethan had woken early that morning, which seemed to have upset the normal routine of the household. He could have sworn he'd heard Greg's voice from the kitchen when he was standing outside, but now he was nowhere to be seen.

"No, I don't have homework, Father." Even if he had, it would have been pointless, rote repetition of the nonsense his teachers had spouted yesterday.

"Where are you going?"

"To school."

The only response was a frown. Ethan tried to leave the room, but his father's tweed-suited bulk blocked the way.

"Perhaps you could help by washing the dishes."

With a sigh, Ethan began soaping the dishes in the sink, feeling the eyes of his parents on him. Through the window he watched the reddening sky. What if he was late? Would the boy he had spoken to at the lockers wait for him? Even working as speedily as possible, washing the dishes took ten minutes. When he had finished, his mother and father were seated once again at the table.

"Father, I have to leave."

"It's early. Where are you going?"

"Why, what time is it?" According to the kitchen clock it was five o'clock, but it must be wrong; when Ethan had first come downstairs it had been half past.

"It's early. Where are you going?"

"I told you. Out."

"Where are you going? Do you have homework?"

"Father, I'm going to . . ." He tried to think of something that might satisfy him. "To wash the car."

His father's expression flickered, for several moments becoming indistinct and blurry like an old TV with a bad signal. Then it settled on a broad smile. "That would be a great help to your mother and me."

.00　01100101　01111000　01110100　00100000　01000010　01110010　01100101　01100001　0110101

"Morning, young Ethan!"

The postlady's call came between bursts of whistling as she struggled up the hill on her bike. She must have got up early this morning too. Ethan passed her at a jog.

The hams hadn't yet been laid out at the butcher's shop. The butcher was ready at the window, though. He winked, happy as ever.

Ethan slowed down on Rectory Road, pretending to be engrossed in the map of the village. When he had first arrived in Touchstone a fortnight ago, he had pored over the map, but since then he hadn't given it much attention. It was easy enough to locate Ilkley Grove on the map, but surprisingly difficult to trace his route from there to where he now stood. The mapmaker hadn't connected the roads, as if he or she had been uncertain how they joined up. The housing estates appeared isolated, like floating islands. Many of the roads that spiderwebbed from the high street led nowhere.

He turned at the sound of an engine and watched the red saloon car pass, then the school minibus. It was dim enough that the bus driver ought to have switched on his headlights.

He stopped. *Four . . . three . . . two . . .*

A passengerless taxi appeared at the junction. The driver's eyes were fixed on the road.

Now the coast should be clear. Even so, Ethan looked along the road twice in each direction before he stepped from the pavement and onto the footpath.

Nothing happened. No repercussions, no calamity.

With newfound confidence, he followed the path as it wound through the park, past a cluster of featureless houses, until it became a dirt track. The track led to a small farm comprised of a tiny brick house and a barn. A pony paced to and fro within a fenced-off area. Ethan stopped for a moment to watch it. Its mane appeared shiny and rigid. The grain in a trough lay untouched. The pony walked in a tight circle as if it were slowly chasing its own tail.

"Morning, horse," Ethan said.

The pony continued circling. The grass beneath its feet had worn away to reveal a perfect halo of packed soil.

Ethan was about to leave when the pony's body juddered. Pinpricks of light appeared in its patterned flank. Within moments, the animal had become little more than a speckled outline, like a constellation of stars.

With a crackling, popping sound, the pony disappeared entirely.

Ethan rubbed his eyes, uncertain what he'd witnessed. When he opened his eyes again, the pony shook its mane and continued walking in circles. Ethan frowned. He must be exhausted, or something.

The path led towards a copse of trees at the summit of the hill. When Ethan reached halfway he turned in the direction from which he had come. Only the tallest buildings—the church and the school sports hall—jutted above the horizon. The housing estates were square and blunt, as if they had been dropped onto the meadowland at random locations, and just as he had noticed on the map, the roads were oddly connected, turning back on themselves and crisscrossing inefficiently. Beyond the high street the land tapered to nothing. For the first time, Ethan saw that the village was on a peninsula; vivid blue water surrounded Touchstone on three sides. In fact, water and land met at a point not far beyond the school, though he had never noticed the sounds or smells of the ocean. The sea stretched as far as he could see, melting into the flat blue of the sky.

He resumed his climb and soon reached the edge of the copse. It was dark within. Was it safe? He told himself that he didn't have any choice.

It wasn't only the darkness that made the place eerie. He bent down on one knee and brushed at the ground with the palm of his hand. It was perfectly smooth. Even though he could see fallen leaves and twigs, he couldn't feel them. Now that he looked more closely, the trees appeared to be arranged at regular intervals. Maybe they had been planted by hand. In fact, they looked regular in every possible sense. Even the arrangement of branches and leaves appeared the same from tree to tree.

A glimmer of light shone through the gloom. He moved towards it, at first treading carefully and then walking normally when he realized the leaves underfoot produced no noise.

"And here he comes, finally," a voice said, accompanied by a slow handclap.

Ethan stepped out from the copse into an open space. Beyond it, the hill fell away sharply towards a landscape of meadows that varied only in their shade of green.

"Hi there." It was the same boy from the lockers. He wore a green cap with a stubby brim, making him look like a Cub Scout. "We're glad you came."

Five other people stood behind him. They were all Ethan's age or slightly older. He recognized a couple from school. A girl with her dark hair in a ponytail was in his science class, as was the heavyset boy with the shaven head. His thick arms were folded over his chest and he scowled at Ethan. Beside the line of trees, an Asian girl played with a lattice of string wound between her fingers.

But Ethan's attention was fixed on the last member of the group, who hadn't yet acknowledged him. This small, wiry-looking boy seemed entirely focused on a game of his own. He was leaning back at an odd angle, which wouldn't have been strange if not for the fact that there appeared to be nothing behind him to lean upon. He was absorbed in throwing and catching a tennis ball. Again and again, he tossed it away from him. Each time, the ball ricocheted off thin air to return to his hand.

00100110 01101110 00100000 01101110 110...
0010 01101001 01110100 01110100 01100101 01101110 00100000

001 00100000 01010100 01101001 01101101 00100000 01001101 01100
010 01101111   00101110 00100000 01001100 01100001 01111
111 01110101 01110100 00100000 01100001   01100100 00100

01100101 01110011 01101001 01100111 01101110 00100000 01100
01001010 01100001 01110010 01100101 01100100 00100

01110000 01101001 01110010 01101

01000011
0101

01000101 01010010 01000011

01101000   00100000 01110111
00100000 01101000 01110101
00100000 01101001 01101110 00100000
01100101 00100000 01100001 01101001
00100000 01110010 01101001
01110100 01100101 01100100 00100000
00100000 01110100 01101000 01100101
01110010 01100011   00100000
00100000 01110100 01101000 01100101
01110010
01100111 01101000 01110100
01110010 01101111

01101111 01110101 00100000 01100010
01110101
01110100

0011   00100000 01110111 01100001 01110001   011
10010 01101001 01110100 01110100 01100101 01101110 00100000 0110
11001 00100000 01010100 01101001 01101101 00100000 01001101 0110
01010 01101111   00101110 00100000 01001100 01100001 011
01111 01110101 01110100 00100000 01100001 01101110 01100100 0001
00100 01100101 01110011 01101001 01100111 01101110 00100000 0110
11001   01001010 01100001 01110010 01100101   0010
010011 01101000 01100001 01110000 01101001 011
01111 00101110 01000010 01101001 01101110 01100001 01110010 0111100
          01100110
          C11APIEO

CHAPTER FIVE
Out of the Innards

The shouts and thudding sounds of the rioting became a dull roar in the distance as Lex moved away from the apartment. The moon was three-quarters full and bright enough for Lex to pick her way through the streets without a torch. Though this made her less conspicuous, each dark alley became a source of potential threat.

She was an idiot; she shouldn't be outside. James would have convinced her to wait until morning. Except he'd gone and got himself arrested, hadn't he? Leaving her alone with only her whims to guide her. She gnawed on her already ragged fingernails. It would only take half an hour to get back to the flat. If the gangs remained on the main streets she might avoid giving away her hideout.

But she needed to make something happen.

She had slept fitfully on the ancient sofa in the flat. When she had awoken, she had realized with a sense of surprise that her dreams had involved not only James, but Ethan. Their faces had swum in the darkness, merging together.

10001
01101000
1 00101110
0 01010100
1 01110010
0   110
0 01101000
00101100
0 01100101
0 01101111
01100001
1 01100110
0   111
1 01110101
01101001
0 00100000
1 01100001
0   011
1 01101000
0 01100001

They—or rather *he*, brother and victim merged—held something. A lilac folder. Sheets of paper labelled *Project Q*.

Stupid subconscious. She had got the message. James was locked up, sure, but she had pretty much known that already, but whatever had happened to him had been his own doing, ultimately. He had known what he was getting into.

She had to face facts. James was no longer the only person haunting her conscience. Now there was Ethan too, his cheek streaked with his own blood.

"Stop it. Just stop it." She couldn't recall when she had begun talking to herself.

Blearily, without showering or eating, Lex had sat before her terminal, watching the green cursor blink. Then she had set to work.

The file on Ethan was more detailed than James's. The Department for Conviction crest was relegated to the top left corner, while the Mercy logo, its "M" a caricatured set of weighing scales, was prominent above the photo of Ethan. He looked terrified, but that was nothing new. The collar of his jumper was ripped too, and nobody had even cleared the blood from the wound on his cheek. The hope that he had been shipped home by his dad had faded fast.

Subject: Ethan James Wright. The middle name felt like a cruel irony.

Apprehended: Zone 2 upper west, L block. She snorted. Whoever had logged the report couldn't even bring themselves to identify it as the Mercy HQ. She supposed it wasn't in anyone's interests to note that their own HQ wasn't, after all, an impenetrable fortress.

Charge processed.

Charge jurisdiction: MERCY. Five letters that made Lex's stomach feel hollow.

Sentence processed.

Sentence jurisdiction: MERCY.

Nature of sentence: [redacted].

The rest of the screen was filled with a text equivalent of static, rows of dashes and forward slashes. Whether this represented encrypted information or a glitch, Lex had no idea.

The gnawing sensation in her belly increased. When James had been taken, she had responded the only way she knew how—as a journalist. She had hunted for a primary source, or as close to one as she could find. When Ethan had stumbled into the RealWorld forum he had exposed himself in a way that no conspiracy nut would have dared. Had she felt sorry for him at all? She couldn't even remember. He'd been a prize, that was all, a lucky break. And Ethan had been so desperate for answers that he'd volunteered the information about his dad without her needing to use any of her manipulative journalist tricks.

So she had coaxed Ethan into getting what she wanted. Pale and shivering, at the Mercy entrance, his dad's ID card burning a hole in his pocket. And then—

And then he'd been taken too.

And it was entirely her fault.

No matter how she framed the issue, she wasn't going to be able to chalk Ethan's fate up to bad luck. She was responsible for him. And her nightmares were enough to prove that she had more of a conscience than she liked to admit.

James was way beyond her reach. In all likelihood, Ethan was too. But she had to know for sure.

As the sun began to rise Lex passed the last of the high-rises and derelict shops and approached the low roofs of the suburbs. She checked her map, making sure to keep to the periphery of the suburban estates. She hadn't ventured beyond the Innards since James's disappearance. The gangs had been hard at work here. Any houses lacking reinforced doors and windows had been raided. The roads were strewn with fragments of glass and discarded possessions. She knelt to pick up a framed photo showing an elderly couple on the deck of a ferry, gaudily dressed in Hawaiian shirts and garlands of flowers.

00   01100101   01111000   01110100   00100000   01000010   01110010   01100101   01100001   0110101

"Can I help you?"

The iris of the CCTV camera twitched and dilated to focus on Lex. She squinted against the dawn sunlight while simultaneously trying to offer her most pleasant, unthreatening smile.

"I'm not sure I've got the right Gate," she said. "I'm looking for Ethan?"

Several seconds passed before the woman's voice came again from the speaker. "Are you school friends?"

Lex chided herself for not having neatened herself up or changed her clothes. Her leather jacket wasn't helping her to look any younger. "Sort of. I mean, we go to the same, um . . . computer class."

"Ah." This obviously sounded half-plausible. "I'm sorry. Ethan isn't home. He's— Well, your teacher will probably have a chat with you at some point. I'm sorry."

Lex sensed the opportunity slipping away from her. "We were supposed to meet. After class, I mean, a couple of weeks ago."

Another pause. There were strict rules about who ought to be let into the Gates, and Lex met none of the criteria. But fretting about a missing child would make anyone desperate.

The lock emitted a sharp click.

"We're number fifteen, up on the rise," said the speaker.

Lex had never been behind any of the Gates before. It had the appearance of a fairy-tale land, with its immaculate lawns and litter-free roads. She realized that she was striding, ready to run; she straightened her spine and managed to approximate a casual pace. She passed a school with children playing hopscotch outside classroom windows strung with paperchains.

It's not real, she told herself. *Don't be seduced.* The Gates were a ghostly image of the old world, a pretence. Despite their wealth, these people lived behind high walls because they were terribly afraid.

Ethan's mom was waiting at the door. Her eyes were large and pale as water. Her long black hair was pinned up, but several strands had fallen free. She looked Lex up and down. Maybe she was struggling to imagine her son having a friend like this. Lex put on the politest face she could manage.

"You'd better come in."

The house was a bungalow, like all the others in the estate, but it stretched further back than the façade suggested. Refusing to add a second floor was a statement of wealth—why build upwards when you could sprawl across expensive acres of real estate? Lex could feel warmth rising from the copper-coloured tiles of the hallway floor, even through her boots. The walls were decorated with paintings. Some depicted flowers and landscapes, but a larger canvas at the end of the corridor caught her eye. It showed a birds-eye view of a city centre—no, *the* city centre, the Innards as it was before Mercy—in greys and browns. Faceless figures filled the streets.

Ethan's mom directed her into a sitting room. Lex noticed smears of blue paint that marked the cuffs of the woman's white shirt, and the front was marked with a faint blue handprint.

"Would you like a drink?"

Lex nodded, genuinely grateful, and Ethan's mom disappeared into the depths of the house.

In the corner of the sitting room was a huge TV; no surprises there. Beside it was an expensive-looking stereo. Other than that, the room was plain, with more paintings and a few family portraits showing Ethan flanked by his mom and Cecil Wright, whose boyish face Lex recognized from his ID card photo. On the coffee table was a vase containing flowers with wilting petals. When she returned with the drinks, Ethan's mom followed Lex's gaze to the flowers. Her eyelids flickered as though she might burst into tears.

"Here you go. Freshly squeezed," she said. She placed one glass onto the table before Lex and nursed the other herself. Lex sipped, thankful for something to do with her hands. The orange juice was thick with pulp. It had been years since she had tasted anything so real.

"So, you're a friend of Ethan's." That same hesitation again, when she said his name.

Lex nodded. *A friend? More like his worst enemy.*

"I'm Caroline."

"Alexandra Raymond."

"I don't remember him mentioning you before."

He was probably the kind of kid who confided in his mom, or the kind of kid who didn't have much happen to him, or both.

"We met only recently," Lex said, "but we've become close." She noticed Caroline's weak smile. "He's a good—" *Don't say "kid."* "—friend."

"Yes. He's a good boy, always has been. That's why . . ."

Lex tensed. This was it.

Caroline chewed her lip and looked down at her glass. "He didn't say anything to you?"

"About what?"

"I didn't notice anything. His own mother!"

Lex adopted what she hoped was a politely curious expression.

"I'm so sorry. You probably think I'm very silly. I'll explain. Just two weeks ago, Ethan didn't come home. And then it was three days before we knew what had happened."

Lex knew how those three days must have felt. "What *had* happened?"

"It seems that he was somewhere he shouldn't have been. I don't know much more than that, though they hinted. Even my husband—" She glanced at the photo above the TV set. "They're not telling us anything, really."

"Ethan's in trouble? Where is he?"

"He's not here." Flecks of mascara had become lodged in the laughter-lines at the corners of her eyes. "They say he's in prison." She placed the glass on the table. Then she began to weep, silently and heavily.

Lex hesitated, awkward and uncertain. Finally, she moved to the sofa and held the woman's shaking hands in her own. Caroline's body lurched with sobs.

Lex waited until she had recovered, then said in a quiet voice, "Could I see Ethan's room?"

Caroline wiped her eyes with a sleeve and nodded.

Lex followed Caroline's hunched shoulders past a chrome kitchen and a sparkling white bathroom.

Ethan's bedroom was far bigger than hers, but it felt smaller. Its shelves were jammed with books, two rows deep. A hardback book had been left splayed open on the unmade bed and another peeped out from underneath the pillow. The few gaps on the shelves held figurines of spacemen and alien monsters. They were all painted in bright colours—presumably by Ethan himself, judging from the unwashed plastic palettes and brushes scattered on the desk.

A small telescope was fixed upon a tripod before the window. It pointed up and out of the room, above the roofs of the neighbouring houses. Pages torn from books containing illustrations of star constellations were stuck along the bottom of the window.

Lex felt a wave of sadness; she was surprised at the intensity of the feeling. The truth threatened to spill out of her mouth. She wondered if she might be sick.

A sharp sound came from the hallway. Lex wiped her forehead. It was clammy and cold.

"Alexandra, this is Ethan's dad."

Cecil Wright was taller than the photos suggested, and his clean-shaven face wider, as if his features stretched too far around his head. He smiled crookedly and removed his ugly black hat, which had a brim that seemed far too wide for his head. His glasses were smeared with fingerprints.

"My wife says that you're a friend of Ethan's?"

Lex wasn't sure if he was challenging her. She nodded.

"Then you're a friend of ours too. You've heard what's happened, I assume."

"Yes. But I don't understand it."

"No." Ethan's dad looked about him as if wondering where to put his hat. He held it before him in both hands. "Neither do we, Alexandra. Neither do we."

Lex bit her tongue. *You do understand it*, she thought. *You understand it completely. You sit in your office with a black marker pen, blanking out all the details of your secret projects. And now your son is mixed up in it all and you don't care one bit.*

Caroline caught her reflection in a mirror mounted on the wall. "Goodness, I look a mess. Excuse me while I change out of this shirt." She retreated into another part of the house.

"Your wife said that Ethan's in prison," Lex said to Cecil. She winced. Too eager, too direct.

"So it seems."

"For how long?"

"It's . . . unclear. But he'll be back soon enough, I trust."

"Do you know where he's being held?"

Ethan's dad crossed to a bookshelf and picked up a painted figurine of a NASA astronaut. He turned it over in his hands without looking at it. "I don't see that it matters much."

"I suppose not. But—" It was worth the gamble. "But what about Mercy?"

The astronaut disappeared within Cecil's fist. He stared down at his hands as if surprised that he could envelop the whole thing. "What do you mean?"

Lex tried to sound casual. "I suppose it was Mercy who conducted Ethan's trial? I mean, I've seen on the news about the extra courts, faster sentencing, all that." She jammed her hands into the pockets of her leather jacket. Her fingers curled around a rectangle of smooth plastic; she shuddered as she realized that it was Cecil's ID card. Should she try and get rid of it? She could deposit it somewhere in the house for him to find later. Perhaps she could leave it on Ethan's desk—it wasn't as if he could get into any deeper trouble. She pulled the card halfway out of her pocket, ready to drop it. Cecil looked up and she tucked it in again.

"Does it matter?" he said.

"You work at Mercy, isn't that right?"

Cecil narrowed his eyes. "What did you say your name is? And how old are you?"

"Alexandra Fullman." She had already given her real surname to Caroline. This was getting messy. "I'm sixteen."

Cecil looked doubtful.

"Okay, I'm nineteen really. Ethan mentioned several times that you worked at Mercy. He's really proud of you, Mr. Wright."

Cecil seemed to soften a little. Lex felt words bubbling up, words she shouldn't say but couldn't possibly hold in. "But it seems strange, about Mercy. That the very corporation that arrested Ethan are the ones who operate the courts. The same people who ended up sentencing him. Doesn't that seem wrong to you?"

"What do you know about all that?"

"I've heard rumours, that's all."

Cecil placed the figurine back on the shelf, adjusting it so that it stood in exactly the same place as before. Now his expression was strained, as if he was peering into bright light from the depths of a tunnel.

"I think that you should leave now."

Yes, she absolutely should leave. She was amazed that she hadn't got herself into a far worse situation. She nodded.

"But tell me one thing," she said, cursing herself inwardly even as she spoke. "How can you stand there while your employers press charges against your innocent son, then sentence him however they see fit, without anyone to keep them in check? How can you be so casual while Mercy has made certain that your son is trapped for who knows how many years in a cold prison cell?"

Cecil appeared stunned. Lex braced herself, expecting him to lash out at her, or force her to reveal what she knew, or phone Mercy to let them do the job for him. But he had become even more distant than before, as if he was only half-awake.

"No," he said slowly, "not in a prison cell. At least there's that."

"What do you mean?"

Cecil didn't reply. He drifted over to the desk and placed a hand on the telescope tripod. He gazed out of the window at the sky. "He always loved watching the stars."

"What do you *mean*?" Lex repeated. "About Ethan not being in prison?"

Cecil's entire body shook. He fixed Lex with red, raw eyes. "I said that you should leave."

00100000 01101111 00100000 00100000 01110100 01110100 01101001 00100000 00110000 00110001 00110001 00110001 00110001 00110000 00100000 00110001 00110001 00110000

0010 01101001 01110100 01110100 01110100 01100100 01100010 01100101

001 00100000 01010100 01101001 01101101 01100101 00100000 01101101 00100000 01001101 01101100 01100

010 01101111   00101110 00100000 01001100 01100001 01111

111 01110101 01110100 01110100 00100000 01100001   01100100 00100

011101 01101000 01100111 01101001 01101001 01100111 01101110 00100000 0110

01001010 01100001 01110010 01100101 01100101 01100100 00100

01110000 01101001 01101010 01110010 0011

001 011011100 01101001 01101110 01100001 01110010 01111001

01000011
0101

01000101 01010010 01000011

01101000   00100000 01110111
          00100000 01101000 01110101
00100000 01101001 01101110 00100000
01100101 00100000 01100001 01101001
          00100000 01110010 01101001
01110100 01100101 01100100 00100000
          01110100 01101000 01100101
01110010 01100011   00100000
00100000 01110100 01101000 01100101
                   01110010
01100111 01101000 01110100
          01110010 01101111

01101111 01110101 00100000 01100010
                   01110101
                   01110100

"He wasn't worth the wait, was he?" the boy with his arms folded tightly over his chest said. The freckles on his cheeks and nose seemed at odds with his bulky body, as if he was a toddler that had suddenly expanded.

"Give him a chance," the ponytailed girl said. "Hi. I'm Libby, and that sarcastic brute over there is Russell."

"I'm Anita," said the other girl, without looking up from her string game. Her dark hair was styled into a neat bob. She had knotted her school tie the wrong way round, so that only the short end was visible.

The small boy wearing glasses stepped forward. He shook Ethan's hand with stiff formality. "I didn't get to introduce myself yesterday. I'm Kit Carruthers. People call me Kit-Car."

"They do not!" Anita snorted.

"Yes they do," Kit said. "Back home, I mean. Sometimes."

"It's good to meet you all," Ethan said. "I'm Ethan Wright."
He glanced over at the only person who hadn't yet spoken—the boy absorbed in throwing and catching a tennis ball.

"Don't mind Miller," Libby said. "He'll talk when he feels like talking."

The boy threw the ball again. Ethan flinched as it bounced, apparently hitting nothing.

Ethan felt he should say something. "I didn't know we were allowed tennis balls. Or any toys, really."

A couple of them laughed. After two more bounces, Miller regarded Ethan levelly. "It's a perk, dimwit." His voice was a nasal whine.

Ethan decided immediately that he didn't much like him. "What does that mean?"

Miller scowled, then resumed throwing and catching the ball.

"You haven't had any perks?" Kit said, filling the awkward silence. "How long have you been here, anyway?"

"Two weeks. Two weeks and two days."

"Seriously? Sorry it took so long for us to spot you. You're good at blending in."

Ethan frowned. While Kit seemed to view this as an insult, blending in had been entirely Ethan's plan the whole time. "I've seen you before, most of you."

"But you didn't spot us?"

"Spot that you were . . . No, I had no idea."

Libby's face crumpled. "You thought you were stuck here on your own?"

Ethan shrugged and nodded.

"You poor, poor thing! That must have been dreadful."

Anita made a retching noise and scrambled to her feet. "Enough of the caring-sharing act, Lib. The new kid's going to make us late for school."

Miller glanced up. "Maybe that's what he wants. Maybe that's why he's here. Maybe he's one of *them*."

"What do you mean?" Ethan said. "No! I'm not one of them. I'm one of you." He paused. "Unless *you're* them."

Anita cackled with laughter. "Get a grip, idiot. He's messing with you."

Ethan felt his cheeks redden. "How long have you all been here?"

"I arrived six months ago, more or less," Libby said. "It's hard to keep track without calendars. Only Russell was already here before me, isn't that right, Russell?"

Russell grunted confirmation.

"Only the day before me, though," Libby continued, "and Anita showed up later that week. Miller was a month later, then Kit, not long after that."

"It's been so long since then, we were certain there wouldn't be more," Kit added. "I guess we got lazy about keeping an eye out for newbies."

Ethan drew a deep breath and tried to formulate the question he had wanted to ask all along. "So what is this place?"

"Touchstone," Libby replied. "Where only the best will do and where your new family will make your life the dullest kind of nightmare."

Ethan felt a rush of guilty relief that he wasn't the only person being forced to live with strangers who insisted they were family. "But whereabouts in the country are we?"

Libby narrowed her eyes. "Hold on. You mean to say you really don't know? They didn't tell you at the briefing?"

"I don't think I had one of those." His arrest at the Mercy HQ felt a lifetime ago, as did the flurry of activity afterwards, when he was delivered from the uniformed guards to the authorities. He was unsure what had happened next. He had asked for his parents again and again, but after a while he had simply stopped asking. He had been brought to Touchstone at night, when he was sleeping. He didn't remember a journey.

"It would have been after your trial, when they were preparing you for arrival."

"It all happened so fast. I'm not even sure which bit was the trial, to be honest."

Kit rubbed his chin. "Sounds like it's getting worse out there. Mine was short, but at least they went through the motions. No trial, no briefing . . . It's no wonder you figured you should keep your head down."

"But you're all the same as me? You're all—" Ethan struggled to find a different word, one that wouldn't sound foolish to describe their circumstances "—prisoners?"

"Course we are. This is a prison, isn't it?"

Ethan looked around at their surroundings. The sun had risen fully now. The ground was a shifting carpet of dappled yellow and green as sunlight strobed through the copse.

"I guess," he said without conviction. "So, what did you all do? To end up in here?"

They all glared at him. Libby raised her hands a placating gesture. "Cool it, guys." To Ethan she said, "We don't talk about that. It wouldn't help anyone."

"We need to stick together," Kit added. "One for all and all for one."

"Oh. Okay. Sorry."

The only sound now was from Miller's ball, which continued to bounce off thin air.

Kit's eyes followed the direction of Ethan's gaze. He laughed. "I guess this is the first time you've been to the limits?" He stood beside Miller, who stopped throwing the ball and glared up at him. "It's actually pretty cool. Watch this."

Still watching Ethan, Kit reached up and tapped three times with his knuckles, as if knocking on a wall—except there was nothing there. Each knock produced a dull metallic thud from the air. Then Kit turned and leaned backwards. Rather than toppling down the hillside as Ethan had expected, his shoulders were stopped by some invisible surface and his legs slid forwards on the smooth ground until he sat in a reclining position like Miller. Now he was leaning at forty-five degrees, suspended in mid-air. "Come over here and take a look for yourself."

Ethan raised his hands like a sleepwalker as he drew close.

Kit smiled. "A couple more steps."

Then Ethan felt a hard surface against his fingertips, even though all he could see were the meadows that stretched far beyond the hill. He splayed out his fingers and felt a cool surface beneath his palms. He knocked, softly at first and then sharply. The dull sound echoed oddly around the clearing.

"Is it glass?"

Miller snorted with derision.

"You're way off," Kit said. "Look more carefully at the view."

The meadows were almost uniformly green, each one a consistent shade across its entire width. The more Ethan looked, the less detail he could make out. Instead of dividing fences between the fields, he saw smudges of brown lines.

"The view doesn't look so impressive after all, does it?"

"What is all this?" Ethan whispered.

"I can't imagine how confusing it is without having been briefed," Kit replied. He pushed against the invisible wall to stand. "It's just the edge of the skybox, that's all. Think of it as a video screen. It's not in their interest to program an infinite amount of procedural landscape. The village has water on three sides, so that's simple enough—there's no view other than sea, sea and more sea. At this corner of the skybox they figured we'd be fooled by a suggestion of green fields that go on and on." He grinned. "In fairness, it obviously did fool you."

Ethan blinked rapidly, trying to dispel the illusion. He failed.

Anita slung her rucksack onto her shoulder. "I'm serious, you guys. I'm going to school. If you want to stay here until the bots come looking, that's your problem."

00   01100101   01111000   01110100   00100000   01000010   01110010   01100101   01100001   0110101

Russell and Anita strode ahead as they all made their way down the hill. Libby walked with Ethan, and Kit jogged awkwardly to keep up. Ethan glanced behind him to see Miller bringing up the rear, shambling slowly with a sour look on his face.

Kit seemed proud to be acting as tour guide. "You see, the trick is not to think of yourself as *being* some*where*. While you're here, try to imagine yourself as *in* some*thing*." He rapped his knuckles on the fence that ran alongside the path. "This isn't real. This whole place doesn't exist. We're not here."

Ethan stared at him.

"It's a sim, a simulated environment."

Ethan wished Kit would stop talking. A simulated environment? A village that didn't exist? When he had been deposited in Touchstone he had understood that he was being punished. The dreary routine of school, the awful people in his new house that called themselves his family. It was an unusual way to punish him for the break-in, certainly, but he had no experience with the justice system. He had supposed that they knew best. His dad worked for Mercy, after all. They couldn't be all bad.

"But it's—" he began. "I mean, it's all so—"

He gazed up at the sky. Was it flickering? Some patches looked oddly flat. He blinked and looked away. Russell and Anita were watching him with amused expressions.

"God, he's dumb," Russell said. "It's just a video game, that's all."

"That's a vast simplification," Kit said. "But I suppose Russell's more or less right. It's just a videogame."

"Except one that's no fun," Anita added.

Kit nodded. Still addressing Ethan, he said, "We're here to be taught a lesson. We're here because someone's decided we should learn about good behaviour, public decency and manners." He recited this list in a plummy voice, like an actor on stage.

Ethan knew he was being foolish when he said weakly, "So *none* of this is real?"

Anita groaned.

"But . . . what about us? What about me?"

Kit placed a hand on his shoulder. "I know this is a shock. But your body in here isn't the *real* you. You're out there somewhere—" he pointed upwards "—plugged into a computer. I know it feels real, as if you're really here. And to all intents and purposes, you are, but only because your mind *thinks* you are. You can think and move, and you have to go to the loo and all that. If you don't eat, for example, your mind will believe that you're starving and it'll act accordingly. Shut you down."

Russell thumped Ethan in the stomach, winding him. "And you can feel pain, too."

Ethan struggled to straighten up again, grimacing. Russell grinned.

"So we're trapped here to be taught a lesson," Ethan managed to say. "But what about when we've learned it? What happens then?"

Kit shrugged. "I guess we'll find out when they've had enough of us."

"Hold on," Ethan said. "You said 'they.' And Anita called them 'bots.' So is it our new families who are trying to teach us to behave differently? And the teachers at school?"

Anita slapped her forehead. "Are you serious? You believe they're real people?"

Ethan wavered. "I noticed them acting strange. My father—I mean, the man who calls himself my father—he's weird. So you're saying he's part of the video game? The sim?"

"*Finally*," Anita said to Russell in a stage whisper. "He's getting it. Maybe he's not as stupid as he seems."

Miller came up from behind. "*Nobody* could be as stupid as he seems." He barricaded the path. "Look. Does nobody else think that this is a bit suspicious? This new guy suddenly showing up after months? It's a trap, I'll bet."

Ethan felt the blood drain from his cheeks as they all turned to reappraise him. "No. I swear—"

Miller's stern expression evaporated. "I'm only yanking your chain, noob."

The others laughed with obvious relief. Ethan forced himself to laugh halfheartedly too. Miller stepped aside to allow his friends to set off again, but, unnoticed by the rest of the group, he gave Ethan a hard glare and an ugly sneer.

Ethan hurried after the others.

00011 01111001 00100000 01101110 01100110 00111110 110
010 01101001 01101000 01110100 01110100 01100101 01101110 00100000

001 00100000 01010100 01101001 01101101 00100000 01001101 01101100 01100
010 01101111   00101110 00100000 01001100 01100001 0111
111 01110101 01110100 00100000 01100001   01100100 00100

01100101 01110011 01101001 01100111 01101110 01101110 00100000 01100
01001010 01100001 01110010 01100101 01100100 01100100 00100

01110000 01101001 01110010 00110 **0110**

01101001 01101110 01100001 01110010 01111001

01000011
0101

01000101 01010010 01000011

01101000   00100000 01110111
00100000 01101000 01110101
00100000 01101001 01101110 00100000
01100101 00100000 01100001 01101001
00100000 01110010 01101001
01110100 01100101 01100100 00100000
00100000 01110100 01101000 01100101
01110010 01100011   00100000
00100000 01110100 01101000 01100101
01110001C
01100111 01101000 01110100C
01110010 01101111

01101111 01110101 00100000 0110001C
01110101C
0111010C

1001 00100000 01010100 01101001 01101101 00100000 01001101 011
)1010 01101111   00101110 00100000 01001100 01100001 011
)1111 01110101 01110100 00100000 01100001 01101110 01100100 001
)0100 01100101 01110011 01101001 01100111 01101110 00100000 011
1001   01001010 01100001 01110010 01100101   001
010011 01101000 01100001 011 10000 01101001 011
)1111 00101110 01000010 01101001 01101110 01100001 01110010 0111100

01100110

C11APTEO

CHAPTER SEVEN

The Fagin

Lex didn't dawdle after she left Ethan's house. It was getting late, and darkness would bring fresh dangers. The elongating shadows made the empty suburbs even more eerie than usual.

"Hold it, little miss."

Lex froze.

"Who do you work for?"

She straightened up slowly. She didn't reply.

"Answer me! Who's your carer?"

Carer. The Fagins had a peculiar idea of their position in society. They enjoyed thinking of themselves as mentors to disaffected city youths.

"Booker," Lex said finally. "I'm with Booker."

The Fagin paced around her in a circle. The low sunlight outlined the creases in her face and made her hair golden. She was older than most of the Fagins, perhaps over sixty. Lex had seen her before. Her name was Gillespie; she had become notorious due to a land-grab a few months ago.

Maybe Gillespie hadn't foreseen Mercy cops ending up in the middle of the gang fight, but it had been no accident when an officer was killed. She had made her gang of youths cop-killers as well as looters, and yet they'd do anything for her, to keep on her right side.

"Is that right?" Gillespie's voice was high-pitched. A talking weasel. Lex nodded. "He's right behind me."

"So this is recon, is it? Scouting out new digs? Maybe I should be worried."

"Nah." Lex felt a flash of pride at her convincing nonchalance. She indicated the debris piled up against the abandoned houses in the suburb, the smashed windows. "Booker's got no use for this neighbourhood. This whole place is shot."

Gillespie chuckled as she surveyed the desolate estate. "It is, it is. And you know what else is shot? *Booker*. Shot him myself, on this very street two days ago." Suddenly, her hand gripped Lex's right forearm. "So, tell me again. Who do you work for?"

Lex winced. The Fagin was surprisingly strong considering her age. She gasped, and said, "He didn't tell me his name."

Gillespie snorted. "No carer works anonymously. Reputation is everything. So, shall we agree that you're alone?"

Lex writhed, trying in vain to free herself.

"Well you work for me now, all right? A Gillespie girl, that's what you are. Bet you can squirrel into a property through the tiniest of spaces, a little thing like you. Let's get you home to meet the others, shall we?"

If Lex let herself be taken to the Fagin's den, she'd have little chance of escaping. All of the gangs had something in common: a strict code in which each member was responsible for two others. Each of them was ready to pounce if anyone attempted to leave or disobey orders, fearing punishment if they let either of their charges get away. She'd never be left alone.

Gillespie gripped even tighter. She was strong enough to drag Lex behind her, and Lex had also spotted a stolen Mercy pistol strapped to her belt. Outrunning her wouldn't be an option, even if she was able to break free.

Instead, she made a show of giving up. She bowed in submission and allowed herself to be escorted away.

"That's right, child. You're keen to meet your new friends, aren't you?"

Lex rummaged in her jacket pocket with her free hand and pulled out the map she'd used to find her way to Ethan's house. Holding it against her thigh with her palm, she manipulated her fingers awkwardly to begin ripping the single sheet into thin strips. By the time Gillespie noticed what she was doing, ribbons of paper had already fluttered away on the breeze.

"What've you got there?" Gillespie grabbed a fistful of shreds of paper. They were too torn to be legible, but they were clearly identifiable as parts of a map. "Got yourself a secret, do you?"

Lex shook her head vigorously, her lips tight. She would have to play this carefully.

"Tell me, girl! What are you after? Where were you going?"

For a second Lex allowed her eyes to stray towards the ruined estate. She dug the nails of her free hand into her palm and squeezed her eyes shut to produce tears. Hot streaks stung both of her cheeks. She made herself shiver, then stopped, fearing it was too theatrical.

Gillespie's features softened, though Lex wasn't fooled for a second. The Fagin pulled her to her bosom. Lex stifled the urge to push her away. Her sickly-sweet perfume was nauseating.

"Don't you cry, child." Her voice was more sinister now for its soothingness. "Tell old Mrs. G all about it."

"I . . . No, I can't."

"This is Booker's doing, isn't it? He sent you, before he died?"

Lex waited—it was best not to appear eager to offer answers—and then nodded slowly.

"He's gone. It's awful, but Booker's gone. I'll watch after you now."

A pleading look. A tentative smile. Lex hated herself for playacting.

"Spit it out, child. What did Booker send you to fetch? What did the map show?"

Lex murmured, "Loot. A prize."

"Must have been real special."

She nodded. "He said I was the best, when I work alone. Said I should keep apart from the rest of the team until I figured out where it was. And then I did. And now—" She let out an exaggerated sob. "I didn't know he was dead."

Gillespie reached out to smooth her hair. Lex shuddered, for real this time.

"You're under my care now. Nothing to worry about. But we have to get started on the right footing, don't we? I need you to tell me what it is. What was this loot of Booker's?"

So far so good. But having got this far, Lex struggled to think what her next move ought to be. What was this imaginary loot? What might a Fagin prize highly enough to go out of their way to find?

She began speaking hesitatingly, hoping inspiration would strike. "It's a leftover from the old days, hidden. The . . . the lord mayor's staff. Four foot long, studded with jewels." The jewels were an unnecessary detail. It was its symbolic status that Lex was banking on. Power and authority. All Fagins yearned for validation.

Gillespie stiffened. Her eyes were shining. "A fine prize indeed! So where is it?"

Beyond the roofs of the bungalows and semidetached homes of the estate rose a single taller structure. She pointed. "The fire station. That's where they hid it."

Gillespie regarded her silently. Then she yanked Lex's arm and began to drag her back into the estate.

Lex felt a wave of relief when she saw the heavy chains across the entrance to the fire station. They looked too strong for any cutters to break.

"So," Gillespie said, "did Booker's plan cover those locks? Got yourself a key, do you?"

When the station was operational, the tall tower attached the main building would have been used for firefighting practice. It was little more than a shell now. Anybody that did loot the building wouldn't even bother venturing up there. Its only glassless windows were at the very top of the tower.

"Booker said I was resourceful," Lex said. She pointed upwards. "I can climb."

"A regular little cat burglar." Gillespie tapped her long fingernails on a wrinkled cheek. The nails were dark red, false and peeling away to reveal the glue beneath. "Well then. You're going to get on up there after all. You're going to bring that staff to me. And then we can be the best of friends. Got it?"

Lex hoped that her expression suggested her resigned acceptance. "No funny business, though. I'll be right here watching you."

Gillespie let go of Lex's arm only when they had reached the base of the tower. She pulled the pistol from her belt.

Lex scanned the tower for a handhold. Her bluff had been called. There was no playacting being able to climb a building, but she took to the task well. Despite the threat of the Fagin below, she registered a glimmer of pleasure, deep down. Before the riots, when their parents had been alive, she and James would climb the oak tree in the garden of a holiday cottage they visited each spring. Lex had always been the better of the two of them. One day she had climbed all the way to the thinnest branches at the top and had tied James' favourite skull-and-crossbones bandana up there. He'd been furious, of course, but he hadn't let it show, acting as though he could have shimmied up to collect it whenever he liked.

She reached the roof of the main building. From there she would be able to stretch out to the nearest handhold on the tower and continue her climb.

Except that wasn't the plan.

She looked down. Six metres or so below, Gillespie gazed up, clearly impressed at her easy ascent.

Lex straightened and faced the tower, as if she was about to hop onto it.

She took a breath.

She leapt. But not towards the tower. Instead, she soared through the air, away from the building entirely.

She did her best to curl into a ball as she hit the ground. Broken glass nipped at her flesh as she rolled forward. She barrelled into Gillespie, knocking her legs from under her and making her give a wheezing shout.

Without checking whether the Fagin had recovered herself, Lex clambered to her feet and darted away, scrabbling at the corner of the fire station to pull herself around it. She ran in a zigzag pattern in case Gillespie still had hold of the pistol.

She cast about for a hiding place. She had to fight the temptation to try and outrun the Fagin. There was no telling what kind of aim the old woman had.

Planks and corrugated metal sheets that had once reinforced the entrance to a nearby house lay abandoned on its scrubby lawn. Lex dragged a sheet towards the wall of the house, propping it up at a shallow angle and then jamming it in place to be protected on one side by thorny bushes.

She rolled underneath and lay motionless, regaining the breath that had been knocked out of her by her landing. Protecting her face with one arm, Lex peered out of her hiding place.

Within seconds, Gillespie appeared at the corner of the fire station. She was nursing her left arm, which was studded with broken glass that penetrated the sleeve of her coat. In her right hand was the pistol.

The Fagin ran straight past Lex's hiding place, howling with anger.

10001 CHAPTER EIGHT

1101000 The Inspection

Ethan experienced a flash of panic as his new friends approached the mass of pupils on the high street: their heads bowed and their pace slowed until they were indistinguishable from the other children. Only a glance from Libby reassured him. She smiled briefly, alive and alert. Ethan fell into step behind her.

As they trooped past the canteen and through the main entrance, Ethan allowed himself occasional glances at the surrounding pupils. Now it seemed obvious that they weren't human. Something had always seemed off about life in Touchstone: the clockwork routines of the village's inhabitants, the too-perfect surroundings, the featureless sky. What he had mistaken for the willing obedience of his classmates had actually been simple programming, and the bots could no more break free of their routine than Ethan could decide to stop breathing.

At the thought, he placed a hand on his chest to feel his ribs rise and fall. If this wasn't reality, why *was* he breathing? He felt whole and real. His hand moved up to his cheek to feel the smooth skin. It had always puzzled him that there had been no scar from where the Mercy security guard had hit him. Perhaps there were some details missing in the sim, after all.

The crowd of pupils swept into the assembly hall. Ethan lost sight of the other prisoners and was surrounded by unfamiliar, expressionless faces. Robots. Bots. Jerky movements and chugging, simple minds. His skin prickled. He resisted an urge to run to the front of the hall and do something, *anything*, to prove to them all that he was alive in a way that they could never be. Cartwheels along the stage, perhaps. Anything that the bots wouldn't find programmed into their own memory banks.

Libby reappeared at his side. "I didn't want to leave you alone so soon after we'd found you."

The pupils settled and the hall was filled with the eerie silence of hundreds of bodies making no sound.

Three adults entered in single file. First was Miss Earnshaw, followed by the head teacher, Mr. Tooley. He wore an old-fashioned cloak that flowed about him like a black waterfall. Ethan was transfixed by the flapping fabric, now aware that its every movement had been programmed. Mr. Tooley was balding and his few strands of hair had been scraped over his shining scalp. Surely that was too specific a detail to have been invented—had he been based upon somebody in real life?

An obese woman with a pile of dark curls brought up the rear of the short procession. She appeared immediately out of place. At first Ethan put it down to her round, almost jolly face contrasting the severe expressions of the other teachers, but she was moving oddly, too. Whereas Miss Earnshaw and the head teacher walked at a steady, monotonous pace this woman scurried in fits and starts, moving swiftly despite her heavy body.

Ethan realized that Libby was watching him. "You've noticed, then?" she whispered.

He nodded, though he wasn't at all sure he knew what he *had* noticed.

"It's easiest when you see them moving," Libby continued, hiding the movement of her lips with a hand. "Or if you see into their eyes. There's no disguising the eyes."

"I don't understand."

"You asked the wrong questions earlier. What you should have asked is this: Who's watching us, to make sure we learn our lesson?"

The three adults took their places at the front of the hall. Mr. Tooley retrieved an old-fashioned fob watch from his pocket and compared it to the clock on the wall. He cleared his throat and began to speak, but Ethan's found himself watching the obese woman instead of listening to the head teacher. Her face twitched throughout Mr. Tooley's announcements about the importance of punctuality and dedication. She looked as though she was struggling to keep her mouth still. Her eyes darted around the hall as if she was searching for something.

A change in Mr. Tooley's tone of voice made Ethan suddenly alert. "I have an additional announcement, students. As is customary at this point in the school calendar, we welcome to our establishment an esteemed visitor." The heavy woman beside him rose halfway from her seat and then thudded down again. "Allow me to introduce, to those of you who have not yet had the pleasure, Mrs. Benedict of the Sub-Department of Inspections and Corrections."

"Inspections and Corrections." Ethan couldn't imagine a more unappealing combination of words. He realized that the pupils around him were clapping. He joined in just as the applause stopped.

Mrs. Benedict rose from her seat again with difficulty. "Thank you for your generous welcome, students. I have always enjoyed my visits to Touchstone High School. And I'm certain that my stay will be as pleasant and straightforward as usual." Her voice trembled and was too quiet to address such a large hall.

"However," she continued in an even lower voice. "My records indicate that there continue to be, ah, *incidents* at this school. And I think we can all agree that a life without incidents is a life to which we should aspire. My presence here is not to enforce the rules but to witness them being enforced. Above all, you must continue with your studies as usual and imagine that I am not here."

Her face, which had been slack and unmoving during her speech, came suddenly under her control. She gave a dazzling smile, displaying rows of white teeth. Once again, her eyes darted around the room. Ethan shuddered as he felt the weight of her gaze upon him.

Ethan watched Mrs. Benedict stumble into Miss Earnshaw's desk at the front of the classroom.

"Look at her, waddling like a toddler," Libby muttered. All this time, all these dreary science lessons, Libby had been sitting at the desk in front of Ethan's. He wasn't the only one who was good at blending in.

"It's weird," he replied. "As if she's not used to walking."

"Good. So, do you see it yet?"

"See what?"

"Mrs. B. Look closer."

Ethan thought of Mrs. Benedict's trembling voice as she had addressed the assembly hall. Now the heavy woman watched the pupils as they took their places. Ethan stiffened as her gaze fell upon him. Her eyes shifted around constantly.

"She's real," he said. "She's human."

Libby nodded. "What else?"

"She's never done this before. It's her first time in the sim."

Libby appeared impressed. "It took us months to figure that out. And there's more than that. That body's only an avatar. When any of the prison wardens need to appear in the sim, 'Mrs. Benedict' is pulled off the shelf, ready to be wheeled about like a remote-control car."

The idea of this friendly-looking woman being little more than a camera operated by someone entirely different made Ethan's skin prickle.

Miss Earnshaw turned to write on the blackboard. The last of the bot pupils entered the classroom, followed by Russell. After making sure that neither Miss Earnshaw nor Mrs. Benedict were watching him, Russell raised both of his middle fingers, gesturing at their backs. Ethan tensed, expecting repercussions, but nothing happened. Russell slumped into a seat several desks from his own.

Mrs. Benedict was sitting awkwardly on Miss Earnshaw's stool, engrossed in the class register. The other pupils within Ethan's field of vision were already writing in their exercise books.

"What happens if she catches someone doing something wrong?" he whispered to Libby.

"You don't want to know."

He shuddered and concentrated on his work. Under the title *Why local government matters* he copied a phrase from the blackboard: *Local government provides invaluable services, including . . .* He began a bullet-pointed list: *rubbish collection, parks and leisure services, road repairs, local police.*

A sound to his left startled him. Russell was leaning forward in his seat, arm outstretched and holding a plastic ruler. He tapped the head of the boy sitting at the desk in front of his. The boy had an eager expression and his tongue protruded from his mouth as he wrote in his exercise book. He flinched each time the ruler tapped the back of his head, but then returned to his work. How could Ethan have not realized that this boy, and all the others, were fake? The flinch was only a response to an interruption to his programmed routine, a mechanical reaction. Even so, Ethan felt sorry for him. Russell sneered and struck with the ruler again, more forcefully this time. The boy jerked and his eyelids flickered rapidly.

"Russell!" Libby hissed. "Cut it out, moron."

Russell shot a look at Libby but continued prodding at the bot's head.

"She'll catch you at it," Libby whispered.

Russell gave an exaggerated who-cares shrug.

Something blocked Ethan's view. Mrs. Benedict stood directly before his desk. "Students, what is the meaning of this commotion?" Her voice was somehow both warm and grating at the same time.

Ethan simply stared upwards at Mrs. Benedict's twitching face. He tried to force himself to look down at his exercise book. Mrs. Benedict bent forward until her huge face hung inches from his own, and Ethan felt as though he was being scanned by an enormous satellite dish.

"Have I discovered some kind of . . . troublemaker?" she said in a low voice.

Ethan's mouth moved wordlessly. He felt hypnotized by her eyes. They seemed in constant motion, even though they remained fixed on him. Something within her dark pupils shifted in a constant pattern, a suggestion of jagged peaks like the teeth of cogs. He could see the rise and fall of individual pixels—perhaps they reflected the bandwidth required to keep the prison warden within the "Mrs. Benedict" avatar. More strikingly, the movement reminded Ethan of the workings of old-fashioned clocks, full of cogs and jerky, precise movements. If he fell into those dark eyes he would be torn apart by the teeth of clockwork wheels.

Finally, Mrs. Benedict twisted to look at his exercise book. "Miss Earnshaw," she said in an expressionless tone, "please come here."

Ethan gripped the edges of the desk. Obediently, Miss Earnshaw appeared alongside the inspector.

"Look at this student's work," Mrs. Benedict said.

Miss Earnshaw moved to stand behind Ethan, looking over his shoulder. He felt hemmed in and vulnerable.

"Would you agree," Mrs. Benedict said, "that this list demonstrates good understanding of the importance of local government?"

Ethan glanced at the door, trying to judge how many steps it would take him to reach it.

"Yes," Miss Earnshaw said. "This is a very good list, Mrs. Benedict."

"Quite right. Therefore I think our young student deserves recognition, does he not?"

Ethan wasn't sure how to react. He jumped as Miss Earnshaw's hand snaked around from behind. He looked down to see that she had pinned a badge at the top of his tie. It was grey, a couple of centimetres wide, with a single word printed in yellow in the centre: MERIT.

"I understand that this is your first perk," Mrs. Benedict said. "It may be small, but keep up the good work and there will be more of them, and more valuable ones. Congratulations."

Ethan had never felt less pleased at being congratulated. The inside of his mouth felt dry and raspy.

The silence was interrupted by a snigger. Somebody coughed, not entirely masking the word "swot." Mrs. Benedict lurched to track the sound.

Russell. At that moment, Ethan could have hugged him.

Mrs. Benedict's huge head swung from side to side as she searched for the source of the interruption. She slid from Ethan's desk. After a minute of silence punctuated only by the sound of her skittering footsteps, she seemed to give up. Out of the corner of his eye, Ethan saw her settle into an empty seat before the wide window.

"Miss Earnshaw, please continue with the lesson."

The teacher came to life. She moved to the blackboard. "Draw a horizontal line in your copybooks. Now, take dictation, pupils. Romulus and Remus, sons of the god Mars, were the founders of Rome. After their birth they were abandoned in the river Tiber and were then brought up by wolves."

Russell gave a snort of laughter. Too loud. Ethan clenched his fists. "*Wolves? Are you kidding?*"

Did Russell have some kind of death wish? Ethan noticed Mrs. Benedict straighten in alertness. She was sitting almost directly behind Russell's desk.

Miss Earnshaw continued, "Ignorant of their true origins, both twins developed a large following. When they discovered the truth, they decided not to wait to inherit their mother's city. Instead, they founded a new city of their own."

Russell yawned loudly and theatrically.

Mrs. Benedict rose from her seat. Her neck swivelled again as she attempted to locate the disturbance. She was zeroing in on Russell from behind.

Ethan felt frozen to the spot. He should make some kind of distraction to force Russell to turn and see Mrs. Benedict behind him. But that would mean risking punishment himself.

Russell picked up the ruler, reached out and began to tap on the boy's head again.

Mrs. Benedict sprang forward and clamped a hand onto each of Russell's shoulders. His face blanched as he was lifted clear from his seat. His feet dangled limp, inches from the floor. Without a word, and with Russell held aloft before her, Mrs. Benedict swept jerkily out of the classroom.

As he was carried away, Russell stared at Ethan. The look in his eyes was a mixture of shock and anger.

"—a fifteen-hundred-word essay titled '*The importance of Romulus and Remus to Roman culture*,'" Miss Earnshaw continued. Her flow of speech hadn't been interrupted at all.

0 01100101 01111000 01110100 00100000 01000010 01110010 01100101 01100001 0110101

The rest of the day passed in a fog. Libby had bustled about, informing each of the other prisoners about what had happened. At lunchtime they all ate at separate tables. If Ethan hadn't already known which pupils were real and which were bots, he wouldn't have been able to tell them apart. Several times, Mrs. Benedict strode through the dining room, her head swaying like a radar dish.

The final lesson of the day was personal development with Mr. Cooper. Lean and hawk-nosed, his body was constantly tilted as if he experienced gravity in a different direction to everyone else. The lesson was dreary. Mr. Cooper lectured the class in a monotone voice, referring to a large flipchart showing a cross-section of the female body. Below the hips all of the labelled parts of the diagram were blurred and illegible, and each time Mr. Cooper made reference to any specific area his voice dropped to an inaudible mutter. Ethan felt grateful when the school PA system crackled into life, drowning out the teacher's drone.

"This is an announcement to all pupils," Mr. Tooley boomed over the crackling PA system. "Following the school bell you will all assemble beside the all-weather football pitch to receive further instructions."

Minutes later, the bell rang to signal the end of the lesson. Mr. Cooper stopped his lecture mid-flow and sat staring into empty space, as inert as a statue.

Ethan allowed the crowd of bot pupils to sweep him outside. The red sand of the all-weather pitch was dotted with pools of rainwater, as was always the case, even though it had been sunny all week. The idea that some computer programmer had deliberately designed this faulty, waterlogged pitch seemed ridiculous.

The pupils formed lines corresponding to their school years. A teacher stood at the head of each line. Once the entire school population had arrived the teachers began to stride away, perfectly in sync with one another, with their snaking lines of pupils following close behind in military formation. They trooped in silence along the school fields and towards the centre of the village.

Soon the school buildings disappeared behind the tennis courts. The pupils merged into single file on the paved pathway that ran alongside the church graveyard. For the first time, Ethan examined the gravestones. None of the engraved names were legible. The weeds and clumps of daisies grew at precisely regular intervals.

The line wound around the corner of the church, and as Ethan rounded it he saw the pupils ahead of him had come to a halt. They now made a wide half-circle in the public square before the church, facing the clock tower. Ethan took his place at one end.

Mr. Tooley and seven other teachers stood before the doors of the church. Beside the head teacher was Russell, shivering but with his shoulders raised in sullen defiance.

"Pupils," Mr. Tooley bellowed, "it is my regretful duty to inform you that one of your colleagues has been found in flagrant disobedience of the school rules. This boy's offences include—" his voice altered in tone, as if changing to a different track on a CD "—speaking up in class, taunting a fellow pupil and additional insubordinate behaviour. We are fortunate that Mrs. Benedict was able to take the matter in hand."

Perfectly on cue, the studded wooden doors to the church swung open. Mrs. Benedict appeared, blinking in the afternoon sunlight. She crossed to Russell and shoved him in the back so that he stumbled forward to stand alone in the centre of the horseshoe of pupils. Mr. Tooley and the teachers stepped forward to close the ring around him.

"Your school, and the village of Touchstone, rely on rules in order to operate efficiently, for the benefit of all," Mrs. Benedict announced. Her voice had grown in confidence since that morning. "These are rules to which we have all subscribed, and represent standards against which we will all be judged. The very fabric of our society relies upon this. Therefore, when one of us transgresses our own rules, we must decide for ourselves what is and is not acceptable."

She scanned the crowd. Ethan guessed she was searching out the human prisoners—this was all for their benefit, after all. When her eyes met Ethan's, he squirmed under the intensity of her stare.

"Let me make this clearer still," she continued. "What this boy has done is *not* acceptable. It follows that punishment is required."

Russell stood immobile in the centre of the ring. While his face was angled towards the ground his eyes were raised, giving him an almost devilish appearance. With a start, Ethan realized that Russell was staring directly at him. He knew, somehow, that Ethan could have warned him about Mrs. Benedict when she was looming behind him in the classroom. That Ethan could have prevented this punishment, whatever it was.

Russell mouthed three silent words: "Just you wait." Then he turned so that Ethan could only see his broad back.

"Not this time!" Russell shouted at Mrs. Benedict. "Not this time, you old witch!" He pushed up his sleeves to reveal muscled arms.

Mrs. Benedict watched him impassively. With slow, deliberate movements she reached into the pocket of her dark jacket and retrieved a round object that glinted in the sunlight. When she pushed at it with her thumb, part of it hinged upwards.

Despite his bravado, Russell took only a single, tentative step forward. Mrs. Benedict glanced down at the object in her hand, peering through her half-moon spectacles. It was an old-fashioned fob watch.

Russell took another step. Mrs. Benedict looked up at the clock tower. The minute hand on the huge dial was a fraction off vertical.

"No! I won't let you!" Russell lurched towards Mrs. Benedict like a coiled spring being released. His right hand was raised in a fist.

Mrs. Benedict glanced at the fob watch again. In any other context, her smile might have appeared indulgent.

Ethan gritted his teeth, waiting for Russell's fist to make contact.

But it never did. Ethan heard a soft click as the minute hand of the church clock reached the twelve o'clock position. Russell froze in mid-run. His right arm hung upright, wavering as though he were a puppet on strings. Ethan couldn't see his face. Russell's arm lowered, painfully slowly, until it dangled stiffly at his side.

"Russell Reynolds, are you quite well?" Now Mrs. Benedict's voice oozed with maternal concern.

When he finally replied, Russell's speech was slow and his words were enunciated carefully. "I am perfectly well, thank you, Mrs. Benedict."

Mrs. Benedict looked at the horseshoe of pupils, but instead of making an announcement she spoke only to Russell. "Then you may go. Your parents will oversee you and will report to me in due course."

The bot pupils began to melt away in the direction of the village shops and homes, but Ethan stayed in position. Russell turned towards the village centre too. He walked towards Ethan with light, careful footsteps. Ethan half expected the boy to thump him as he passed. Instead, Russell gave him a broad smile, though his eyes were cold and emotionless. Ethan saw a suggestion of circular motion and flickering pixels within each dark centre.

"Good afternoon, Ethan," Russell said in a flat voice. "I look forward to seeing you tomorrow morning in maths class."

Ethan felt sick with revulsion. Whoever was standing in front of him was no longer Russell. He couldn't decide whether he wanted to reassure the boy or to shake him until he returned to normal.

"Don't touch him." It was Libby's voice. "Walk away. The teachers are all watching you."

Ethan hesitated, then did as she said. They walked together towards the high street behind Russell.

"Is he a bot now?" Ethan said, whispering even though they had left the church and the teachers far behind.

"No. Worse. That Benedict woman put him on autopilot. For a couple of days, I reckon."

"But where is he? The real Russell, I mean?"

Libby sighed. They both watched Russell walking slightly ahead of them.

"He can still see and feel everything that's going on. But he can't control his own body. When they do this to you, you're still in there. Trapped. Watching through your own eyes, shouting silently in frustration. Believe me, it's torture."

1011 01111001 00100000 01100001
0010 01101001 01110100 01110100 01100101 01101110 00100000

001 00100000 01010100 01101001 01101101 00100000 01001101 0110(
010 01101111   00101110 00100000 01001100 01100001 0111
111 01110101 01110100 00100000 01100001   01100100 0010(
        01100100 01110011 01101001 01100111 01101110 00100000 0110(
        01001010 01100001 01110010 01100101 01100100 01100100 0010(
                            01110000 01101001 01110010 01101001 01110010 0110

        01110010 01110010 01101001 00100000 01110010 01110010 01110110

01000011
010

01000101 01010010 01000011

01101000   00100000 01110111
            00100000 01101000 01110101
001 00000 01101001 01101110 00100000
01100101 00100000 01100001 01101001
            00100000 01110010 01101001
01110100 01100101 01100100 00100000
        01110100 01101000 01100101
01110010 01100011   00100000
00100000 01110100 01101000 01100101
                      01110010
01100111 01101000 01110100
            01110010 01101111
            01110010 01101111

01101111 01110101 00100000 01100010
                      01110101
                      01110100

CHAPTER NINE

Cogs

MERCY.

An array of twisting, pixelated cogs crowded the screen. Circles within circles, all intermeshed.

Processing.

Processing.

The cogs grew larger and larger, accumulating pixels until the screen became entirely black.

Denied.

Lex rubbed her temples. She'd been banging her head against this virtual wall for hours, since escaping Gillespie. The Mercy portal wasn't yielding an inch. It was time to try another tactic—what James would have called the "side door." His argument was that the front portal would always be well guarded, and the back door, buried deep, is where anyone would expect a hacker to attack. But there was always a side door, a way for legitimate techs to enter safely. Techs were lazy, James said, and wouldn't stand for entering password after password. Lex's fingers tapped at the keys as she probed for some new, uncharted route. The screen filled with green text.

The wall of meshed circles reappeared, spilling beyond the edges of the monitor to suggest a vast clockwork barrier that protected the Mercy servers. Lex felt a wave of dizziness. She massaged her eye sockets with hands cold from typing.

How long had she been working? It was dark outside. She was exhausted, having spent the afternoon and evening crouched beneath the corrugated metal sheet, not daring to creep out after her brush with Gillespie.

She felt an insistent thump in her stomach. Cecil Wright's words kept returning to her: "Not in a prison cell. At least there's that." But if Ethan wasn't in prison, where was he?

Processing.

In a bleary daydream she imagined Ethan, in some remote factory, lying prone on a conveyor belt. *Processing.* A defective product to be stripped of its faulty parts, fixed, renewed. The cogs on the computer monitor became spinning whirlpools.

Denied.

Give up. Take a shower. Rest.

The mouse cursor hovered over the X in the corner of the command window.

No. Ten more minutes. Try something new.

Soon the screen was crowded with browsers. In place of the Mercy portal, the banners of tabloid news homepages and local press websites cast a red hue onto the walls of the flat.

Someone couldn't just disappear. Even Mercy couldn't remove someone from the world without trace.

Wait. There.

The *City Examiner* local news website was barely functional, its readership having dwindled to almost nothing. Whilst other sites updated hourly, the last *Examiner* post had been a week ago. But there it was: *Convictions include gated community youth.* The short article included a list of people tried in court on that day. There were fifteen in total, some teenagers but mostly adults. Ethan's name appeared at the bottom of the list. There were only names, though, no details about each conviction. Sloppy reporting. No wonder the site was going bust.

She set to work with renewed energy, directing exploratory attacks at the *City Examiner* site. Her code burrowed into crevices like rats, searching for weak spots.

Six minutes later, she was in. The security system was comically simple. James could have managed it with his eyes shut. She scrolled through files, browsing the site's internal folders. The first batch were system files. The thought crossed her mind to hack the entire site and shut it down to teach the *Examiner* a lesson about security. *No. Down, girl.* Towards the bottom of the list were a string of folders all prefixed 'Z_' to keep them arranged together alphabetically. *Z_drafts. Z_edits. Z_legal. Z_reports.*

Lex double-clicked *Z_reports.* The window filled with document titles arranged by date. She switched windows to the news article, then again to the document with the corresponding date. The text document contained the same list as the original article, with no more detail. The only difference was that at the top of this document was the Mercy logo. It wasn't much, but it was a first sniff of the correct scent. Her hands darted over the keyboard as she flicked between windows, comparing and evaluating. The report must have been emailed from somewhere within Mercy. All she had to do was follow the trail to its origin.

Time passed. It could have been an hour. It was probably more.

Bingo.

There were no spinning cogs this time but in her addled state she imagined them anyway, unmeshing and giving way with a creak, allowing her to pass. She was in.

The document filled the screen. It was almost blinding in its whiteness.

Mercy Corp. Strictly confidential.

Trials 3 Oct.

Mercy processing site Al-8. Zone 1 west.

Abramov, Sergei. Age: 48. Conviction: unauthorized dwelling, Zone 2. Representation: third-party. Sentence: 3 yr standard.

Carson, Paul L. Age: 25. Conviction: shoplifting grade C. Representation: elected proxy. Sentence: 10 yr redbrick.

The word "redbrick" made her skin prickle. She scrolled down to the end of the list.

Wright, Ethan. Age: 15. Conviction: breach of peace. Representation: nil. Sentence: Q prelim test, pending redbrick, yrs tbc.

Breach of peace was almost comical in its vagueness. Mercy obviously couldn't bear to admit, even to themselves, that she and Ethan had successfully broken into the company's own headquarters. But *Representation: nil*—that was something. A first nugget of real evidence that trials were being conducted without defence lawyers. From Mercy's point of view, defending accused parties could only slow down the system. Wouldn't it be so much more efficient to simply convict, announce the sentence and then move on to the next person?

It was far from the watertight proof she needed, but it was a sign that she was on the right track. Relief, along with fatigue, swept through her body.

Q prelim test, pending redbrick, yrs tbc. Ethan's was the only sentence that wasn't a straightforward jail term, whether in standard prisons or the high-security redbricks. *Pending redbrick, yrs tbc*. The length of Ethan's full sentence in a converted redbrick prison was *to be confirmed*.

But the phrase *Q prelim test* was the key. It must refer to Project Q, the title on the lilac folder in Cecil Wright's office. So Mercy was in the process of conducting preliminary tests into Project Q, whatever it was. Something new, something to be evaluated.

With Ethan as a guinea pig.

Her vision blurred again. This was a small victory, enough for tonight. *Take a shower. Rest.*

10001 CHAPTER TEN

1101000 Trapped

When Ethan woke, his forehead was damp with sweat. He had had awful dreams during the night. He had been trapped in a narrow room not much larger than himself. It had been almost entirely dark. The only light came from a tiny grate, through which he could see the faces of people who peered in. Libby, Kit, Lex and his parents—his real parents—had spoken to him through the grate, but he hadn't been able to say a word in reply.

Russell. The dream was about Russell. It had been two days since his punishment at the church. Two days in which he had been a prisoner in his own body. Looking out at the world from his dark cell, lacking the free will to move a single muscle.

Clattering sounds from downstairs suggested that his family was preparing breakfast. Or perhaps those sounds were merely recordings to rouse Ethan from sleep? Perhaps when he wasn't in sight the family members simply froze or even disappeared. They only existed to keep him in line.

His bedroom was dimmer than normal. Without leaving his bed he stretched up to lift a corner of the curtain. Dark clouds filled the sky, each rimmed with light. What was the phrase? Every cloud has a silver lining. Except that the lining of these clouds was more of a sickly yellow.

He had once been told that weather and differences in pressure could affect people's dreams. Maybe that was why he had slept so badly. But what *were* dreams, here in the sim? This entire world was a kind of dream. More to the point, which version of Ethan had actually been asleep—the Ethan avatar trapped in Touchstone, or the one out there in the real world, plugged into the computer? Had time actually passed since he closed his eyes, or had the virtual reality software only simulated the effects of sleep?

He shuddered and rolled out of bed. There was no use having thoughts like that. He was stuck in Touchstone and there was nothing he could do about it.

When he entered the kitchen his family was silent. His plate was already piled high with rashers of bacon. He helped himself to toast and made a sandwich; he had to admit, the bacon tasted good, even if it wasn't real.

"Hey Ethan," Greg said, snapping into fidgety movement, "whatcha think of my fort?"

Ethan glanced out of the window. Ragged planks of bare wood rose above the hedge that separated the lower and upper lawns. The fort hadn't been there yesterday. If Greg really had built it, he must have been working throughout the night.

"It's great," he replied.

"Father thinks so too," Greg said. "Isn't that right, Father?"

Ethan glanced at the imposter who called himself his father. Whoever he was, he looked thoughtful and tired. It was strange to think that a computer program could look tired.

"Father thinks so too," Greg repeated. "Isn't that right, Father?"

His father didn't react. He didn't even seem aware of the rest of them sitting around the table.

His mother cleared her throat. "It's dark this morning."

Ethan was surprised. She barely ever spoke at mealtimes, unless it was to offer more food. As far as he could see, the computer programmers were sexist and stuck in the past. When he had come downstairs he had been intent on ignoring his family as long as possible, but the uncertainty in his mother's voice made him relent. "Maybe it'll rain," he replied.

She blinked, considering the idea, as if rain was something she had heard about but never seen. "If it rained . . . would we be all right here in the house?" She looked genuinely afraid.

"Sure. You'd be all right out there too, as long as you have an umbrella."

His father spoke for the first time that morning. His loud voice made Ethan jump. "Ethan, remember that you have school today."

"I have school every day."

"And do you have an umbrella?" his mother asked.

"No. I suppose I'll get wet."

"You should take an umbrella."

"You must go to school on time."

"I *know*. I've got plenty of time. It's only—" Ethan looked up at the clock. It read a quarter to eight. "Huh. You're right—it's later than I thought. I'd better go."

"But dear," his mother said to his father in a halting voice, "he has no umbrella."

"If it rains, I will hide in my fort," Greg said gleefully. "The roof is made of tin and no rain can get in. I'll sit in my fort and I'll invent magic tricks and if you're lucky I'll let you come inside too. Do you want to come into my fort, Ethan?" Greg stood on the bench to get a better look out of the window.

"I don't have time," Ethan said. The thought of being trapped in such a small space with Greg, for any amount of time, made him shudder. He glanced at the clock again, which now read five to eight. He stuffed the rest of the bacon sandwich into his mouth and retrieved his coat from the back of the chair. He pushed past his father, who had become motionless once again.

His mother rose and smoothed her hair with shaking hands. "Go to your room, Greg. And stay out of my way. I must have time to search the house. There is an umbrella here somewhere. There must be."

Greg's bottom lip stuck out petulantly. He dropped down from the bench. To Ethan, he said, "You wait. You'll wish you had a fort when you see mine."

Ethan actually gasped at the spite in the young boy's voice.

Greg ran at full pelt towards the kitchen door. Ethan winced, expecting a crunch of impact, but Greg simply kept running, melting into the surface of the door as if there were nothing there. The thump of his footsteps came from the staircase beyond.

Neither parent had noticed. His father was studying a newspaper that Ethan was certain hadn't been there a moment ago. His mother paced in circles around the breakfast debris.

1010100   01100101   01111000   01110100   00100000   01000010   01110010   01100101   01100001   01

After school Ethan climbed the hill to the clearing beyond the copse. He found Miller and Anita sitting on tree stumps, their heads bent in conversation. As Ethan approached, Anita jerked and stared up at him, startled. Miller smirked.

There were no other stumps so Ethan sat cross-legged on the ground. Anita looked as though she might be about to speak, but after a glance from Miller she clamped her lips together. Ethan shuffled in discomfort, then busied himself experimenting with leaning against the invisible wall of the skybox.

He was grateful when Kit and Libby entered the copse. Not for the first time, he noticed something strange about Kit's movements. He walked hesitantly, stumbling occasionally and knocking against the branches of trees. It reminded Ethan of Mrs. Benedict.

Libby raised an eyebrow at the sight of the three of them sitting silently. "If I knew this was going to be a party, I'd have brought a cake."

"Sod off, Lib," Anita said.

"Oh, come on. Sulking isn't going to help Russell."

Ethan's attention remained on Kit, who walked on the spot for a few moments after he came to a halt, giving the strange impression that his actions and his forward movement were unrelated.

"All we can do is wait," Kit said. "We all know what Russell's going through, and it's awful, but there's nothing we can do." He sat down with some difficulty.

Anita glanced at Miller. "Maybe not. But there's somebody who could've stopped him being punished in the first place." She let the statement hang in the air.

Ethan felt his cheeks glow. It was fair enough that he was being accused.

"That's nonsense," Libby said. "You should have seen the way Russell was carrying on in class. He's got a death wish. Don't ask me why, but it's as though he *wanted* to be caught."

"That doesn't sound like Russell to me," Miller said, oozing fake concern. "Not our Russell Reynolds, full of life and energy." He jabbed a finger at Ethan. "What's your take on this, new boy?"

Ethan gulped. He was certain his glowing face broadcast his guilt. He began to stammer. "I don't know. I don't know how Russell feels, really."

"Well I can fill in the details for you, noob. Right now Russell feels angrier than ever before. Except you'd never know it to look at him, of course. The poor thing. Suffering." He seemed to enjoy the way the final word sounded: he repeated it, enunciating each syllable carefully. "*Suffering.*"

"Don't be cruel, Miller," Libby said.

Anita was on her feet now. "It's not cruel, it's true! I saw Russell at lunchtime. He was sitting on a bench, staring out at the field, looking at nothing in particular. But when he looked at me, I swear I could see the real Russell there, deep down in his eyes. I could tell he wanted to shout out, jump up, *anything*. But he only smiled at me and answered my questions with 'yes' or 'no.'"

The worst of it was that Ethan agreed. He had been in classes with Russell for the last couple of days, but Russell had paid him no more attention than any of the bot pupils. He'd been attentive and helpful in each lesson, answering questions that Ethan was sure the real Russell couldn't have answered. Yesterday, he had even sat with Ethan in the canteen at lunchtime and offered him his unopened bag of crisps. In short, he had been unrecognizable.

Anita glared at Ethan. "I think he was tricked."

"Don't be an idiot," Kit said. "It's Russell's own fault and nobody else's. He's been in a self-destructive mood for weeks. It's like he's given up." Kit struggled to his feet but his legs buckled abruptly. Ethan rushed to grab him by the waist before he fell, but he waved Ethan away, scowling. In a strained voice he said, "I'm fine. Leave it. I'm fine."

Ethan saw that Libby was watching Kit with a worried expression. Miller and Anita appeared not to have noticed his stumble.

"If I was Russell," Miller said in a deliberate, thoughtful tone, "I'd be very upset with anyone that might have anything to do with me being punished." He swung his rucksack onto his shoulders. Then, brighter, he continued, "But I suppose we'll have to wait until he's released to find out, hey?"

1010100 01100101 01111000 01110100 00100000 01000010 01110010 01100101 01100001 01

The next morning, the sickly yellow sky, and the fact that Ethan was in a rush, made everything feel slightly off. The postlady looked a little more unsteady than usual on her ascent of the hill towards Ilkley Grove. A single pale ham had been laid on the fake grass display in the window of the butchers. Ethan was surprised at his sense of relief when the red saloon car, minibus and taxi passed him as usual as he walked along Rectory Road. At least they were dependable. He hurried through the village centre.

At the church he slowed when he recognized the person standing before its doors. Mrs. Benedict surveyed the stream of pupils impassively, then looked up at the clock tower. The doors of the church opened automatically to allow her entry. Ethan stifled a shudder at the woman's strange gliding motion and was thankful when the doors swung smoothly closed behind her. He prayed that it signalled the exit of Mrs. Benedict—or rather, the Mercy employee who operated her—from the sim.

In the graveyard behind the church he came across a group of pupils standing in a huddle, and kept his distance until he recognized Kit, Libby, Miller and Anita.

"What's going on?"

Libby and Anita parted to reveal Russell in the centre of the circle. His eyes were rimmed with purple. He looked desperately tired.

"He's just come back, ten minutes ago," Libby said.

Ethan tried not to show his anxiety. "Are you okay?"

When Russell didn't reply Ethan wondered if Libby might be mistaken, that he was still on autopilot. Finally, he spoke in a cracked, dry voice. "I'm not *okay*, no. You wouldn't have lasted a day in my position, trapped like . . ." He tailed off. His hands clenched into fists.

"He says you ratted on him," Anita said with a trace of delight.

Russell's dark eyes were fixed on Ethan. "Yeah, he did this to me. It should have been him being punished, the bloody sneak."

"So, did you? Did you do Russell in?" Miller's tone was more amused than accusing, but when he addressed the others his face was a picture of concern. "We should watch out for this one. If Ethan can do this to Russell, he might do the same to any of us."

"I didn't do anything!" Ethan protested. "I just . . . Mrs. Benedict was right there. There was nothing I could do. I was scared."

"Oh, you were scared, were you?" Miller scoffed. "Well that's all right then."

Abruptly, Russell sprang towards Ethan. Libby and Anita clutched at his arms and Kit dived to put himself between the two boys. Miller stepped to one side. Ethan couldn't tell whether it was to avoid getting hurt himself, or to give Russell more room to attack.

"We don't have time for this," Kit hissed. "Do I have to remind you that we're right beside the school grounds?"

"Yeah. My geography class is calling to me. Yeesh." Anita twisted her hair and affected a look of boredom. A sly look appeared on her face. "Maybe you guys can settle this argument later, in the forest."

Ethan shuddered. Would he really be expected to fight Russell? He'd be pounded into the ground. He would have no chance of defending himself against the older boy's strength.

Russell reluctantly allowed himself to be led towards the school by Miller and Anita. Libby and Kit hung back with Ethan.

"He'll get over it," Libby said.

"I guess."

They plodded in silence. Ethan couldn't bear it. He wanted to fill his mind with something other than the prospect of a beating delivered by Russell. As he stared at the ground, a series of jagged cracks in the pavement reminded him of the disconnected roads on the map of Touchstone.

"Hey Kit, I wanted to ask you something. Why is it that the different parts of the village don't fit together? It's as if there are bits missing, all over the place."

Kit grinned. "I'm glad you asked, because I happen to know the answer. Remember Russell calling this place a video game? He's more right than he realizes. It was built for leisure, once upon a time. Ever wonder why everything's so green and pleasant here? It was designed for families to come and take their holidays. A controlled environment where everyone was safe."

"Why would they do that?" Ethan said. "Why not go somewhere nicer in the real world?"

Libby laughed. "When was the last time you went on holiday? Abroad, that is."

The idea of Ethan's parents leaving home, even for a short time, was unimaginable. His dad worked almost every day. He shrugged.

"Right, and it's not only you. With fuel prices the way they are, nobody goes abroad these days. So sims were built to give rich-but-not-crazy-rich families a way to take a wild holiday without having to travel."

"But this isn't wild. It isn't even abroad. It's just a dull English village."

"Yeah, you're not wrong," Kit said. "But someone must have appreciated it, I guess. There were other more exotic sims than this, mind you. Tropical paradises, Wild West towns, moonbases, you name it. But as for this place . . . you can put it down to nostalgia. I suppose some people found it easier to relax in a weird artificial simulation of the sort of place they grew up in than on a sun-drenched beach."

"It's pretty hard to imagine feeling relaxed in Touchstone."

"Well, it wasn't called Touchstone back then, for a start. The reason this place feels so cobbled together is that it *is* cobbled together. The developers made quick and dirty changes. A few tweaks here and there, snipping out bits of the code. It was supposed to be a town, not a village, twice the size it is now. There was an outdoor swimming pool, a cinema, all sorts of stuff. I bet it was all right."

"So why did they do all this?" Increasingly, Ethan felt stupid and slow.

"As far as I can tell, it happened in stages. Maybe those rich-but-not-crazy-rich families turned out not to be so nostalgic after all, and didn't take to the place. Or maybe they weren't quite rich enough, once the riots forced most of them to abandon their property. Either way, this sim wasn't popular with guests, so stage two was to make it into something more appropriate. A museum. School kids would show up here to learn about the good old days when the baker always said hello and everybody had their own flock of sheep, that sort of thing."

"And then they adapted it again, as a prison for us."

"Exactly. We're in stage three. Somewhere along the line, somebody decided this sim was suitable for teaching us a thing or two about behaviour and manners."

A thought struck Ethan. "How do you know all this, anyway?"

"It's all there, if you know where to look. All I—"

Libby held up a hand. "Hey, keep it down for a second. Do you hear that?"

A whining sound carried across the school fields. As they approached, Ethan recognized it as a broadcast over the PA system.

"—to announce that this afternoon we will be holding our monthly sports day," Mr. Tooley's voice boomed. "All pupils will assemble on the school fields directly after lunch."

Libby and Kit groaned.

"What's so bad about a sports day?" Ethan asked.

Kit was disconsolate. "You'll see soon enough."

01000110 01111001 00100000 10011110 1101

0010 01101001 01110100 01110100 01100101 01101110 00100000

001 00100000 01010100 01101001 01101101 00100000 01001101 01100

010 01101111   00101110 00100000 01001100 01100001 0111

111 01110101 01110100 00100000 01100001   01100100 00100

01110011 01101001 01100111 01101110 00100000 01100

01001010 01100001 01110010 01100101 01100100 00100

01110000 01101001 01110010 0110

01101110 01100001 01110010 01101001

01000011

0101

01000101 01010010 01000011

01101000   00100000 01110111

00100000 01101000 01110101

01101001 01101110 00100000

01100101 00100000 01100001 01101001

00100000 01110010 01101001

01110100 01100101 01100100 0010000

01110100 01101000 01100101

01110010 01100011   0010000

00100000 01110100 01101000 01100101

0111001

01100111 01101000 0111010

01110010 01101111

01101111 01110101 00100000 0110001

0111010

0111010

01100110

CHAPTER ELEVEN

CHAPTER ELEVEN

Project Q

Lex spent another day in a sunlight-less blur. Her mole code burrowed through the internet, collecting clues from news services, internal reports and emails, sniffing out references to Mercy initiatives and anything that might relate to Project Q. As the code chugged away she concentrated on another terminal running an image editor.

The mole finished its task at the same moment that she completed her fake ID. She printed the results onto thick card and hung it on a white string beside the monitor.

Drawing upon the mole's new findings, she typed up her notes so far in the hope that a conclusion might leap out at her.

Project Q / Q prelim test

Direct government funding. £20m+

Extent of Gov. involvement = financing / identification of problem. Problem = young, repeat offenders.

2 yrs ago: Gov. call for proposals.

Successful bid = Mercy. Test phase this yr, rollout next yr.

Project linked to concern about prisons? Courtroom trial process becoming faster and faster, so more prisoners than ever before. Therefore running out of cell space to house them all.

Initial emphasis of project = rehabilitation of offenders to relieve pressure on prisons.

Emphasis changed over time? Hints at more than rehabilitation? Mercy employee emails refer to 2 benefits:

i) Educating offenders, ready to reintroduce them to society

ii) Saving space & costs per prisoner

Lex scrolled up and down the page, puzzling over the information. How could a project that aimed to re-educate young offenders save the government money? Surely there had to be classrooms and tutors on top of the usual costs of food and accommodation for each prisoner. She flicked through the windows containing data the mole had dredged from its sources. She must have missed something.

References to food cost. Savings, but how?

Mention of "nutrient feed." No more prepared food?

This was becoming stranger and more sinister all the time.

Odd reference in Mercy email. Junior employee discussing "the process." Says she has been through it herself. Nutrient feed = "delicious." Casual tone, joking.

Mention of size of room (why not "cell"?) needed. 10 square metres for every 8 prisoners.

That couldn't possibly be right. She tried to picture the size of the cell. It was smaller than the living space of her tiny flat. How could eight prisoners be held in a room that small?

Staff required: 2 skilled

Prison wardens required: 0 permanent roles, 1 transient

What kind of prison didn't require any prison wardens? Whatever it was, Mercy believed that they had designed a prison so cheap to run and requiring so little space that it would solve all of the problems of overcrowding. The government would be delighted.

She scoured the mole's files once more but could find no more useful details. She'd reached the limit of what she could achieve by hacking. It was time to go out into the daylight again.

CHAPTER TWELVE

Sports Day

The PE teacher, Mr. Jeffers, announced through a megaphone that cross-country running would be the first event. Bot pupils came forward at once, eager to participate. Ethan felt somebody push him from behind. It was Miss Earnshaw. She gave him an encouraging smile.

He waited at the starting line on the playing field. Four other boys and five girls joined him, all bots. Standing beside him was the young-looking boy who had been teased by Russell.

Ethan scanned the crowd of onlookers at the tennis courts for Kit, who gave a subtle thumbs-up sign.

Ethan had never met Mr. Jeffers before. Perhaps he spent his days skulking around the sports hall—Ethan's school schedule included no PE lessons. He wore a blue baseball cap that matched his tracksuit, and his face was lined and weathered, as if to demonstrate how much time he spent outdoors squinting into the sunshine. In contrast, his white trainers were spotlessly clean.

"I want a good, fair race," Mr. Jeffers shouted. He swung his whistle on its string as he marched up and down before the waiting contestants. "The entire track is marked with yellow cones, a two-mile route exactly. Anyone who oversteps the line of cones will receive a penalty. Anyone pushing or using foul play will also receive a penalty. Understood?"

Ethan made a mental note to pay careful attention to the route. He didn't want to find out what a penalty involved.

Mr. Jeffers raised an arm. "Ready!"

The runners lowered themselves into their starting positions.

"Steady! Go!" Mr. Jeffers' arm dropped and he blew his whistle for good measure.

They set off, swiftly arranging themselves into a line to take the first bend. Ethan kept to the middle of the pack. The yellow plastic cones made a wide loop to the other side of the football field, beyond the tennis courts and towards the overgrown, weed-filled edges of the lower field.

Ethan didn't care where the route took him. He relished the cold air that stung his cheeks and whistled past his ears. His long legs pounded the ground as regularly as clockwork. Most sports filled him with anxiety—they usually quickly became bad-tempered grudge matches or outright fights—but he had always been good at running. For the first time since he had arrived in Touchstone his body felt uninhibited.

When Ethan had been younger, once a week he and his dad would visit the park within their Gates. Ethan always challenged his dad to a race around the perimeter of the park and he always won. When had his dad no longer needed to slow down on the last stretch to allow him to pass? Maybe only during the last few years. But one time his dad had made excuses about not having time to go to the park, and they hadn't raced each other since.

There were only two pupils ahead of Ethan now, a red-haired boy and a tall girl whose shoulder-length plaits swung as she ran. How far around the course were they? Perhaps a mile, half of the route already. He felt a swell of pride that he hadn't yet felt any of the discomfort of a long run. He wished the spectators gathered at the tennis courts were able to see down here into the lower field.

There was no reason why he shouldn't be able to overtake those last two runners. That would show the other prisoners, as well as all those teachers programmed to have such low opinions of him. He filled his lungs with cold air as his legs pounded faster and faster. He passed the red-haired boy, who didn't even acknowledge his presence.

It took another hundred metres to reach the lead girl. There, the route wound into the long grass at the edge of the field. Ethan had to squint to make out the yellow markers obscured by reeds and brambles, and he made sure not to overstep any of them as the grass whipped at his bare legs. When he reached the girl she turned to look at him. It was the same bot who always said hello to him at the end of the high street each morning. Her arms looked thin in her baggy sports kit and her eyes were almost hidden by her dark fringe. For the first time, Ethan noticed how pretty she was; he wondered again if real people had acted as templates for the bots. His pace faltered. Then he lowered his head and accelerated, feeling almost apologetic about overtaking the girl.

The route led him out of the long grass. Now there was nothing before him but an open field dotted with yellow markers. He felt more alive than he had since he had arrived in Touchstone—even more alert, he realized, than he had been the night he and Lex had broken into Mercy's HQ. He glanced over his shoulder. The boy and girl who had previously been in the lead were now lagging at a comfortable distance. The other runners were specks in the distance.

He wouldn't raise his arms in triumph when he crossed the finish line. Instead, he would impress everyone by remaining cool and calm, as if he enjoyed this sort of triumph all the time. He grinned. Only a quarter of a mile left. He wasn't even out of breath.

Gradually he became aware that the rushing of air on his face had lessened. The flowers that dotted the hedge to his right were no longer streaks of colour. He looked down. His feet thudded on the ground as easily as before, yet his pace had definitely slowed.

He sensed someone approaching from behind. The red-haired boy was close, staring impassively ahead. Ethan tried his best to accelerate. His lungs were full of air, his breathing came easily and his limbs felt strong, but despite all this, he couldn't break away from his pursuer. Instead, he lost even more ground. The red-haired boy was now at his shoulder. Ethan pushed hard but could tell that he was still decelerating. The boy swept past, producing a rush of air. Despite his best efforts, Ethan dropped back more and more until other runners passed him. The girl with the dark fringe was now in fifth place but, compared to his speed, she ran at an incredible pace.

Another girl, who had until recently been only a dot in the distance, passed him. She was wheezing and one of her legs swung with a strange loping motion, and yet she was able to run far faster than Ethan, as well. What was happening? How could he suddenly be performing so badly?

Of course. In his excitement and enjoyment, he had almost forgotten where he was. Or more importantly, *what* he was. This wasn't really his body. He had no idea what his avatar was capable of, physically. His body was computer code, a simulation of his real self. That simulation, that computer code, was in the hands of Mercy's prison wardens. And they wanted to teach him a lesson.

His pace slowed even more, but this time is was due to his sense of defeat. Another runner struggled past him up the hill to the final stretch. Now Ethan was in ninth place. He slowed to a jog, then to little more than walking pace. A plump boy approached from behind, panting with exertion.

"Hi. Nice to meet you," Ethan said. "Why don't you go on and I'll bring up the rear?"

The boy didn't react. His heavy feet thudded on the ground as he staggered on.

As he watched the boy lumbering ahead of him, Ethan felt a sharp pain in his stomach. A stitch? No, he was barely exerting himself anymore. The pain bloomed and grew in intensity as it reached his chest. This wasn't normal. He came to a standstill. The pain became a severe buzzing ache and his arms shook as if he was being electrocuted.

This pain had nothing to do with his fitness. He thought again of the prison wardens. They were doing this to him. But why?

He grimaced as the buzzing sensation reached his head. In his confusion, he stumbled a few steps forward. The pain lessened momentarily, then returned with greater intensity when he stopped again. Tentatively, he walked a few steps and the pressure in his head subsided enough for him to think clearly. He broke into a jog. His mind cleared and the pain was now restricted only to his limbs and chest.

This was the lesson that he was being taught. He wouldn't be allowed to win the race, despite his best efforts—but neither would he be allowed to give up. As long as he remained in last place, the pain would continue. A terrifying thought crossed his mind. If the race finished and he lost entirely, what punishment would he receive?

He had wasted several minutes. Though it was clear that the overweight boy before him was still struggling, he was already far ahead. Ethan took a gulp of breath and ran.

He watched the grass slip slowly beneath his feet. The pain now centred in his chest. It felt as though his ribs were being pushed together by some external force. He was dimly aware that the yellow markers had taken him around the corner of the lower field. This must be the final stretch of the race. He heard applause as the first runners crossed the finish line.

It wasn't all that far. He had to keep going at all costs.

More spectators had gathered on the slopes to watch the race. Their applause was polite and equally enthusiastic for each contestant. Mr. Jeffers stood at the finish line with the head teacher and Miss Earnshaw, his whistle and stopwatch raised. At a distance halfway between Ethan and the finish line was the overweight boy, the only other contestant still running. Ethan's legs were weak from exertion. The pain in his stomach began to spread once again into his limbs. He felt lightheaded and sick.

He told himself to stop looking up. Just one more push.

The applause became a background hum that merged with the buzzing in his head. His muscles strained but he was still moving terribly slowly.

The whistle blew. The spectators clapped politely. The pain in Ethan's stomach disappeared abruptly. Strength returned to his limbs and his pent-up energy sent him toppling to the ground. As he fell, he saw the plump boy cross the finish line behind him, a look of resignation on his red, puffy face.

Mr. Jeffers bent down to Ethan.

"A valiant effort. Perhaps, with more application, you will do better next time. But in reward for your efforts, take these coloured shoelaces."

Ethan gazed up at the smiling, weathered face and held out his hand to accept the gift. He nodded weakly at the teacher.

Lesson learned.

0   01100101   01111000   01110100   00100000   01000010   01110010   01100101   01100001   0110101

"So you get it now?" Kit said.

He and Ethan sat leaning against the wire fence of the tennis courts, facing the all-weather pitch.

"I get it. They're determined to put us in our place. That's why the lessons are full of droning nonsense. We absorb it and repeat it to the teachers, even though it doesn't make any sense. And that's why we can't win any of the sports events, but we aren't allowed to lose either."

"You're a quick learner."

"And so the idea isn't to teach us anything in particular. It's to make us obedient."

"Yep. Not much different to the bots, except the bots can only exist here in the sim. Although Mercy isn't only keen on punishments." He pointed down at the rainbow-coloured shoelaces that Ethan clutched in his right hand. He laughed. "In theory they're supposed to be tempting us with carrots as well as beating us with a stick. Do your chores and you'll be rewarded with perks. Perform well in school, get some perks. It doesn't count for much, but I guess it gives a weird sense of achievement. There's no telling how long we'll be stuck here, so it all matters." As he spoke his fingertips rubbed a badge pinned to the inside of his lapel. Like the one Ethan kept in the pocket of his jacket, it was engraved with the word *MERIT*.

Ethan felt sudden concern for Kit. Despite his cynicism, the way he stroked the badge told a different story. Surely nobody could feel that the trivial perks were worth anything? Perhaps Kit had been in the sim long enough to start getting worn down.

As if he was able to read Ethan's thoughts, Kit said thoughtfully, "People end up going one of two ways to survive. Either you find something within yourself to hang on to, or—"

"Or you lash out at everyone, like Russell." Ethan raised himself from the grass bank to search for Russell, but he was nowhere to be seen. He noticed Miller sitting at the foot of the bank, twirling a grass stalk in thoughtful silence.

They watched the bot pupils laying out yellow markers on the pitch.

"I don't know whether I'd have managed on my own," Ethan said. "I'm glad you all found me. Thanks, Kit-Car."

"Nobody calls me that really."

"It suits you."

Kit cleared his throat. "Looks like the high jump is next up. I wonder who they'll pick on this time?"

Each of the events so far had involved a single human prisoner. Anita had attempted the hurdles. Although she was tall, she had knocked over several hurdles and had come fifth, a perfectly average attempt. Kit had taken part in the two-hundred-metre race. He had looked uncomfortable from the start, limping as though he had struggled through a marathon already. He had yelled in exertion during the final stretch to achieve eighth place, only fractionally ahead of two of the most unfit-looking children that Ethan had ever seen.

The high jump apparatus had appeared at the centre of the all-weather pitch. Ethan hadn't noticed anyone carrying the thick landing mats which now lay three deep. Perhaps they had appeared when no humans were looking.

"Oh no," Kit muttered. "This isn't going to be pretty."

A group of four pupils had assembled at the far end of the pitch, performing warm-up stretches. Among them was Russell. His thick arms bulged from the sleeves of his shirt. He was staring along the length of the pitch, but Ethan couldn't tell if he was looking at the high jump apparatus, at the crowd or at Ethan himself.

Mr. Jeffers was instructing the contestants, too far away for Ethan to hear. Then the teacher retreated to stand beside the bar of the high jump. The contestants formed a line. At Mr. Jeffers' signal the first girl set off at a sprint, her gangly legs taking immense strides. At the take-off line she propelled herself upward, her trailing foot tucked in so that she sailed comfortably above the bar. The crowd applauded and the girl rolled off the mat to take her place at the end of the line. She showed no signs of satisfaction at her attempt.

A sporty-looking boy traced an almost identical path through the air as the first girl. Then it was Russell's turn.

Ethan and Kit watched in tense silence as Russell sized up the high-jump bar. He lurched forward, but even as he ran his eyes were fixed on Ethan's. His upper lip curled. He reached the take-off point and launched himself upwards. The bar clattered onto the gravel as Russell hit the mat, landing flat on his back.

The crowd applauded again, with no more or no less enthusiasm as they had had for the attempts of the other contestants. Russell plodded to the end of the line with his shoulders raised.

"I can hardly stand to watch," Kit said.

The final bot contestant was a stout girl, though she jumped with grace equal to the others. Miss Earnshaw and Mr. Jeffers moved to either end of the metal bar. It disappeared, then reappeared several inches higher. The first two contestants had second attempts, each barely clearing the bar.

When it came to his turn, Russell rolled his neck and bent to stretch each leg. In normal circumstances, his added strength would have made him a stronger contender than any of the three bot contestants. It must be unbearable to him that the programming of his avatar stopped him from competing normally.

Without warning, he burst into full speed. He raced in a wide arc past Ethan and Kit, each of his paces worth two of Ethan's own. He leapt and, once again, the bar hit the ground with a clang. Russell hit the mat face first, then rolled off in a single fluid movement. He thumped the mat with his fist, then roared, staring up at the sky with his hands on his hips. He glared at Mr. Jeffers sullenly but took his place at the end of the line of contestants.

The final girl cleared the jump easily, pogoing from the floor to sail over the bar. The bar teleported to a position a few inches higher. The tall girl launched well but then nicked the bar with her back foot. When she rolled off the mat she glanced down at the fallen metal bar without any hint of disappointment. The sporty boy made exactly the same mistake and simply strolled away into the crowd.

Russell remained motionless even when Mr. Jeffers blew his whistle. His neck rolled again and Ethan saw his lips move, though he couldn't hear the words. Then he lowered himself into a starting position. He began running at a slow, loping pace, but by the time he reached the take-off point his strides were immensely long. Ethan saw the muscles on his back leg grow taut as he jumped.

Ethan waited for the clatter of the metal bar.

Russell's back arched and he sailed over the bar in a graceful arc, clearing it with inches to spare. He landed squarely on both feet, bouncing lightly on the mat with the momentum of his jump. He looked up at the bar.

No applause came from the crowd of spectators. The only sound Ethan heard was Kit's sharp intake of breath. Even Russell, having come to rest on the mat, seemed unsure what to do next.

Ethan looked to the far end of the pitch where the final bot contestant waited. The stout girl wavered, then began walking along the field, leaving the all-weather pitch and the school buildings behind.

"What on earth happened?" Ethan whispered.

Kit didn't reply. His attention was fixed on Mr. Jeffers, who hadn't yet reacted to Russell's successful jump.

The teacher stepped towards Russell. His voice cut through the silence. "A valiant effort. Perhaps, with more application, you will do better next time. But in reward for your efforts, take this school cap." A soft hat, the same colour as his own baseball cap, appeared in his hands. He placed it carefully on Russell's head.

Russell was nonplussed. His eyes scanned the crowd, and at first Ethan thought he was seeking him out. But the shaven-headed boy was looking elsewhere, towards the foot of the grassy bank. Ethan followed his gaze to see Miller standing slightly apart from the rest of the pupils.

It was the first time Ethan had seen Miller look happy.

0011 011 1001 00100110 00100000 011 0 1100
0010 01101001 01110100 01110010 01100101 01101110 00100000
1001 00100000 01010100 01101001 01101101 00100000 01001101 0110
1010 01101111   00101110 00100000 01001100 01100001 0111
1111 01110101 01110100 00100000 01100001   01100100 0010
011 011 01101001 01100111 01101110 00100000 0110
01001010 01100001 01110010 01100101 01100100 0010
01110000 01101001 01110010 01110010 0010 0110
011 01001 01110010 01111001

0100001
010

01000101 01010010 01000011

01101000   00100000 01110111
00100000 01101000 01110101
00100000 01101001 01101110 00100000
01100101 00100000 01100001 01101001
00100000 01110010 01101001
01110100 01100101 01100100 00100000
00100000 01110100 01101000 01100101
01110010 01100011   00100000
00100000 01110100 01101000 01100101
01110010
01100111 01101000 01110100
01110010 01101111

01101111 01110101 00100000 01100001
01110010

01100110
C11AP1EO

10001 CHAPTER THIRTEEN
1101000 An Interview with Mercy

"State your name and purpose."

"Karen McAdam. Journalist, *City Enquirer*." Lex held up the fake ID and smiled at the camera as sweetly as she could manage.

She prayed she wasn't making a mistake. Was it suicidal to return to Mercy's HQ? Even though the press entrance was on the opposite side of the building to the main entrance, she felt an uneasy sense of déjà vu. Above and to her right she could see the vent from which she had jumped. She only hoped that Mercy hadn't been able to identify her from the CCTV footage of the break-in.

The jacket she wore had belonged to her mother. It was a little threadbare and missing its lowest button. Would it pass muster? She had no idea what journalists—*proper* journalists—wore. The jacket was crumpled too. She had kept it stashed in her bag for most of the journey, not wanting to draw attention to herself within the Innards.

She hadn't wanted to give the gangs any reason to identify her as anything out of the ordinary.

The speaker grille she was speaking to was fixed to the wall above a small brass plaque engraved with the words, *Mercy Corporation, Corporate Affairs*. It crackled again. "Please answer the question. State your purpose."

"I'd like to speak to someone about Mercy's new initiatives for young offenders."

"We don't have any statements to make at this time. Please move along."

"Who am I speaking to?"

No sound came from the speaker for a few seconds. "Please move along."

Lex made an exaggerated what-a-shame expression. "Okay, okay, I'm going. I suppose I'll have to do some vox pops on the streets. Maybe someone out there has heard something about Project Q." She turned on her heel and strode along the paved pathway.

Four steps. Five. *Don't turn around.*

A click came from behind. The speaker crackled into life. "Please enter, Miss McAdam. The door is unlocked." The voice was louder than before, with a suggestion of alarm. Lex returned to the entrance. A thought flashed through her mind: if only James were here to see this. This was top-notch journalism.

The lobby was large and plain, lacking any furniture other than an unmanned counter. Daylight streamed through long windows patterned with yellow and red glass, giving the room something of the feel of a chapel.

"Please continue along to the press room," the voice said, clearer now.

Lex couldn't see any speakers on the walls. She entered a corridor beside the counter. The first door along it was labelled *PRESS ROOM*. After a moment's hesitation she continued walking along the corridor. The next door was marked *STAFF ONLY*. She gave it a light push. Locked.

"Please return to the press room," the voice said. There must be hidden cameras. Lex performed a pantomime of confusion before doubling back.

The door to the press room opened at a touch. Two red sofas lined adjoining walls decorated with framed cuttings of news reports.

She scanned the headlines, which included *Government Announces Turnaround in Riot Crisis* and *New Justice Measures Reduce Sentencing Wait.*

"A representative will join you momentarily," the disembodied voice said.

Thirty seconds later, the door opened. A man emerged. His pale grey suit was wide at the shoulders, making his torso appear unnaturally square. He was young, no more than five years older than Lex herself. Handsome too, in a straight-laced sort of way. His face was long and his eyes were the shape of almonds.

"Matthew Solomon." He extended his hand. Silver cufflinks reflected the white of the strip light.

"Karen McAdam." Lex felt a strong intuition that she wasn't the only person using a false name. "From the *City Enquirer.*"

"A wonderful publication."

Lex almost laughed. Was there a trace of irony?

"Please, do take a seat."

She perched on one of the red sofas, tucking her legs to the side. She couldn't get used to wearing a skirt. Matthew sat at a right angle to her. He splayed one arm out, but his casual body language was undermined by his fingers tapping against the seat back. Was it a sign of impatience, or nervousness?

"So, Miss McAdam. To what do we owe the pleasure of your visit?"

"I've been doing some snooping." She noticed his tight smile and added, "Just asking around. I'm doing a piece about the riots. How they started, the initial reaction of the government and Mercy's more recent initiatives."

The fingers stopped tapping.

"It's more of a 'people piece' than anything," she said hurriedly, "about folks leaving their homes due to the riots. The factual stuff is mainly for background detail. It's what our readers want to hear about. The human angle." She leaned forward. "We really have no choice. Don't tell anyone I told you, but the *Examiner*'s circulation is down fifty percent. Now we have to cater to the interests of the readers we have left."

This seemed to satisfy Matthew. His fingers drummed on the fabric again. "I understand. So how can I help? Mercy's involvement is well documented, as I'm sure you're aware."

"It is? I suppose so. I'm new at the *Enquirer*, you see. I only graduated six months ago."

Matthew's eyes flicked down—perhaps he was reconsidering her age—then returned to meet her eyes.

"So I need to do some catching up," Lex continued, "and I thought to myself, why not go straight to the people who understand the riots best of all? I do hope I'm not wasting your time."

"Of course not! Anything we can do to aid the press is valuable work." But his expression betrayed his true feelings. Yes, she absolutely was wasting his time. She'd have to get to the point soon, or she'd lose his attention entirely.

"I'm being overly modest, probably. I guess I have a decent understanding about the trials. What's most interesting to me is looking to the future. What's in store? I'd love the article to include a few details about the improvements Mercy is hoping to make. More police on the ground, even smoother sentencing and trials, Project Q and rehabilitation, public outreach, all that sort of thing." She watched him carefully, noticing his eyes widen for a fraction of a second. "Did I say something wrong?"

"Wrong? No." He gave a broad grin. Too broad to be believable.

"It's Project Q, isn't it? Sorry, I knew I shouldn't have listened to them."

"To whom?"

"Street kids. I was out canvassing for opinions. Fat lot of good it did me, though. I thought it sounded stupid. I guess they were just trying to feed me a story that came across as super-top-secret!"

Matthew laughed, but his eyes were cold. "I'm sure that's the case. Tell me, Miss McAdam . . . would you know where to find these children again?"

"Oh, I'm sure I could, with a little digging. And I intend to, to give them a piece of my mind!"

"There'll be no need for that." He wiped his hands carefully on the fabric of his trousers. "Miss McAdam. May I call you Karen? I'm going to tell you something. I hope you will appreciate that I am doing so in strict confidence."

Lex allowed herself to show the delight she genuinely felt. "A scoop?"

"Perhaps, but all in good time. I'm going to make a suggestion,

Karen. A business offer, if you will. Project Q is a term with which I'm familiar—"

Lex clapped her hands together. "Wait until the folks in the office hear about this!"

"No, Karen. Your colleagues mustn't hear anything about this. And of course, that goes for your readers too. What I am suggesting is an offer of an exclusive story. But in exchange for exclusivity, you must agree not to report on the story until I—until we—give you the go-ahead. Do we have an agreement?"

"Of course! Wow-wow-wow. Only six months on the job and I get an exclusive!"

Matthew took a deep breath and rose from the sofa. When he looked down at Lex he had restored his salesman's expression, calm and cool. "Project Q is one of the most exciting new developments here at Mercy. And, when the time is right, your readers will be thrilled with our progress. Tell me, Karen—what is this country's principal malaise?"

"I'm sorry . . . 'malaise'?"

"Trouble, Karen. Problem, sickness."

Lex adopted a thoughtful expression. "Well, there's the economy. At least, that's the start of it. I guess the main problem has to be the city riots, the gangs."

"I agree. And what is the biggest challenge as regards the rioting?"

"Well, catching all the gang members and then sentencing them quickly. That's why I'm here, isn't it? And that's what the government has contracted Mercy to do."

"That's a short-term measure. You're right, though. It has been a great challenge for Mercy, on behalf of the government, to ensure that the situation is under control. But catching criminals and sending them to prison . . . if that's all we do, we'll always be chasing after them. We'll always be behind the problem rather than in front of it. So my question is, what can Mercy do to improve this situation?"

Lex couldn't resist giving an honest answer. "Well, how about addressing the problems that made people riot in the first place? The fact that they're poor, and have no prospects, and they believe that their government has abandoned them."

Matthew was sizing her up again. "Would that we could, Karen. Those issues, sadly, are out of our hands. But we at Mercy view the problem as relating to society as a whole. This country lacks a feeling of pride. Our young people possess no sense that they *belong*, or that they have anything to protect and cherish. I'm talking about public spirit."

"Picking up litter, you mean, that sort of thing?"

"You're being flippant, I can tell. But yes, that sort of thing. There has been a degradation of standards within the United Kingdom, Karen. I am in no position to speculate upon the reasons. But we at Mercy believe that this country could once again become fine and peace-loving, if only our young people could be brought back on side, so to speak. And there's the rub. Locking up young people will not solve the problem. They should be rereleased into society at the earliest opportunity."

Lex held her tongue, stifling all her real objections before saying instead, "But hasn't that been tried before? Won't young offenders only go and join gangs again once they're freed?"

"Quite right. And to prevent that, they must be educated."

Lex shuddered involuntarily. She had never heard the word "educated" uttered with such menace. "You mean . . . reminding them of all those things that they should be proud about?"

"No, Karen. Our young people are disillusioned. They can't be simply *told* things anymore. They need to learn these things themselves, from direct experience. They need to learn what is right and what is wrong."

"But how?"

"The government has performed countless educational studies. In the past, education was always about more than simple school lessons. Young people learned how to behave because their entire society supported them in doing so. They picked up litter, to use your example, because they were instructed to do so not only by their teachers, but by their family, by their neighbours, by strangers. They were polite because impoliteness was not tolerated, either at home or in public. That is the way that young people learn, Karen. We must develop a way to return to those values." Matthew stretched, appearing to be enjoying himself. "And Mercy, I am happy to say, has done exactly that. Have you heard of virtual world holidays?"

Lex nodded slowly. Suddenly, everything was beginning to fall into place.

"We've partnered with a company that provides this type of service. Project Q is a test case, the culmination of our research. It provides a perfect, coherent world in which young offenders can reside. Houses, a school, everything. It's beautiful, Karen, genuinely idyllic. Its residents should consider themselves very fortunate. For the length of the test period they will be tutored, encouraged and, to a degree, coerced. And when they are released, they will be reformed characters."

The word "coerced" echoed in Lex's mind.

Her mouth felt terribly dry. "It sounds . . . ambitious. So, these young people. They're actually locked up somewhere, plugged into a computer?" She tried to recall the details she had noted down following her hacking foray. Eight people in a ten-metre-square room. Packed like sardines. Cost and space savings. A steady nutrient feed from a drip. "Is it safe?"

"Of course. It's the exact same technology as the VR holiday sims, except adapted for a longer, um, visit. Safety is a primary concern, and one that is at the forefront of the minds of our government colleagues."

That was an odd thing to emphasize. "So do I take it that the government is somewhat nervous about this Project Q? They're a little less enthusiastic than Mercy?"

Matthew's smile wavered. She had hit a nerve. "It's simply good sense. Representatives of the government are free to visit the virtual world at regular intervals. They appear within the simulated village as one of a number of adult avatars."

"But they're not present throughout?"

"They are busy people, Karen. Inspections are scheduled each month. In fact, the final inspection ended only yesterday."

"Final? So the project is nearly at an end?"

Matthew's easy smile reappeared. "You're eager for your exclusive report, I see! Yes, yes, it's almost complete. Less than a month from today our young offenders will exit the test sim and we will understand to what degree they have improved."

Lex's heart raced. "And then they'll be returned to society? They'll be freed?"

He laughed. "These are not just any young people, Karen. They are serious criminals, some of the most notorious repeat offenders. And remember that this is only a test case to prove that the sims work, to prove that we can profoundly affect the outlook of these vulnerable and disaffected youngsters. No, they will not be freed. They will be sent on to more traditional institutions as is appropriate."

"And then?"

"And then the government will review the situation. If all goes well, the sims will be rolled out to all young offenders, for longer timescales dependent on the severity of their charges. When their sentences are complete, they will be assessed to ensure that they are indeed reformed. And then, yes, they will be returned to their normal lives, though I suspect we will find that they will approach their responsibilities in a rather more wholehearted manner."

Lex felt her face redden with anger. So, this was the truth. Up until now, Mercy's attitude had been to lock offenders up and throw away the key, regardless of whether they were guilty or not. In the future, they would instead be brainwashed and pushed out onto the streets once their personalities had been satisfactorily altered, their spirits crushed.

And throughout all of this the government was prepared to sit back and watch. What gave them, and Mercy, the right to alter people to suit them? For all their rioting, the gangs weren't the ones who destroyed the country. It was smiling, suit-wearing creeps like Matthew Solomon that had ruined society, before scurrying out of the cities to the safety of their country mansions.

Lex realized she was actually shaking with rage. She had to get out before she gave herself away.

"Well. It's about time I skedaddled." Her lips were trembling and she struggled to keep her voice level.

Matthew appeared surprised. "I must be certain that you won't reveal any details of this project."

She daren't look him in the eyes in case he saw her anger. "I promise. I need the scoop. I'm desperate." Her voice faltered at the truth of this last comment.

It did the trick. "If you return here a month from today, I will provide you with far more comprehensive details. Metrics of success, photographs. I may even be able to arrange a tour of the sim, once the test has ended, of course. Imagine that!"

"Yes. Thank you," she managed to say. "I'm sorry, I really have to go now."

Matthew rubbed his chin in confusion. Lex burst into the lobby and then outside, sucking in lungfuls of air. She sprinted to the gates of the Mercy compound. In her hurry to leave she barged into a passerby, almost dislodging his wide-brimmed black hat. The man spun away from her, muttered an apology, and strode away in the opposite direction.

100001 10 011010 00100000 100110 1101
0010 01101001 01110100 01110100 01100101 01101110 00100000
.001 00100000 01010100 01101001 01101101 00100000 01001101 01100
.010 01101111   00101110 00100000 01001100 01100001 0111
.111 01110101 01110100 00100000 01100001   01100100 00100
01100101 01110011 01101001 01100111 01101110 01101110 00100000 0110
01001010 01100001 01110010 01100101 01100100 00100
01110000 01101001 01110010 01110010 0110
01101001 01101110 01100001 01110010 01111001

01000011

010

01000101 01010010 01000011

01101000   00100000 01110111
00100000 01101000 01110101
00100000 01101001 01101110 0010000C
01100101 00100000 01100001 01101001
00100000 01110010 01101001
01110100 01100101 01100100 0010000C
00100000 01110100 01101000 01100101
01110010 01100011   0010000C
00100000 01110100 01101000 01100101
01110010 01100011
01100111 01101000 01110100
01110010 01101111

01101111 01110101 00100000 0110001C
01110101
01110100

01100110

C11APTEO

10001 CHAPTER FOURTEEN
1101000 Holes and Loopholes

The next morning, Ethan found Kit and Libby deep in conversation at the main entrance of the school. They looked up as he approached.

"Is it okay to talk out in the open?" he said.

Libby shrugged. "We've got bigger things to worry about. We were waiting for you to show up. Strength in numbers."

"Why? What's happened?"

Libby and Kit exchanged looks. "Come and see for yourself."

Ethan hurried to catch up with Libby as she led them towards the sports hall. "It's something to do with Russell and the high jump yesterday, isn't it?"

She didn't answer. She pushed open the heavy, rusted door. The interior of the sports hall was vast and the air felt no warmer than outside. Ethan saw a climbing wall studded with plastic handholds and hung with ropes. Basketball nets cast spiderweb shadows under the flickering fluorescent tube lights. The enormous space echoed with voices and the squeak of shoe soles on the polished floor.

At the far end of the basketball court, Russell, Miller and Anita surrounded some kind of squat object. They were jogging around whatever it was and chanting, as if they were performing some kind of strange ceremony.

Kit only raised his eyebrows in response to Ethan's puzzled expression. "Come on then," Libby said. "Let's get this over with."

They made their way along the length of the basketball court. Now Ethan could see that the three prisoners at the far end of the hall were wearing peculiar outfits. Russell sported a denim jacket which was a little too small for his bulk, and each of his footsteps produced a thud due to his heavy black boots. Anita wore a tasselled Peruvian hat woven with purple and white zigzags and matching woollen gloves. Miller's eyes were hidden behind dark sunglasses.

In the centre of the group, Mr. Jeffers oscillated on a swivel chair, gazing up at each prisoner with an expression that suggested encouragement or even pride. He nodded vigorously as they jogged around him.

"—and last night I did all my geography homework," Anita was saying, "and Mr. Connelly marked it ten out of ten!"

Mr. Jeffers smiled indulgently. "A valiant effort. Perhaps, with more application, you will do better next time. But in reward for your efforts, take this scarf."

A red woollen scarf appeared in his hands. Anita yanked it from him. "I wanted purple, to match the hat," she muttered as she shoved it into a pocket. She continued circling the teacher.

"Mr. Jeffers," Russell said, "I ran a hundred metres at twice the speed of light. What do you say to that?"

"A valiant effort," the teacher said, beaming. "Perhaps—"

Before he could finish, Russell snatched something from his hands, holding it close to his face to see it in the dimness. It was a pack of cards. Russell paused, looking from the pack of cards to Miller and back again.

"I'll take that," Miller said casually, holding out his hand. Russell passed it over and Miller slipped it into his jacket pocket. Then he noticed Libby, Kit and Ethan. "Look who's come to play. And they've brought their new best friend too. How sweet."

"Miller, you have to stop this," Kit said. "We don't know what the repercussions might be."

It was Anita who answered. "Are you kidding? This is a-maz-ing! All you have to do is tell Mr. Jeffers that you've been good, and—*alakazam!*—he rustles up a perk. Why would we stop? I've already got three sets of gloves and I'm holding out for a necklace."

Russell stood behind Mr. Jeffers. With his eyes fixed on Ethan he flicked at the teacher's head, in the same way that he had taunted the boy in their science class. Mr. Jeffers flinched and then beamed again.

"Poor Mr. Jeffers isn't feeling well," Russell said with exaggerated sadness. "But we'll look after him, won't we, Miller?"

Instead of answering him, Miller addressed the three newcomers. "We're having fun. It's been a while. Do you have a problem with that?"

It was obvious that Libby sensed it was a losing battle. "We wanted to let you know that classes are about to start. You've had your fun, but don't push it. Are you coming?"

Anita shifted uneasily from foot to foot. "I guess we better." She kicked at the PE teacher's chair, making him spin slowly on the spot. "I just wish the other teachers were half as much fun as old Jeffers."

Russell looked to Miller for instruction. Miller shrugged. Without another word they all began walking towards the main school building, leaving Mr. Jeffers alone in the half-dark of the basketball court.

00   01100101   01111000   01110100   00100000   01000010   01110010   01100101   01100001   0110101

The morning's lessons were as dreary as usual. In geography, Ethan traced outlines of a map of Europe, but each time he finished the task, the teacher, Miss Derbyshire, insisted that he begin again. The following session was maths, in which Miss Earnshaw instructed the class to copy endless tables of logarithms into their exercise books. Ethan half expected Russell to act out again but he remained sullenly silent, playing with the cuffs of his ill-fitting denim jacket.

At lunchtime Ethan waited until the head teacher had passed through the canteen from his office towards the classrooms, as he always did, then took a place at Libby's table. He caught her eye and gestured in the direction of Russell and Anita, who were sitting together at the far end of the room.

"Yeah, I thought they'd go to the sports hall as well," Libby said. "Thought they'd be keen to return to their favourite new pastime of taunting Mr. Jeffers."

Ethan craned his neck to look around the room. Kit gave a shy wave from a table at the front of the hall, then left his seat to join them.

He slumped with a grimace into his chair. "Are you thinking what I'm thinking?"

Ethan nodded.

"Are you guys going to let me in on the secret?" Libby said. "What's up?"

"Miller," Ethan replied. "He's not here."

"It isn't just that," Kit said. "He wasn't in our design and tech class either. Something's definitely going on. D and T is the only lesson he actually enjoys. He plays with the drill when the teacher's not looking."

"Do you think he's been put on auto?" Libby said, horrified. "Maybe Mr. Jeffers finally cottoned on to what was happening."

"No idea." Kit glanced at Russell and Anita, who sat in tense silence. "But it looks like those guys are worried too."

They all spun at a sharp noise. The outer door of the canteen had opened and slammed against the floor-to-ceiling window, shaking it violently. As Miller sauntered in, Ethan saw that he had accumulated even more perks than before. As well as the sunglasses he now wore a padded coat that might have suited an Arctic explorer. Its pockets bulged with more items. An old-fashioned teacher's mortarboard perched on his head at an angle.

"Come with me if you're human!" Miller shouted, "We're getting out of here."

The bot pupils watched him with polite expressions. None of the prisoners moved, as if they too were bound by programming.

"We can't leave," Anita hissed. She nodded towards the canteen staff who were busy ladling food onto the trays of queuing pupils.

Miller sneered. "Hey, you over there!" he called in the direction of the kitchens. "We're leaving. Do you have a problem with that?"

The canteen staff stared at Miller impassively.

"Come on, you bloody cowards," Miller said, addressing the prisoners. "I've had just about enough of this place."

"What is the meaning of this?" The voice boomed from the rear of the hall. Mr. Tooley strode into the canteen from the direction of his office. Ethan frowned. Hadn't he exited at the opposite end of the canteen hall only moments ago? His cloak swept behind him as if he were some kind of ghost. "Miller Williamson! Explain yourself!"

Miller stood his ground. If anything, he looked even more nonchalant than before. He reached into a pocket of his new coat and retrieved the pack of cards he had taken from Russell. He opened the packet and shuffled the cards slowly as the head teacher approached. "Mr. Tooley! It's wonderful to see you." He removed his sunglasses and tucked them into his breast pocket. "I was only this moment explaining to my friends that we're leaving."

The head teacher shook with barely contained rage. "Do I need to remind you, Mr. Williamson, of the school's policy when dealing with insubordination? I must warn you that this outburst of yours represents the lowest possible regard for authority. Furthermore—"

"I'm going to have to stop you there," Miller said calmly. "There's something I'd like to show you."

He rifled through the cards, selected one and held it up: the Jack of Clubs.

"I was instructed by Mr. Jeffers to bring this to you. As you can see, it's a note explaining that my friends and I have to leave the school immediately."

Mr. Tooley seemed gripped with indecision. He took the playing card, turned it over in his hands, then looked again at Miller in obvious confusion.

"Mr. Jeffers was very clear in his instructions. If you have any concerns, you should take them up with him." Miller adopted a serious, mature tone. "Mr. Tooley, we really must leave right now."

The head teacher spun on the spot, gazing around the canteen. Ethan saw streaks of pixelated colour zigzag across his face before settling to become a crimson blush—but whether it was anger or embarrassment, he couldn't tell. Finally, Mr. Tooley said, "Very well, Miller. I understand. Be on your way then."

A grin spread slowly across Miller's face. "You heard the man. Let's be on our way."

Tentatively, with his eyes on Mr. Tooley, Russell rose from his seat. The head teacher didn't react at all. Russell moved to stand with Miller and they were soon joined by Anita. Miller grinned and then looked to Libby, Kit and Ethan, raising an eyebrow.

"What do we do?" Kit whispered.

Libby sighed. "Someone's going to have to keep an eye on him." She rose slowly, watching Mr. Tooley carefully until she was satisfied that he wouldn't react.

Kit refused to move until Ethan pulled him gently to his feet. "Come on. It's like you said, Kit. All for one and one for all."

01010100   01100101   01111000   01110100   00100000   01000010   01110010   01100101   01100001   0:

Miller strode confidently towards the village centre. Russell stomped behind him and Anita jogged to keep up. Ethan, Libby and Kit followed at a distance.

"It's a test, I swear it is," Kit muttered.

"How could it be?" Ethan said.

"We have no idea what the wardens might be up to. It'd be easy for them to make it look as if the teachers' programming has broken."

"To see how we react?"

"Exactly. And look at us! We've taken the first opportunity to break all the rules. We're in for it, I'm telling you."

"Is Mrs. Benedict still here somewhere?" Libby asked.

They crossed the church square where Russell had been punished.

Ethan pointed at the church. "I saw her go in there. Yesterday morning. Maybe that means she's left?"

"Yeah. Maybe."

They all looked up at the clock tower, as if Mrs. Benedict might be looking down on them.

Ethan shuddered. "What's Miller playing at, though? He's acting as if he has a plan."

"He's a nutcase," Kit replied. "If he does have a plan, it's bound to be a plan that'll get us all into serious trouble."

"Come on, we'd better catch up with them," Libby said.

They ran to catch up. Russell and Anita looked pleased simply to be out of school early, while Miller had a clear sense of purpose. Libby jostled his elbow. "So, what's the story?"

"We'll have to go back sooner or later," Kit added.

Miller's sunglasses reflected discs of sunlight where his eyes should be. "We're just out for a bit of fun. Isn't that right, guys?"

Russell whooped and punched the air.

"Too right!" Anita said. "Except . . . where is everyone?"

They had reached the high street. All of the shops were dark and the streets remained empty. Perhaps, during school hours, the village centre simply shut down.

"If a tree falls in a forest and nobody's there to hear it, does it make any sound?" Ethan said to himself.

"Perhaps they're all having an afternoon siesta," Miller said. "So we'd better wake them up." He crossed to the nearest shop, a key maker and cobbler, and battered on the glass front with a fist. "Hey! Mr. Cobbler! Wakey wakey!" The window shook with each blow.

The other prisoners hung back in stunned silence.

"Mr. Cobbler must be a heavy sleeper. I'll try someone else."

The neon cod that hung in the window of the fish and chip takeaway was unlit and the interior of the restaurant was dark. Miller thumped on the glass. "Chippie! Mr. and Mrs. Chippie! We all want chips!"

Libby tried in vain to hold him back. "Miller, seriously. You're going to land us in deep trouble. Let's go back to school before things get nasty."

Miller gave a scornful look and rattled the handle, but it didn't give way. He took a step away from the shop. At first Ethan thought he had decided to leave well alone, but then he barged the door with his shoulder. After a second hit it gave way, bursting open. The jangle of a bell echoed louder than the crash of the door against the glass front. Miller stepped inside and felt for a light switch. White light bathed the restaurant and the neon cod flickered yellow.

"Coming in?"

Anita's hands clasped together in fear. Even Russell held his ground.

"Just me then? Fine." Miller slammed the door.

Through the window they watched him approach the steel counter. He slapped both palms down, then banged on the cabinet that warmed the cooked fish. Ethan noticed that it was full. Did food in the sim have to be cooked, or did it magically appear hot and ready to eat?

A kind-looking, plump woman appeared behind the counter. On top of her flowered dress she wore a white apron stained with golden grease. She regarded Miller with bemusement.

Miller's words were muffled by the glass. The restaurant owner looked as though she was trying but failing to speak. Her mouth twitched and she looked increasingly uncomfortable. Finally, Miller produced the pack of cards and handed one to her. The woman hesitated, then nodded and moved to the warming cabinet. She produced a small cardboard box.

Miller returned to the group. He opened the box to reveal chips swathed in ketchup and a cloud of heat. He waved it about. "No takers? Your loss then." Whistling between munches, he continued along the high street.

Kit groaned. "This is going to end badly."

By the time they reached the end of the high street, the sim had registered their presence. Shop signs flickered into colour. Ethan watched Miller, expecting him to become alarmed, but he appeared delighted.

"Finally," he roared, "some friends to play with!"

Shoppers appeared from alleys, as if they had all been waiting out of sight. Miller wagged his index finger to point at bots in turn, coming to rest pointing at an elderly man. The old man's back was hunched so that his head pointed towards the pavement. His grey beard reached almost to the belt of his trousers. He dragged a canvas shopping bag on wheels behind him.

"Excuse me, sir," Miller said, blocking his path. "My friends and I were hoping that you could help us."

The old man looked up with some difficulty. His eyes were milky pale. "Young man," he said in a slow, considered tone, "you should be in school, you and your young friends."

"It's our day off."

The man gave a hollow laugh. "And if I speak to Mr. Tooley about this? What would he say to that?"

Miller bent as if he was going to whisper into the man's ear. When he spoke, though, it was at a thunderous volume. "Mr. Tooley's dead!"

The old man staggered in shock. Ethan heard Anita giggle.

"Poor old Mr. Tooley," Miller said mournfully. "They've put Mr. Jeffers in charge now. Us pupils, we love Mr. Jeffers. Isn't that right, gang?"

Russell cheered and Anita clapped her hands.

"Leave him alone, Miller," Ethan said, "He's done nothing to you."

"Shut it, noob." Miller bent down to the old man again. "Anyway, that's not what we wanted to talk to you about. My good friend Anita is trying to learn a dance, but she's forgotten all the moves. Anita, remind me, what was the dance?"

Anita's forehead creased in thought. "Um, the waltz? No, the tango!"

After some consideration Miller said, "I don't think that was it. Oh! I remember. Sir, you would be doing us all an immense favour if you could show us the moves to the birdie dance."

The old man peered up at him, baffled.

"Do it, old timer. Flap your arms like a chicken." He held up a playing card. "As you can see, Mr. Jeffers insists that you do exactly as I say."

At first it seemed as though the old man would walk away. He fidgeted, looking up at Miller. Then, with agonizing slowness, he placed his hands on his hips. His elbows jutted out as he raised and lowered his arms spasmodically.

Anita began humming a tune, comically slowly to match the old man's painful movements.

Russell snorted with laughter. "That's the worst chicken impression I've ever seen."

"He's right," Miller said to the old man. "Do it faster."

The man's eyes widened. His arms flapped more and more vigorously.

"Stop it! Stop it, Miller!" Libby shouted. She leapt forward to support the old man as he slowed to a halt.

Miller lifted his sunglasses. His eyes were dark.

Ethan placed himself between Miller and Libby. "Back off." He hoped that he sounded more confident than he felt.

Miller gave a lopsided smile. Ethan saw a flash of real cruelty in the expression.

Then Miller cocked his head.

A strange sound came from the direction they had come. A low hum, like approaching thunder.

"I think we may be too late to return to school." Kit pointed along the high street.

A handful of bot pupils had appeared at the far end of the street. More and more children joined them.

"Maybe Mr. Tooley let them all leave too?" Anita said hopefully.

Libby snorted. "They don't look all that happy to be out of school early."

It was true. The bots were always serious looking, but as they drew closer Ethan could see real anger in their expressions. They strode purposefully along the length of the high street. There were many dozens of them now, perhaps a hundred. The rumble of their feet was matched by their monotonous chatter.

Kit was trembling. "What are they saying?"

Ethan strained to hear. The bots were chanting the same phrase over and over again. "Return to school, truants. Return and be punished. Return to school, truants. Return and be punished." They were now more than halfway along the high street.

"Wow," Libby said. "That is absolutely the least appealing invitation I've ever had."

"We're not seriously going to go back to school with them, are we?" Anita said.

Ethan surprised himself by being the first to make a decision, even if it was a cowardly one.

"No. We're going to run."

They raced along the remaining stretch of the high street and onto Rectory Road. At the junction, Russell slowed and turned to face the tide of bots.

"What's to be afraid of? They're only kids. I can take them."

"Are you serious?" Kit said. "They're not kids, Russell! They're part of the simulation. They're part of the same software as the adults. If they catch us, the teachers catch us. And have you got such a short memory that you're not afraid of what the teachers can do to us?"

Russell chewed his lip, then set off again at a run.

"My house isn't far from here," Anita panted. "We could hide there."

"They know where we live," Libby said. "They'll be able to home in on us straight away. We need to go somewhere where we stand a chance of staying hidden."

Ethan and Miller exchanged looks. "The forest," they said simultaneously.

They veered off the pavement and onto the path that cut through the park. Behind them, Ethan saw a handful of bot pupils gather at the edge of Rectory Road. Most of them held objects in their hands: schoolbooks, pieces of classroom equipment, stationery. They had stopped chanting.

"Maybe they won't follow us now that we're off the main route?" He knew it was wishful thinking.

Russell sniggered. "Stupid bots! They didn't put up much of a fight."

Kit was studying the bots with interest. Their faces twitched as though they were being bothered by insects.

"It looks as if they're listening to something," Ethan said.

Kit nodded. "But I don't think it's us they're listening to. I think they're receiving instructions. About whether to follow us up here, maybe."

The bots became motionless again. Then, all moving with the same deliberate slowness, they turned to gaze up at the human prisoners.

"This doesn't look good," Kit said.

The closest bots set off along the track at a run. The rest followed, evenly spaced in military fashion.

"Return to school, truants. Return and be punished." The voices, slightly out of sync, overlapped to become a hypnotic, menacing drone.

"Run!" Ethan shouted. He turned to find that the other prisoners had already sprinted up the hillside. At the farm with its circling pony, he caught up with Kit, who was panting as he began to climb the hill. The bots were closing the gap. If Kit kept running at that speed, they would soon catch up with him. He reached out to pull the other boy along after him.

"RETURN TO SCHOOL, TRUANTS!"

They were halfway to the forest. The other prisoners had slowed to a halt.

"Stop! Think about what we're doing," Libby said between gasps. "If we go to the clearing, they'll know about our only hiding spot."

"Do you have a better idea?" Miller said.

Ethan gulped for breath. "Libby's right. And there's another thing. We'd be trapped in the clearing. It's the corner of the skybox, remember."

The footsteps of the bots accumulated to become a deep rumble. The ground beneath Ethan's feet shook. He and the other prisoners watched inert as the bots began climbing the hill, neatly spaced apart as they ran.

"RETURN AND BE PUNISHED!"

"So . . . what *is* the plan?" Anita said.

Russell splayed and flexed his fingers. "We stand and fight, dummy."

"We haven't a chance." Anita slumped heavily onto the grass.

"Maybe we never did," Libby said.

The bots swarmed up the hill. The nearest ones brandished their textbooks and rulers as if they were clubs. The rumbling sound grew louder and louder. Ethan realized that the noise wasn't only due to the bots.

He looked up.

"Hey . . . have you noticed the sky?"

The sky had filled with dark clouds, each shot with streaks of luminous yellow that pulsed like veins.

"It never rains, but it pours," Kit said quietly.

Ethan looked from the sky to the oncoming bots. There really was no escape.

"RETURN TO SCHOOL, TRUANTS!"

None of the prisoners spoke. They braced themselves against the oncoming attack. Ethan balled his hands into fists. Whatever the bots were going to do with them, he wasn't going to go down without a fight.

The sky rumbled again. Yellow light sparked within the clouds, momentarily tinting the ground a sepia colour.

"RETURN AND BE PUNISHED!" The words were barely distinguishable now, overlapping to become a metallic shriek.

The hillside shook with a combination of the thunder and the stampede of the bots. Lightning flashed and for a brief second everything became monochrome.

The first wave of bots reached Ethan.

He swung his right fist wildly and held his other hand before his face to guard it.

Something made sharp contact with the side of his head. He retched at the pain.

And then the world stopped.

One of the bots, a young boy, hung over him with a pair of compasses raised ready to strike. The bot was motionless, even down to his eyes. Ethan looked around. The other bots were immobile too. They were fixed in impossible positions, some mid-leap and defying gravity.

The sky continued to flicker yellow, but Ethan realized that its rumbling had ceased at the same moment the bots had frozen. Another sound had taken its place. At first he thought it was only a ringing in his ears.

"It's the school bell!"

The bodies of the frozen bots emitted sparks of colour. It reminded Ethan of corrupted video on a computer screen, tiny sections freezing and changing colour. Pixels blinked off, making parts of arms, legs and faces transparent. With a noise like an engine shutting down the bots flickered once more, then disappeared in swift sequence. Books and stationery rained down to the ground.

But not all of the bots had gone. A single girl remained, facing the human prisoners. It was the thin girl with the dark fringe, the same one Ethan had raced against at the sports day. Above her head she held a heavy hardback book. Her arm wavered and she lowered it. She blinked in confusion.

"Hi," she said in a faltering voice. "It's nice to meet you all."

00 01100101   01111000   01110100   00100000   01000010   01110010   01100101   01100001   0110101

The shock of the disappearance of the bots, coupled with the arrival of a newcomer, left all of the prisoners dumbfounded. They stared at the girl, who appeared equally stunned. The sky continued to pulsate with yellow light, casting juddering shadows onto the hillside.

Ethan finally found his voice. "Are you—" he was going to say "human," but changed his mind "—all right?"

The girl looked down at herself and then at the hardback book in her hand. It dropped to the ground, splaying open.

"Yes. I'm all right."

Ethan turned. "And everyone else?"

Kit lay prone on the grass. Anita cowered with her hands protecting her head. Russell and Libby were crouched, prepared to defend themselves at any moment.

"I could've taken them." Russell dusted himself down and shrugged his denim jacket into place.

"Sure," Libby said.

"What actually *did* happen?" Anita said.

"We had a lucky break, that's all."

There was more to it than that. Ethan glanced at Kit for confirmation as he said, "The bell summoned the pupils to school. They'll have been reset to whatever part of their routines they should have been in."

Kit nodded, obviously impressed.

Ethan scrutinized the newcomer again. "You've been here a while, haven't you? I've seen you. We've spoken, but only to say hello."

The girl's nose wrinkled. Ethan thought the action made her even prettier, somehow.

"Why didn't you say anything?" he said. "I mean, properly."

"I didn't know. I didn't know that I could." Her voice was dry and croaky.

Libby trotted over to her. The girl was much shorter than she was. Libby stooped so as not to tower over her. "You mean whether the rules would allow it? The rules don't allow anything much at all."

Miller appeared from further up the hillside. He must have run all the way to the copse when the bots attacked.

"How long have you been here, then?" he said to the girl in an accusatory tone.

"I don't know. A long time."

"We've all been here for months, other than Ethan," Kit said. "I recognize you too. Have you really been here the whole time?"

The girl nodded. "A long time."

"You poor thing." Libby clasped the girl's shoulders. "We've all had each other for support. Even Ethan only had a couple of weeks before we found him. And there you were all that time, scared and on your own."

"She wasn't on her own, she was in the middle of a pack of bots," Miller said scornfully. "The bots that were trying to kill us, remember?"

The girl shuddered in Libby's arms. "I'm sorry. I didn't know what was happening."

Ethan tried to adopt an encouraging tone. "I bet it was terrifying. I can't imagine what I would have done either, if I was still trying to blend into the crowd when the bots went nuts like that."

"When you left the canteen, Mr. Tooley sent the other pupils after you," the girl said. "It was awful. When they were chanting they sounded as blank as usual, except . . . Except they hated you too. I didn't know they were capable of it." Her eyes shone with tears.

Libby squeezed her shoulders. "Hey. You haven't told us your name."

The girl's eyes continued to well up. She stared down at the ground.

"It's okay. You don't need to be scared now. What should we call you?"

"I'm called Maldemaire," she said in a thick voice.

"Nice. Strange, but . . . Sorry. I mean, it's nice."

The girl hesitated. "People call me Mal?"

Libby hugged her again, tighter.

Mal was still looking downwards. Ethan followed her gaze to the hardback book she had dropped. The French vocabulary guide lay on the grass with its pages spread, showing cartoon illustrations of a boy and a girl in conversation. In the top image, a speech bubble emerging from the boy's mouth contained a phrase in blue print. *J'ai mal à la tête.* The same cartoon was repeated below, this time with the girl speaking. *J'ai le mal de mer.* The title of the page was simply *J'ai MAL.*

His eyes flicked up. Why had the girl given a false name? What was she hiding?

"It's lovely to meet you, Mal. I'm Libby, and this is—"

She stopped speaking as an intensely bright light flashed across the sky. The air hummed with electric charge.

Kit was lying on the ground and staring directly upwards. "Do you see that? It's going mental up there."

Ethan's stomach lurched as a low booming sound came from above. The yellow light became brighter and the clouds fizzed with static. But instead of lightning, the flashes of yellow light became a swirling circle, like water running down a plughole. The circle grew larger and larger.

"I know what that is," Kit said, almost to himself. "I know what that is."

He leapt to his feet with more athleticism than Ethan had seen him demonstrate before. "We have to go. Now."

"What is it?" Ethan stared up at the kaleidoscopic swirl, almost hypnotized.

"It's the skybox . . . That thing up there, it's a rupture—an enormous glitch in the sim. This is really, really bad."

The circle grew to become a whirling vortex. It hung directly above them.

"It's going to burst!" Kit cried. "Get away from it!"

The vortex expanded rapidly, its edges crackling and shedding sparks. The centre of the whirlpool fizzed with dark static. Ethan saw a glint of something shining and solid within.

Then everything moved in slow motion. Something—*something*—appeared in the centre of the vortex, swiftly becoming large enough that it took up the entire space above them, its changing size tricking Ethan's eyes so that he wasn't able to focus on the object. The air filled with a groaning noise.

And then the *something* dropped from the sky. In the periphery of his vision Ethan registered that the other prisoners had scattered. He spun to see that only Mal stood immobile, staring directly upwards. Ethan bounded forwards, hurling himself against the girl and knocking her off her feet. They cartwheeled together down the hillside as the ground reverberated with the force of the colossal *something* thumping into the soil, creating an aftershock that made Ethan feel like vomiting.

Abruptly, the noise ceased. The hole in the sky had shrunk again. The yellow lightning around the vortex was now only a faint, dancing flicker.

Ethan's limbs had become entangled with Mal's after they had landed awkwardly on the grass. He eased himself from her, murmuring something like an apology. He lifted his head and winced at a shooting pain in his neck.

Further up the hillside, precisely where they had been standing only seconds before, was a huge wooden ship.

The next morning, after passing the last of the Gates, Lex saw the border crossing for the first time. It was nowhere near as grand as she had been expecting, and a great deal grubbier. The tall, mottled concrete wall that ringed the city was interrupted by a single red-and-white-striped barrier guarded by a uniformed man, partially hidden in the shadow of the wall. His index finger hovered over the trigger of his rifle. Beside the barrier stood a small cabin festooned with security cameras and barbed wire.

Lex forced herself to swing her arms freely as she approached, attempting to appear both confident and casual.

"Hold it, lady," the checkpoint operator said. His wide jaw was thick with bristles. "I ain't seen you before."

"You don't remember me?"

"I remember everyone. But not you."

Lex raised herself to look in to the cabin. On the counter was a blue plastic lunchbox with a label on its lid. "It's Milo, isn't it?"

He looked like a puzzled ape. "Yeah."

"I would have remembered you too." Lex smiled sweetly.

Milo swivelled from the plexiglass window to speak to his colleague, who was filling a kettle at the rear of the cabin. "Mags? Was it you let this one in?"

"Nope."

Lex considered bolting, ducking under the barrier and running the few metres over the border. But she reminded herself about the guard she had seen as she approached the cabin. He had been partially hidden in the shadows beside the reinforced barrier, his index finger held on the trigger of his rifle.

"You'd have your work cut out remembering me. I've been in the inner city for years. Undercover." Lex held up her fake ID card.

Milo's scrunched up and he mouthed words as he read. "With the *City Enquirer*?"

"Among others. Look me up."

He gave her a hard stare, then shifted his attention to his computer terminal. To Lex's surprise, his fingers danced across the keyboard with practiced ease—perhaps he wasn't as stupid as he appeared. He made several grunting noises which sounded like negatives. Lex leaned away from the cabin to peer at the armed guard, trying not to betray any anxiety. Perhaps she had got the timing wrong. It was possible that the border control servers hadn't updated since she'd hacked them the previous evening.

"Mabbett . . . Macabee . . . MacAdam," Milo muttered. "Yeah. Karen McAdam, right?"

Lex nodded.

He bent to read from the screen, then gave a long, low whistle. "You're a busy one, ain't you? *City Enquirer*, government . . . Mercy, even. What've you been up to all this time undercover in the Innards?" When he regarded Lex again his expression was far more appreciative.

Lex stared unflinchingly. "You're right, Milo. I am a 'busy one.' And I don't have time for pointless delays. Are you happy to explain to your superiors, and to mine, that you were the person responsible for preventing me from fulfilling my duties? That you held me against my will in the Innards, for no earthly reason?"

Milo stiffened. "No, ma'am."

After a few fumbled button presses, the barrier raised. Lex didn't dare meet Milo's eyes for fear of undoing her good work.

The armed guard saluted as she passed through the checkpoint.

She forced herself to walk at the same measured pace for several minutes, until she was sure that she was out of sight of the checkpoint operators. Only then did she allow herself to stop and look about.

She saw the world beyond the Innards, the suburbs and the Gates for the first time since her childhood. The real world.

The trees that lined the narrow road towered over her, and small birds darted from branch to branch. The few buildings she could see in the distance were detached cottages, white-painted and idyllic like houses in storybooks. Even here, barely beyond the suburb checkpoint, the air tasted sweet on her tongue. Away from the narrow streets and grimy structures of the city she felt disoriented and light-bodied, as if the effect of gravity had suddenly lessened. She felt free. For now.

)0   01100101   01111000   01110100   00100000   01000010   01110010   01100101   01100001   0110101

When she jumped off the train, she was pleased to discover that the station was little more than a platform and a ticket booth, with a corresponding lack of security. She had spent most of the train journey moving from carriage to carriage in order to avoid ticket inspectors and armed guards. The journey had taken only an hour and a half, but she was exhausted from having to be constantly alert.

Corn stalks taller than Lex herself sprouted from the fields on either side of the lane. Most were grey and rotting, abandoned long ago. Overgrown hedges had narrowed the path so that there was barely space for her to push through. Her introduction to the world beyond the Innards and the suburbs had been misleading. The view from the train window had been mercifully free of high-rises and gangs, but gradually Lex had recognized that the dull stretches of scrubland ought to have been thriving crop fields. Other than small pockets of green that surrounded grand houses, like oases in a desert, the landscape was bleak and scoured of life. She had always supposed that the countryside would be idyllic. It was where anyone with any money had retreated when the riots had begun, but it was clear that the wealthy classes hadn't taken to their new habitat with much enthusiasm. She imagined that they were all holed up in their country mansions, in denial about their surroundings.

It couldn't be much further now, though the height of the rotten corn stalks made it impossible to confirm. Presumably there would be an alternative, more direct route to her destination. Nobody with money would stoop to taking the train, so they would never need to travel along this lane from the station. She pushed through a thick wall of corn and produced a cloud of grey spores. She sneezed and cursed. For a brief moment she caught herself missing the barren Innards.

Abruptly, the route cleared. The lane ended at a junction to a wide road with a surface that looked freshly applied. Lex looked in both directions, then turned right. After a couple of minutes she rounded a bend to find herself standing beneath a huge roadside sign. The thick wall of grass that spilled from the field had been cut back so as not to obscure any part of it. The upper half of the sign was filled with a logo—a letter Q underscored by three twinkling stars, with scattered pinpricks of white to either side. Beneath the logo was a paragraph of white text on a bright green background.

WELCOME TO QUICKSILVR LTD.
Simulations for All Occasions
Take a Break from Yourself!

Beneath the text were illustrations of stylized stick men performing different actions. One figure was dancing and holding a cocktail glass. Another wore an oval face mask, a snorkel and flippers. A third figure was bulked out by an astronaut's spacesuit and its face was partially hidden behind an enormous visor. Further along the road Lex saw an archway decorated with more stick men in other poses.

Following her interview with Matthew Solomon she had immediately begun her research into companies that provided VR holidays. There were several, but Quicksilvr was the longest established and, crucially, the records of its ownership were impossible to source, even with Lex's worm programs working throughout the night. The fact that it began with the letter Q didn't hurt, either.

A sound from behind startled her. On instinct, she dove into the undergrowth on the side of the road. She peered out, doing her best not to disturb the broken grass stalks. A smooth, low hum became the whirr of an engine. She ducked as a large SUV with tinted windows passed her hiding place. The long grass swished in its wake.

Stalks stung her face as she pushed through the undergrowth, following the trajectory of the SUV. Her progress was far slower than when she had been walking on the road. Eventually she found herself at the edge of a circular clearing which allowed vehicles to turn and park before a white brick building. Greek columns surrounded an ornately carved wooden door that appeared out of place against the white façade of the building. Colourful metal signs announced the experiences that guests might enjoy within. *Traverse the Kalahari! Meet Marilyn Monroe! Discover Atlantis!* The black SUV had stopped in front of the entrance.

Lex scanned the front of the building. Though they were well hidden, she could make out the black dots of cameras fixed to the capital of each column. There would be no chance of her entering the building unseen, and she couldn't risk making herself a person of interest. Whoever had arrived in the SUV might be her only lead. If they had already entered the building she would have to wait until somebody came out. She wished that she had thought to bring more food than the few crackers in the pocket of her duffel coat.

She dropped to her haunches as the driver's door swung open. The man who emerged wore a black peaked cap. A Mercy policeman? No, there was no badge. He disappeared around the vehicle. She heard the clunk of another door opening. Laughter echoed around the circular clearing.

Of course. The black-capped man was only the driver. Excited chatter drifted across the clearing; four passengers now stood before the entrance, pointing out to each other the messages written on the signs. Lex could only see their backs. The two men were dressed in identical powder-blue suits. The women wore flowing dresses, one shimmering and peach coloured, the other printed with a floral pattern. Their arms were bare and their hairstyles were complex whirls piled upon their heads. The driver scurried to hold open the door to the building and the guests strolled inside. Their giggling was audible for several seconds after the door closed.

So Quicksilvr really was operational as a provider of VR holidays. That didn't bode well. Was it remotely possible that a sim related to Project

Q, containing Ethan along with other test-case prisoners, might share the building with chattering upper classes enjoying their holidays?

She considered returning home and beginning her research afresh, but the memories of the journey to the checkpoint and the difficulty of avoiding the train guards were enough to convince her to stay. There was still a possibility that this wouldn't have been for nothing. After all, a leisure business might be the perfect cover for illicit activity. Project Q might be hiding in plain sight.

The driver returned to the SUV. After a few moments it pulled away, raising clouds of dust from the gravel track, and revealing a second, smaller car before the entrance. The rustiness and obvious cheapness of this other car made it appear out of place. Lex narrowed her eyes. Was someone sitting in the driver's seat? It might be a trick of the light, but she thought she could make out a figure wearing a wide-brimmed hat.

She pushed a new route through the grass, navigating to the left-hand side of the Quicksilvr building. The car and the clearing disappeared from view. In contrast to the Greek columns of the entrance, the side wall was unpainted concrete. No windows or entrances broke up its sheer surface. Lex gave a soft, bitter laugh; James' side-door theory didn't apply here.

The rear of the building was even less appealing. Grimy pipes snaked along the length of the stained wall. A concrete pipe the width of a tree trunk emerged from the lower part of the wall, supported a foot above the ground by metal struts. Lex followed its path. There, the grass hadn't been cut back, but she saw that patches had been flattened into a carpet of muddy, broken stalks. Chunks of masonry and ragged sections of concrete pipe lay scattered about. The thick pipe wound across the trampled clearing and connected to another, much smaller, building with none of the grandeur of the Quicksilvr guest entrance. It was ringed by a chain link fence topped with razor wire, giving it the appearance of a military compound. Its single door was made of dull, scratched metal and had a closed hatch at eye level.

Ethan was in there, Lex felt certain of it. She edged closer to the only window. She scanned for cameras but couldn't see any. Maybe it was another example of Mercy's complacency, or maybe they were just well hidden. Either way, she wasn't going to turn away now. She pressed herself against the lattice of the fence, which was too tightly woven for her to put her hand through. The window was tantalizingly close but too high for her to see through. If she could only raise herself upwards very slightly . . . She curled her fingers around the wire. She would only need to climb up a short way.

The fence rattled as soon as she put her weight on to it.

"Cutler? Is that you?"

She froze. She couldn't tell where the voice was coming from.

"You're twenty minutes late! I'm bloody starving."

Lex was about to dart into the shelter of the tall grass when a cacophony of noise erupted from within the fenced compound. Something burst forth in a flurry of fur and fangs, hurling itself against the fence. It took her a couple of seconds to identify it as a dog, a German shepherd. It snarled and flung itself at the fence again and again.

A head appeared at the edge of the roof. It was a man wearing a grey uniform. He shielded his eyes to peer out over the long grass.

She was trapped. The guard was watching her only escape route.

She spun around. The dog crashed into the fence again. Its relentless barking scrambled her thoughts.

Get away, she told herself. *Just get away.*

Instead of running into the grass overlooked by the guard, she sprinted in the opposite direction, across the clearing of flattened stalks, looking over her shoulder as she ran. The guard's head bobbed and disappeared; presumably he was climbing a ladder out of sight.

"What you seen, Copernicus? Someone out there?"

The dog barked even louder, working itself into a frenzy.

Lex hesitated in the centre of the clearing, fearing that any movement might attract more of the dog's attention. The guard reappeared at ground level and fiddled with the fence gate, clicking locks into place.

"All right, all right, let's have a look-see."

If he released the dog she might never outrun it. Something jabbed her thigh. It was the sharp end of one of the discarded sections of concrete pipe. Without another thought, she dropped to the ground and pushed her way feet-first into the pipe. Her coat caught on its jagged edge with a tearing sound.

"Go do your thing, Copernicus," the guard said, "but I warn you, if you think it'd be funny to play silly buggers again, I'll . . . well, just you watch out."

Copernicus barked madly. If anything, it sounded more ferocious for being out of sight. Lex heard a skittering sound. The animal must be held on a leash, its paws scrabbling on the trampled grass.

She held her breath as the sound grew louder. She was desperately uncomfortable and the pipe allowed barely enough room for her to fill her lungs with air.

A pair of booted feet came into her line of vision. They shifted as the guard looked in all directions. Copernicus appeared, frighteningly large, straining on its leash and rearing on its hind legs, its deafening barks amplified and distorted by the concrete of the pipe.

Then the dog quieted. Lex mouthed a silent prayer.

She heard a new sound. A snuffling sound. The dog was sniffing the air. It turned in her direction and looked directly into her eyes.

She tried to edge further into the pipe but her feet met its solid end.

The guard yelped in surprise as the dog leapt forward.

Lex closed her eyes and waited for the snap of jaws, the sting of teeth or claws.

But she could only hear a wet slopping sound. She opened her eyes. Copernicus's head was bent to the ground beyond the pipe, its tongue lolling. Drool dripped over a scattering of crumbs. Lex almost laughed out loud. A packet of crackers had fallen from her ripped coat pocket.

"What you got there, Copernicus?"

The boots drew closer and then the guard's legs filled Lex's field of vision as he bent down. The smell of tobacco mixed with the rancid odour of the dog. The guard's podgy fingers scrabbled in the dirt.

"Daft mutt. You got to be kidding me, you greedy bloody pig. You aren't cut out to be an attack dog, are you? All that fuss for a bit of lunch." He prodded at Copernicus's belly, but his animosity had evaporated. "Still. Can't blame you. I'm famished too."

He shifted his weight. Lex blinked, not able to believe that she had been saved by cracker crumbs. But then the guard spun on his heels and crouched again.

"What's this, then?"

His hand grasped at something that lay on the ground. Lex's eyes widened with horror when she realized what it was. It was Cecil Wright's Mercy ID card. It must have fallen from her coat pocket along with the crackers.

"Whaddaya know?" the guard muttered. He turned the card over in his hand, then pulled a walkie-talkie from his belt. It crackled into life. The guard belched before he spoke, and he was close enough to Lex's hiding place for her to smell the stench of meat. "Nilsson fifteen calling in. Is that central?"

The walkie-talkie hissed with static. "Central speaking."

"I'm patrolling the perimeter, Project Q."

Lex closed her eyes, enjoying the sense of validation despite her circumstances. Project Q. She had definitely picked the right place.

"Found me a Mercy pass," the guard continued. "Any thoughts what I should do with it?"

After another bout of fizzing static, the voice at the other end replied, "Return it to the employee at the earliest convenience."

"Yeah, all right." The guard hesitated. "Except . . . it's not just anyone's."

"Go ahead. State the ID number and name."

"Um, ID number is 01287. And here's the thing. It's only the bloody boss."

Lex let out a gasp, then clamped her lips tight. The boss?

After several seconds of silence, the voice on the walkie-talkie said, "Return it to your superiors immediately. They'll pass it on."

"Roger that."

Copernicus had finished lapping up the remains of the crackers. Lex realized that the dog was watching her again. It began barking and straining at the leash. Its muzzle was only inches from her face. Its hot breath stank.

"Found something else, Copernicus? Haven't you already had yourself a good enough snack?"

Lex struggled but found that the narrow pipe had trapped her hands against her thighs. She would have no way to protect herself. She bunched herself as far down in the pipe as she could. Perhaps she could launch herself off the end with her feet. It was hopeless, she knew. What was she going to do, head-butt the dog?

The lower half of the guard's face was close enough that Lex could make out each individual hair on his stubbly chin.

She bit her bottom lip so hard that she tasted blood.

"Nilsson!" The new voice came from the direction of the barbed-wire compound. "Where are you? I've got your lunch."

The guard pressed his hands upon the top of the pipe to look over it. "About bloody time, Cutler, you slacker!" he shouted. He pocketed the ID card and stood up. Lex heard him smacking his lips together. Copernicus howled as he was pulled away from the pipe.

CHAPTER SIXTEEN
Miller's Madness

The yellow sky continued to flicker and rumble around the spinning vortex, which continued to shrink steadily.

The prow of the huge ship pointed downhill, directly at Ethan and Mal. Pixels shuddered across its wooden surface before settling into apparent solidity. Together, Ethan and Mal climbed the hillside. Ethan reached up to touch the hull of the ship. The rough, scratched wood under his fingertips felt real—at least, as real as anything else in Touchstone. He frowned at the realization that his fingers were damp with water. He rubbed them together and felt gritty salt.

The other prisoners seemed to have already forgotten about Mal's sudden appearance.

"This is so cool!" Russell said. Without hesitation he swung himself up the rope ladder that hung beside a row of closed wooden hatches. He disappeared onto the deck.

"It's a bit small, though," Anita said. "I always thought old-fashioned sailing ships were massive. Reckon it's half-size?"

Libby prodded her in the ribs. "Oh, so you're a nautical expert all of a sudden, are you? Oi, Russell! You shouldn't be up there until we've made sure it's safe."

A distant crack of thunder reinforced her point.

"Leave him be," Miller said. "He's like an excited puppy. Anyway, if he comes back alive we'll *know* it's safe."

Ethan said to Kit, "Any chance you have any ideas about what might make a ship appear from nowhere?"

"It doesn't belong here," Kit replied with a shrug.

Miller snickered. "Give that genius a Nobel prize."

"It came from the sky . . ." Kit continued. "It must have come through from some kind of asset repository."

"What does that mean?" Ethan said.

"How technical do you want me to be?"

"Not technical at all."

"Then think of it this way. We're trapped in a sim that's designed to look like an English village from the olden days—"

Anita interrupted. "The dullest village that ever existed."

"—and I'm pretty sure that templates for all the bits and bobs you can see—the houses, the trees, even the shoes you're wearing—are all stored together in a repository, a sort of digital warehouse, ready to be duplicated and inserted into the sim. But maybe the repository contains all the digital assets for other sims too, the ones designed for leisure and holidays. Up there beyond the skybox there could be, I don't know, racing cars, giraffes . . . and ships."

Russell reappeared above them. "You'll never guess what I've found!" he shouted. He bobbed down and emerged with a mass of black fabric. The wind caught and unfurled it, revealing an image sewn upon it in white. "A skull and crossbones! It's a bloody pirate ship!"

Miller grinned and then clambered up the ladder. Ethan and Libby followed, then Anita and, reluctantly, Kit. Mal stood looking up at the ship with a worried expression.

Most of the sails were bound tightly to the masts, but a single expanse of canvas billowed even though Ethan could feel no wind. The bare wooden boards of the deck glistened, reflecting the yellow of the clouds above. Unsecured barrels and coils of rope dotted the deck. At the stern, beyond two tiers of laddered platforms, Ethan could make out the upper part of an enormous wooden wheel. He crossed to the opposite side of the deck and peered over the edge. The wooden hatches on that side were propped open and from each protruded the muzzle of a cannon.

He realized that he and Libby were alone. The other prisoners had disappeared below deck. The words BAD JOKE had been charred into the wood above the hatch. Was that the name of the ship, or a cryptic message?

Miller emerged from the hatch, followed by Anita.

"I'll be taking the captain's quarters," Miller announced. "Do you hear that, Russell? You can be quartermaster!"

"You're not serious?" Libby said. "You can't stay here!"

"I can do whatever I want. Are you disputing Mr. Jeffers' authority?" Miller retrieved the pack of playing cards from a pocket, brandishing it.

"What about the bots? Your pack of cards wasn't going to defend us against them, was it?"

"She's right," Kit said, returning from below deck. "The best thing would be for us to return to the normal routine. It was only the school bell that called the bots off, and that was probably lucky timing. My guess is that their programming would have been reset entirely. Maybe none of them will even have any memory of what happened, even Mr. Tooley. If we act normal, they might leave us alone."

Anita moaned theatrically. "Act normal? I don't want to go back to my house. My family here are fascists. They freak out if I won't shine their shoes or whatever. Can't we stay here? I could sleep up there in the pigeon's nest." She pointed upwards to a basket at the top of the main mast.

"It's called the crow's nest," Kit said.

She shrugged, still staring upwards.

"We really should get away from here," Kit said. "The longer we stay, the greater the chance of the bots getting all worked up again."

"Scared of the little kiddies, are we?" Miller said.

"No, I'm—"

"You are. You're scared of the little kiddies scratching your glasses. You'd rather go to school and play in the sandpit or something. Well go then. And you can take your new girlfriend too." He pointed over the edge of the deck, where Mal watched uncertainly.

Ethan replied on Kit's behalf. "He's not scared of children. Anyway, it seems pretty healthy to worry about the bots going mental and trying to kill us, doesn't it? The more we break the rules, the more likely it is that they'll come after us again."

"It isn't just that." Kit pointed up at the vortex in the sky. "That hole up there only appeared when the sim's routine broke down, after you mucked about with Mr. Jeffers and his perks. We can't risk another rip appearing. Who knows what might drop out of the sky next time?"

Miller looked thoughtful, as if he found the idea appealing. Then he jabbed a finger at Kit. "That's only the half of it, though. You actually *like* it here. You reckon Touchstone is better than the real world."

Kit folded his arms across his chest. He opened and closed his mouth several times.

Miller appeared delighted to have hit a nerve. He shoved Kit's shoulders, hard. "You *love* it here. You're such a geek! Being trapped inside a computer is your dream come true."

"Leave him alone, Miller," Ethan said. "I'm serious."

"And who's going to make me? You?"

"All right, boys," Libby said. "Calm it down. Anyway, Miller, you're nobody to talk. Are you telling me you don't prefer being in Touchstone too?"

The wiry boy raised himself taller. "What the hell do you mean by that?"

"I know more about you than you realize. Most important of all, I know how old you are. It's a wonder Mercy let you into this sim at all."

Ethan had no idea where this was leading. Whatever Libby was trying to do, it was working. Miller was shaking and his hands were balled into fists.

"We forgot to say happy birthday," Libby continued in a cheery tone. "It was only a couple of days ago, wasn't it?"

The clouds flickered once again, casting odd shadows and making Miller's body appear to jerk unnaturally.

"He's eighteen, you see," Libby said, "which means he's no longer a *young* offender—just an offender. He might be yanked out of Touchstone and whisked off to prison at any moment. Real prison. And considering what you did, Miller, it'll be high-security and you'll be there for a long, long time."

Miller appeared unable to speak.

Kit puffed out his cheeks noisily. "So then we should be working together. Make the best of a bad situation. All for one, and all that."

Miller finally found his voice. "All for one? With you goons? I'd rather be chucked in a cell!"

He shoved Kit again, this time catching him off guard. Kit stumbled onto the surface of the deck and his glasses spun from his head to clatter onto the boards. He felt about for them in a panic.

"I told you already, leave him alone!" Ethan yelled.

He had intended only to push Miller away to prevent him from attacking Kit again. Somehow, the angle of Miller's body meant that Ethan's jolt had more force than he expected. Miller fell onto the wooden boards with a thump. He bounded onto his feet immediately, and stared at Ethan in mute disbelief.

A deafening thunderclap sounded directly above them.

The sky flashed a searing yellow.

Then Miller leapt towards Ethan.

00   01100101   01111000   01110100   00100000   01000010   01110010   01100101   01100001   0110101

The last flickers of lightning died away. The clouds became uniformly grey once again.

Ethan held open the curtains of his bedroom window. The fingers of his other hand touched his cheek. No scar and no bruise either.

It was morning and yet it seemed only seconds since he and the other prisoners had been together at the pirate ship. What had happened? The last thing he could remember was Miller leaping at him with his fist raised. Had he hit him? And so hard that Ethan couldn't remember how he got home?

The usual noises came from downstairs, but the house was quieter than normal. He dressed and left his room. He couldn't shake the sense of there being an odd hush, particularly out here on the landing. What had changed?

Of course. The grandfather clock outside the bathroom was silent, its pendulum frozen at an angle. Ethan strained in vain to hear the ticking of any other clocks. The one in the downstairs hallway had stopped too.

The sounds from the kitchen intensified as he crept downstairs. The clatter of crockery mingled with voices that sounded as shrill as birds squawking. Ethan paused with his fingers resting on the handle, took a breath and pushed. As he did so, the voices stopped.

His father stood in a corner of the kitchen with his arms folded over his chest. At first Ethan thought he was staring at him, but then he realized his father's attention was on the unmoving clock. Greg was sitting at the table. His knife and fork were raised, as if he was about to start eating, but he was completely immobile. His mother was frozen in the act of bending over to ladle scrambled egg onto Greg's plate. A strand of hair that had come free from her hairband was as rigid as steel. Some of the egg had left the ladle and was now suspended in mid-air above the plate.

If Ethan passed the threshold of the kitchen, might he get caught up in whatever spell they were under? But he was hungry and he didn't know of any other way to eat before school.

The door creaked as he opened it fully. Abruptly, the bots began to move. The egg fell from the ladle. Greg dropped his knife and fork with a clatter. All three of them turned to Ethan. The house echoed with the sounds of clocks ticking.

His father stumbled towards him with his hands held out like claws. Ethan slammed the door again and fled.

01010100   01100101   01111000   01110100   00100000   01000010   01110010   01100101   01100001   01

He only paused to regain his breath when he had reached the end of the street. The sky had cleared entirely, with no trace of clouds. Standing on tiptoes, he could make out the tips of the trees on the hilltop, but he couldn't see the pirate ship. Was it hidden behind the houses, or had it disappeared? It was hard to be sure of anything this morning. If only he could remember what had happened after they had climbed onto the deck of the ship.

As he passed the postlady it took a second or two for him to realize that, although she was pedalling furiously on her bike, she wasn't moving forwards at all. The wheels spun frictionlessly against the tarmac. When the postlady noticed him she gave a cheerful wave, then returned to her fruitless task.

Ethan watched the windows of the shops warily. His mind filled with images of the butcher waiting somewhere with his cleaver raised. There were no hams laid out on the window display and the lights were off. Ethan glimpsed movement in the shop. The butcher oscillated in the doorway with his body twisted sideways. Each time he stepped forward he hit the door frame, retreated a step, then repeated the action.

The door of a nearby house opened. Ethan braced himself, ready to run at the first sign of trouble. A figure emerged. It was the girl who called herself Mal.

Ethan released the breath he had been holding in. "You gave me a fright. Are you okay?"

Mal blinked in the sunlight. "I'm okay."

"Is this your house?"

She looked up at the curtained windows. "This is my house."

"I come past here every morning and I never saw you." He peered over her shoulder into the dark corridor of the house. "Aren't your parents here?"

Mal didn't reply.

"Sorry. I'll stop being nosy." He coughed to mask his embarrassment. "I guess we should carry on as normal, don't you think? We should find the others. Want to walk together to school?"

Mal's grateful smile made his stomach tighten. She pulled the door of her house closed and joined him on the pavement.

They walked in silence. Ethan glanced at her a couple of times, but her dark hair obscured her face, discouraging any conversation. He couldn't think what to say anyway. Everything that came to mind was a question that she probably wouldn't want to answer.

It was Mal who spoke first. "Did you see the storm last night?"

"The tail end of it, this morning when I woke up. Last night . . . Well, I don't seem to . . ."

"You can't remember either?"

"No! Nothing, after we found the pirate ship. You too?"

She nodded.

"And was anything weird going on in your house this morning? My whole family were frozen, as if their batteries had run out. And the clocks stopped ticking too." Ethan felt stupid mentioning the clocks, even though it had been unnerving.

"The house? No. Everything was normal."

They plodded along Rectory Road. A red saloon car passed by.

"Hey, watch this." Ethan counted the seconds. "I predict that the school minibus will appear in three . . . two . . . one . . ."

Right on cue, the minibus appeared at the junction and pulled onto Rectory Road.

Mal seemed to wake up suddenly. "Wow! You're a magician!"

"And for my next trick, ladies and gentlemen, for your pleasure and delight I will conjure up a taxi." This time he waved his hands in an elaborate flourish, as if he was casting a spell. He timed the gesture perfectly so that the passengerless taxi appeared with the final click of his fingers.

Mal clapped. Ethan was pleased to note that her applause didn't seem intended to be ironic. "I'd never noticed they were so regular."

"So you saw through my magic?"

"The magic wasn't in conjuring up the cars. It was the fact that you noticed in the first place. You're smart." She gave him a playful shove.

Ethan's cheeks glowed. "No more than anyone is. Take Kit, for example. He's the person to ask about how Touchstone really works."

"Is that the boy with the glasses?"

"We never did get around to proper introductions, did we? You must think we're all pretty rude."

"No. Yesterday was all a bit weird."

As they walked, Ethan recounted what he knew about each of the prisoners. Mal listened attentively. Her hair hid her eyes. In his embarrassment, Ethan spent most of the time watching the path rather than looking at her.

"So this Miller . . . you don't know why he was imprisoned here?" Mal said.

"No, or any of the others."

"But it might be something, I don't know, bad? Really bad?"

"The more time I spend with him, the more I'd say that's a distinct possibility."

"And how about you? What got you landed in Touchstone? Do you mind me asking?"

"I don't mind. If I tell you, will you tell me too?"

She hesitated. "No."

"Okay. That's your choice, I suppose. I still don't mind telling you."

Starting from the beginning, he told his story, from the point when he had first met Lex on the RealWorld forum to the morning he had awoken in Touchstone. He didn't mention how scared he been at first of his bot family, especially the father who was so stern, so unlike his real dad. He presumed that Mal had had a similar experience herself.

Mal was lost in thought. "So everything you did was to prove to yourself that your dad's a good person?"

"It sounds stupid when you say it like that."

"No! Not at all. It's . . . it's a good thing. It's wonderful."

Ethan gazed along the empty street. "We used to talk for hours at a time, when we were out walking or camping. He'd tell me about scientists and inventions, space travel and medical breakthroughs. When I was a kid they were just stories. But later on, I saw there was a theme. My dad's stories were all about people helping people. Ideas that made the world better. But that was before the riots."

Mal didn't react. Maybe she lived in one of the Gates too, maybe she had even less of an idea about the state of the inner cities than he had.

"After all that stuff with Mercy and the government, my dad didn't tell those kinds of stories anymore, as if he'd lost faith."

For a second he caught Mal looking at him before her hair fell to mask her face. He thought he saw wet streaks on her cheeks.

"Hey . . . don't, Mal. It's okay."

Clumsily, he reached around her shoulders. She wriggled free and Ethan pulled his arm away as quickly as if he had been burned.

"Sorry," she murmured. "I'm not much used to being near other people. You know how it is."

00   01100101   01111000   01110100   00100000   01000010   01110010   01100101   01100001   0110101

The school day swept Ethan up, and he saw the other prisoners only in glimpses. After the final bell rang he found Libby and Kit at the foot of the sports field. Ethan realized that Libby was waving at someone behind him. He turned and saw Mal.

"You haven't seen them either, I suppose?" Kit said as they entered the high street, keeping a safe distance from the bot pupils that trooped ahead of them.

Ethan and Mal shook their heads. The day had been at once uneventful and eerie. While lessons had continued as usual, Ethan had sensed an undercurrent of menace. Miss Earnshaw had demanded that pupils copy out a single sentence from the blackboard, again and again, for an entire lesson. An "emergency PE lesson" had been announced on the PA system and then cancelled seconds later. At lunchtime the only food available in the canteen had been sponge cake served with glutinous pink custard. Mr. Tooley had patrolled the school constantly, marching faster and faster with each circuit. Most worrying of all, Russell, Anita and Miller had been missing all day.

The pirate ship still loomed on the hillside, all but obscuring the trees. The sky above it had the appearance of a blue bruise around the thin, jagged line where the rip had been.

The four of them began climbing the hill.

"Come no closer!" a distorted voice called out.

They stopped twenty metres from the pirate ship.

Miller appeared at the edge of the deck. He was dressed in an elaborate military jacket complete with golden brocade and medals, and had a tricorn hat jammed on his head. He held a megaphone to his mouth.

"You lot aren't welcome here," he boomed.

"Don't be an idiot, Miller," Ethan shouted. He noticed Libby appeared impressed at his boldness. "Let us come aboard. We have to talk. We've got to figure out what to do next."

Russell and Anita appeared alongside Miller. Russell wore his denim jacket but also sported an enormous pirate hat embroidered with a skull and crossbones, which matched the flag raised upon the main mast. Anita had replaced her outfit entirely. She wore a sequined purple dress that glittered in the sunlight.

"Thanks for your concern," Miller said, dropping his voice to a more conversational tone but still speaking through the megaphone. "But we've already figured out what to do next. The sim's routines have already broken down. There are no rules anymore. So why should we carry on toeing the line? We're going to stay here and have some fun for a change. A pirate's life for us!"

"A pirate's life for us!" his companions bellowed.

Ethan gestured for the others to follow him closer to the ship. He called out to Miller, "There's more than only you three trapped in Touchstone, you know!"

Miller's voice dripped with mock concern. "You're wrong. It's just us three against the rest of the sim. Us against the world! Us against everyone else—the bots and you lot. So we'd *politely* suggest that you go back to your cosy families and your cosy school and get especially cosy with your little kiddy bot friends."

"I knew it," Kit muttered. "He's finally cracked."

"What would it mean if they stayed up here?" Mal whispered. "If we carried on as normal without them?"

"There's no way of knowing. All the routines of the sim are designed with us humans in mind. The bots might react badly to the disruption and go on the attack, like before. We'd all be in danger."

Ethan chewed his cheek in thought. "And if we stay split up into two groups, there's far less chance of either group holding the bots off. We have to at least try to stick together. Miller! I'm going to come aboard, all right? Just me, and only for a minute. We need to smooth things out. We can help you."

"Oh, didn't I mention? We already have help."

On Miller's wordless command, Russell moved to another part of the deck. Ethan craned his neck to see him winding a handle on a bulky wooden structure. A line of rope attached to it looped high over a crossbar of the main mast. At first its other end was hidden by the sail, but then a shape appeared, lowering and rocking jerkily. It was a metal cage. Sitting inside it on a wooden chair with his hands held awkwardly behind his back was Mr. Jeffers.

"What on earth are you thinking?" Ethan shouted. "Another government inspector might appear at any time! And anyway . . . *look* at him, Miller! This is *wrong*. We have no idea what'll happen if you keep him captive!"

Mr. Jeffers seemed unperturbed despite the violent swinging of the cage. He looked as calm as if he was watching a favourite programme on TV.

"I believe I can sum up our feelings in three short words." Miller fiddled with the megaphone and his next words boomed even louder than before. "BRING . . . IT . . . ON."

Ethan took a step towards the ship.

"Stop right there." Miller's calm voice was made crackling and demonic by the megaphone.

Ethan hesitated. Was it a bluff? He took another step.

"You'll be sorry." Miller turned to the cage. "Hey, Jeffers!"

The PE teacher jolted into alertness. He peered through the bars at Miller with an expression of fatherly pride.

"Mr. Jeffers, I think it's about time we showed them what you can really do. Just as we discussed, Mr. Jeffers."

The teacher nodded and smiled. His shoulders spasmed. It looked as though his hands were tied behind his back.

The air before the ship rippled like the disturbed surface of a puddle. The ripples quickly coalesced into something solid—no, *lots* of somethings. Then, with a series of hollow pops, dozens of shapes appeared, blotting out the sun. Ethan squinted up at them. The things were trees. For an eerie moment they all hung in the air before they crashed down, their trunks groaning as they hit the ground.

Somebody pulled Ethan out of the way as several of the trees toppled and began rolling down the hillside.

He and the others hurtled down the hill together, sometimes on their feet and sometimes tumbling head over heels. They stopped at the foot of the hill once the creaking and rumbling noises had subsided.

The pirate ship was now barricaded by a wall of felled trees, their roots and branches twisted in all directions.

01010100   01100101   01111000   01110100   00100000   01000010   01110010   01100101   01100001

"We can't let them keep on doing what they're doing," Kit moaned. "Who knows what they'll get up to?"

Ethan noticed that Kit had to walk at double speed to keep up with the rest of them.

Kit gestured up at the sky. Huge blocks of blue stuttered on and off like faulty strip lights. "The more Miller exploits glitches to get perks, the more he damages the skybox. I'm certain of it."

"What would you suggest, though?" Libby snapped. "Spend an hour or so clambering over those trees, only for Miller to summon up a thousand postboxes or penguins to rain down on us?"

Kit stumbled and Ethan darted to support him, but the smaller boy pushed him away weakly. Ethan thought again of Mrs. Benedict's jerky, hesitant movements. What did it mean?

Libby interrupted his thought process. "Where are we going anyway?"

"We're going to Miller's house," Mal said before Ethan could reply. She looked to him for confirmation and he nodded. Mal was more alert than she let on. Just a glimpse of her eyes made his heart race.

"What good will that do us?"

"You tell them, Mal," Ethan said.

"Well . . ." she began, now sounding far less certain. "With Mr. Jeffers captive, Miller's pretty much got all the teachers wrapped around his little finger. And that means he's able to control the bot pupils too, probably. It's a long shot, but there *might* be some bots who have the power to get him under control—"

"His parents!" Kit butted in. "Why didn't I think of that? Of course! The parental bots delegate our activities, far more so than the teachers. So there's a chance that they won't respond to Miller's playing-card trick."

"That's all very well," Libby said, "but what do we actually want his parents to do? We don't want him put on auto, do we?"

Ethan was pleased that nobody disagreed. He noticed Mal shudder. Hurriedly, he said, "Of course not. But we need to know our options. We might need his parents on our side later." He didn't bother to add "if things get any worse." It was what they were all thinking anyway.

They entered a housing estate that overlooked the farm with its circling pony.

"Miller's house is somewhere around here, isn't it?" Ethan said. "Any idea which one?"

Libby took the lead. Soon they stood at the end of the driveway belonging to a house identical to the others in the estate. The bay windows were dark and the curtains were open, despite the fact that dusk had fallen.

Libby strode to the house and rang the bell. There was no answer. She knocked, quietly at first and then louder. She tried the door. It opened. Ethan, Mal and Kit joined her.

"You're sure this is the right place?" Kit said.

Libby shushed him. "Do you hear something?"

At first Ethan heard nothing other than the familiar overlapping sound of two clocks ticking. Then he became aware of a faint scuffling, pattering sound. "I think it's coming from somewhere towards the back of the house."

They crept into the lounge. As if by silent agreement, nobody switched on the lights. Ethan was unsurprised to find that the furniture was identical in style and arrangement to the suite in his own house. The entirety of the rear wall was plate glass from floor to ceiling, and he could see the chequered linoleum floor of the conservatory beyond. After a few seconds he felt certain that the scratching noise was coming from that direction. He slid open the patio door carefully.

The air in the conservatory was chilly. The linoleum creaked with each of Ethan's steps. A particular smell reminded him of home—his real home in the outside world. It was the smell of damp straw.

He exhaled with relief. "Relax. It must be a pet they're keeping out here. Hey Kit, can you switch on the lights?"

The light reflected from the curved Perspex panels. Ethan winced as his eyes adjusted. Sure enough, there was a rabbit hutch against one wall. He walked over to it but then leapt away with a gasp.

Libby's hand went to her mouth. Kit and Mal looked on mutely, staring down at the hutch.

A young girl was curled awkwardly inside it. Her fingers scrabbled weakly at the metal mesh.

As Ethan bent down, Kit tried to hold him back. "Are you sure you want to do that?"

Ethan glared at him, then twisted the latch on the hutch. The girl continued to flail within her tiny cell without acknowledging him.

Libby and Kit helped pull the girl free. Ethan guessed she was only about twelve or thirteen years old. Her long hair was tied in bunches which remained neat despite her bout of captivity. She stood in silence, not meeting their eyes.

"She doesn't seem too upset," Kit said.

"Are you all right?" Ethan said to the girl.

She didn't reply. She hardly seemed to recognize that she was no longer alone or trapped.

"I bet she never leaves the house, if my kid sister's anything to go by," Kit said. "Perhaps her programming doesn't cover speaking to anyone except Miller or her parents."

The girl began to move. Mal jerked to avoid being touched; her face was a picture of revulsion. Ethan followed the girl as she entered the house. She switched on the light in each room as she made her way towards the kitchen, where she pulled items from cupboards and began preparing a sandwich.

Libby let out a nervous laugh. "I guess she's okay then."

"Yeah, but is anyone else getting worried about Miller's parents?" Kit said quietly.

They split up to search the house, reconvening at the foot of the stairs minutes later, shaking their heads. Ethan glanced up at the ticking hallway clock. It was eerie how similar this house was to his own, and presumably to all of the prisoners' houses. He recognized all of the photos of bland landscapes that hung on the walls. Even without checking to confirm it, he knew that on a shelf to his right was a pale yellow vase that held a single dandelion that never wilted. Across the hallway from where he stood was a cupboard containing a vacuum cleaner and an endless supply of cloths for cleaning the car. And beside the cupboard was another—

"That's strange," he murmured. "In each of your houses, is there another door right here, leading to the cellar?" He pointed at a blank expanse of wall between the vacuum-cleaner cupboard and the staircase.

Kit nodded and Libby said, "Yeah, my father goes down there each evening. Carpentry, or something. I never dared check if he was telling the truth, to be honest."

Ethan tapped on the wall, producing a series of dull thuds. This section was wallpapered in the same style as the rest of the hallway, but on closer inspection he saw that the pattern was interrupted along the edges of a wide, rectangular area. It was exactly the same dimensions as the door that ought to have been there. He continued tapping until a different sound made him pause.

"Do you hear that?" He pressed his ear to the wall. "I swear I can hear voices."

"—did you learn today at school, son?" he heard a muffled voice say.

A higher-pitched voice replied, "It's cauliflower cheese this evening, for those that have finished their homework."

"Yes, and then perhaps you could help by washing the car."

Libby recoiled with horror. "Ugh! They're trapped right there on the other side of the wall."

Kit felt the surface with undisguised interest. "It's amazing. Seamless."

"Won't they run out of air?"

"Course not, they don't breathe. But that's not the point. Somehow Miller's managed to conjure up the bricks and have them placed perfectly to seal up the wall. Using Mr. Jeffers, I suppose. But how he managed to summon a brick wall instead of a random perk, I've no idea."

"The same way he managed to produce a dozen trees to try and crush us," Ethan said. He slumped against the opposite wall. "Anyway, knowing how he did it won't help get his parents out of there. They're stuck for good."

Kit was clearly far less concerned about the welfare of the bots. "Miller's getting stronger all the time. There's no telling what he'll be capable of soon—or what damage it'll do to the sim."

Mal was the last of them to leave. Ethan watched as she reached out to touch the sealed wall of the hallway one last time. When she left the house she pulled the door closed gently as if she were fearful of disturbing its occupants.

1010100   01100101   01111000   01110100   00100000   01000010   01110010   01100101   01100001   0

Ethan awoke gradually. Sunlight turned the inside of his eyelids a rich orange, making the veins appear like forked lightning. The right side of his face was warm. He heard birdsong.

His eyes flicked open. Instead of the usual play of light on the ceiling of his bedroom, above him he saw a cloudless blue sky. He was lying under his grey and white duvet, and to his left he could see his bedside table, lamp and wardrobe—but he and all of these things were in the garden instead of his bedroom.

He saw Greg tinkering with his wooden fort, laughing softly to himself.

Once again, Ethan couldn't remember how he had gotten home. The last thing he could recall was leaving Miller's house, when all four of them had looked toward the hillside to see—

He leapt up to stand on the bed, straining to look over the roofs. Although the pirate ship was hidden from view, the dark rip in the sky above the hilltop pulsated constantly.

He gathered clothes from the wardrobe and pulled them on over his pyjamas, too much in a rush to feel foolish getting dressed out here in the garden. He raced along the side passage of the house without even glancing in at the kitchen window. He didn't want to see what state his bot parents might be in this morning.

As he sprinted along Aldenham Road he narrowly missed the postlady who lurched towards him on her bike. Her hands were raised far above the handlebars and her face was riddled with tics and twitches. The row of shops came into sight. He hesitated, then set off along a different route than usual. He didn't relish the thought of encountering the butcher today.

Mal was waiting outside her house. Her body shook and she looked deathly pale. As Ethan approached she stared at him without seeming to recognize him.

"Where were you?" she said finally. "I was alone."

"I'm here now. I'm sorry. I think the sim reset again."

"I . . . I hate it. I hate it here." She indicated her house. Then her expression brightened a little. "But I was glad to wake up at all."

Ethan frowned. Was that a reference to the sort of punishment that Russell had endured?

"I'm sorry," she muttered. "I feel a bit out of sorts. How about you— are you okay?"

"Confused. I woke up in the garden. Things are getting stranger every time we reset. There's no time to waste."

They found Kit and Libby sitting on a wall at the lower end of the high street.

"Seems like only minutes since we were last together," Libby said with a wry smile.

Kit's hair was sticking up in clumps.

"He'll be all right in a bit," Libby said, patting Kit on the back. "He had a bit of a nasty surprise when he woke up. In a tree."

In a faraway voice, Kit said, "Miller's destroying the sim, bit by bit."

They all looked at the dark line in the sky above the hilltop. It had grown larger and uglier even in the short time since Ethan had left the house.

"What can we do?" Ethan said.

Kit slid off the wall gracelessly. "It's going to get worse. I'm not sure the resets are even a direct response to Miller exploiting glitches in the sim anymore. It's possible the damage has reached a tipping point. The resets might occur spontaneously and randomly."

"This morning most of us didn't even wake up in our bedrooms," Mal said, her voice trembling. "What if one of us wakes up somewhere we can't escape from? We could be trapped, like Miller's parents." Weakly, she added, "If we reset again, what if I don't wake up at all?"

Ethan placed his hand on her shoulder, unsure whether or not she would find it comforting. To his surprise, Mal didn't flinch. She nestled up against his arm.

Kit was lost in thought. "I think I might have an idea."

1010100   01100101   01111000   01110100   00100000   01000010   01110010   01100101   01100001   0

"Where is everyone?" Libby said. They had walked the entire length of the school field without meeting any bots.

"If the world keeps resetting, who knows what other errors might be happening," Ethan said.

"Where are you taking us, Kit?" Mal said.

"The only place I feel totally at home."

The main doors to the school were wide open. Inside, they progressed carefully, checking at each junction of the corridor for bots. Kit led them deep into the building, beyond all of the classrooms, to a room that Ethan had only ever glimpsed en route to his classes.

It contained rows and rows of computers. He saw at a glance that they were old-fashioned and grimy from disuse. Each monitor was an enormous beige box that took up almost an entire desk. The computer towers on the floor left little room for the users' legs. The letters printed on the keyboards were so faded they were almost illegible.

"Does the school even teach computing?" Ethan said.

"Nope," Kit replied. "I reckon this room's left over from the old days, before the school sim was incorporated into Touchstone. It was probably too much bother to replace it with a new classroom so here it is, gathering dust."

"There's something weirdly charming about computer-generated dirt." Libby traced a finger across the top of a monitor and inspected the black mark on her fingertip. "The developers did some neat work when it came to decay."

Kit sat before a workstation and switched it on. He blew on the keyboard, spluttering at the resulting cloud of dust. Once he had wriggled to get comfortable in the swivel chair he looked very much at ease.

"So I'm guessing you've been here before?" Ethan said.

"How do you think I knew so much about Touchstone once being a holiday sim? I couldn't help myself after I found this place early on, soon after I arrived. I only scraped just below the surface, mind you. These rigs aren't conducive to serious hacking."

"Out there in the real world, do you spend a lot of time in front of a screen?" Ethan noticed Libby glance at him, then quickly turn away.

"Yeah, something like that." Kit began typing at an incredible speed, not looking at his fingers as they skittered across the keys. "Anyway, I didn't dare return once I'd seen Libby get punished for the first time at the church tower. Didn't fancy being put on auto."

Green text scrolled upwards on the screen, disappearing from the top faster than Ethan could read.

Mal came to Ethan's side. "I think I understand. It depends whether Kit's right, whether these computers are left over from the days when this part of the sim was less restricted. He's hoping that they're hooked up to the . . . um, I don't know what you'd call it."

"The mainframe. Central processors," Kit said without looking up.

"Right. So there's a slim chance of being able to access some of the central commands."

"Including the reset function?" Ethan wasn't sure whether he should direct the question to Mal or to Kit. Both of them nodded.

"But 'slim chance' is the right choice of words," Kit added.

"At this point, we'll take every chance we have," Libby said. "I feel like Chicken Little, waiting for the skybox to come crashing down."

"All right everyone, shut up now," Kit said. "This genius needs to concentrate."

They retreated to stand by the window, although all eyes were on Kit as he worked.

After ten minutes of constant work, the lines of text stopped moving up the screen to be replaced by two words in a larger font: *DEV COMMAND.*

Kit whooped. "So far so good! I'm into the developer console. All right, you creaky old dinosaur of a machine, let's see what you can do for us." He cracked his knuckles and began typing again.

Mal wandered to a corner of the room and began to draw shapes in the dust layer that covered a desk. Her dark hair obscured her face as usual. Not for the first time, Ethan felt that it was a shame that her fringe so often hid her eyes. He couldn't even recall what colour they were.

"Oh, nice. I've found some references to the bots. They . . . Wow." Kit became engrossed in the information onscreen again, then let out a whistle. "The developers knew their stuff! Those bots out there? They have some seriously heavy-duty AI kicking around inside them. Each persona simulation is amazingly complex. Every single parameter is unique and there are thousands upon thousands of parameters allocated to each bot."

Libby peered at the screen, her nose wrinkled. "So why are they such dimwits? Why do they shamble about like Frankenstein's monsters?"

"It isn't their fault. As far as I can make out, they all have severe limitations imposed on them. Most are only accessing a tiny fraction of their behaviour programming."

"This is all very interesting, but can you hack them? Call them off from attacking us?" Ethan considered adding, "and go after Miller instead, if it came to it," but decided not to.

Kit shook his head. "Sorry, I haven't found a single command for the bots that I can tweak. But respect to the devs, right?"

Libby groaned. "Aren't you supposed to be looking for the reset function? We could reappear back in our houses, or wherever, any minute."

Kit's cheeks glowed. He nodded and began typing again. Minutes passed.

"Getting there . . . Got it!"

They all huddled around his computer. Ethan waited for him to offer an explanation, but Kit simply sat grinning at them all.

"What have you actually done?"

"The reset! I've reset it. Or rather, I've deselected it entirely."

"So we're not going to black out and find ourselves in our houses?" Libby said.

"We shouldn't. In fact, there's no reason that we should have to go to our houses at all. As far as the system's concerned, we're free agents."

Libby snorted. "Free agents in a prison, mind you."

"Don't tease him." Then Ethan said to Kit, "So, what else can you do, now that you've broken in?"

The grin disappeared. "Not much. The reset function is low level. I guess the devs didn't view it as a security issue. Most of the mainframe's stuck behind a firewall, real high-grade stuff."

"What about the perks? It's only the perks that have been giving Miller an advantage. Might they be stored at the lower level too?"

"Hold on, I'll have a look." Kit's hands were already fluttering over the keyboard. Prompts appeared and disappeared onscreen with dizzying frequency. After several minutes, he slumped into his chair. "No chance. There's no mention of perks in the area I can access. It could be that those parameters are stored out there—" he pointed upwards as if to indicate some vague area beyond the skybox "—or they're accessed somewhere else within the sim. Either way, no dice."

"And there's nothing else you can do? Nothing that'd be any use to us?"

Kit looked disconsolate.

Libby put a hand on his shoulder. "You did great, Kit-Car."

He beamed.

Mal peered at the text that filled the screen. She pointed. "What about this?"

Kit shrugged. "What about it?"

"Isn't that another reset function? But this one has an email address field."

It took Ethan a while to spot it. Buried within a garbled section of text was the address, *central@quicksilvr.co.uk*.

Kit flashed Mal a look of appreciation. "Oh, you little beauty!"

Ethan felt a flush of envy at their sharing a secret. "Am I being really dim? What is it?"

"It's the emergency contact! The idea is that if there's a security breach, or if anything happens that the simulation doesn't expect to happen, someone will automatically be alerted. Someone with the email address central-at-quicksilvr-dot-co-dot-uk."

"Are you kidding me?" Libby said. "Hasn't 'unexpected stuff' been happening pretty much constantly these last few days? So where's the cavalry? Where are the emergency services?"

"Fair point. Which would indicate that nobody's been checking that email account. No wonder. This part of the code is ancient."

Ethan gritted his teeth at Kit's constant distractions. "How does this help us?"

"Well, Mal's right—the field is resettable. That means that we can change the email address to alert somebody else. Somebody out there in the real world, somebody who might be able to actually help us rather than send in the Mercy wardens or the government inspectors. And— oh, it gets better! Not only that, I think I might be able to shove in a line of code to patch in an instant messenger client. We could actually speak to someone out in the real world!"

He seemed delighted at their stunned silence. Then his face fell. "There's a catch, though. There's a safeguard. A safeguard on the safeguard. Wow, I'd really like to meet these devs one day. They're smart cookies."

"Kit! Stop geeking out," Libby hissed. "What's the catch?"

"I can only change the contact address once. After that, it'll be set in stone. We'd need high-level clearance to change it again."

Ethan spun around at the sound of hurried, clicking footsteps. Miss Earnshaw was running past the window of the computer suite in the direction of her classroom. A train of bot pupils followed in her wake. Their motions were stop-start, sometimes running, sometimes walking, but always in synchronicity with one another. Their heads lolled drunkenly and their mouths hung open as though they were shouting, though Ethan could hear no noise other than the stamping of their feet.

Libby gasped. "We'll be trapped if they catch us in here. So let's get this done, and let's make our first choice of email address a good one, okay. Who shall we contact?"

They each became lost in their own thoughts.

"I guess it's not worth telling the authorities," Libby said slowly, "given that it was the authorities who sentenced us to be trapped in here at the first place."

"But surely they'd help us if we told them what was going on?" Ethan said. "The glitches, the blackouts, all that?"

The others only gave him hard stares.

"All right, I'm being naïve. I get it. Sorry."

"What about one of our parents, then?" Kit said.

Ethan thought of his dad. Surely he would help? His stomach lurched as he realized that he no longer felt certain of that. If his dad was involved at all in Mercy's sentencing of crimes then contacting him could jeopardize everyone. And there was no telling who his mom might side with. He shook his head sadly.

"My dad's ill, and my mom's . . . well, she's gone," Libby said.

"And my parents were the ones who reported me to the police in the first place," Kit said.

Not for the first time, Ethan wondered what crimes each of them had committed to end up in Touchstone.

Mal's face reddened. "I don't have any parents."

Ethan felt his face glow too. "I'm sorry, Mal."

"There must be *someone* we can trust out there," Libby said, though her tone was more hopeful than confident.

Ethan wished he felt more confident too. He looked at each blank face before he said, "I think I may know somebody."

1001 00100000 01010100 01101001 01101101 00100000 01001101 01101

010 01101001 01101101 00100000 01001101 01101

010 01101111   00101110 00100000 01001100 01100001 0111

111 01110101 01110100 00100000 00100000 01100001   01100100 00100

01100111 01101110 00100000 0110

01001010 01100001 01110010 01100101 01100100 00100

0110

01101001

01000011

010

01000101 01010010 01000011

01101000   00100000 01110111

00100000 01101000 01110101

01100000 01101001 01101110 00100000

01100101 00100000 01100001 01101001

00100000 01110010 01101001

01110100 01100101 01100100 00100000

00100000 01110100 01101000 01100101

01110010 01100011   00100000

00100000 01110100 01101000 01100101

01110010

01100111 01101000 01110100

01110010 01101111

01101111 01110101 00100000 01100010

01110101

01110100

CHAPTER SEVENTEEN

Contact

Lex dashed into the alley beside *Sweetheart's Dessert Parlour*, hurrying to avoid the first spots of rain. One of the boxes she was carrying fell to the ground. She struggled with the locks, dumped the packages onto the coffee table, then returned to the alley to retrieve the fallen one. A movement on the street caught her eye. A dark figure stood alone in the porch of a looted nail salon, facing the alley, a man, judging by his stature. At first she wondered if he might be a Fagin, but they always preferred to announce their presence rather than slink in the shadows. She tried in vain to make out the man's face beneath the brim of his hat dripping with rainwater. Abruptly, he spun on his heel and continued along the street.

She ripped open the box as she re-entered the flat. The slice of pizza had long since defrosted—the supermarket she had stolen it from had been without electricity and its shelves had been empty—and it quickly became bland mush in her mouth. She prayed it wouldn't make her ill.

Hooking open a small freezer with the heel of her boot, she began to load it up with the packages. Juice from a meal-for-one lasagne leaked through the cardboard. A rich, unpleasant smell filled the flat.

In the two days since her narrow escape from the Quicksilvr compound she had spent most of her time accumulating food supplies from abandoned shops. It was a distraction; she had plenty of food stockpiled. The fact was that, having successfully followed the trail to Quicksilvr, she had no clear idea what she ought to do next. Ethan was almost certainly being held within that secure compound. She pictured him strapped to a table and plugged into a computer. But how did knowing that help? It wasn't as if she could storm the building to set him free.

Force of habit made her sit on her computer chair rather than the sofa. She propped both her feet onto a pile of hard drives that James had left there, temporarily, six months ago. Dirt cascaded from her boots as she munched the tasteless slice of pizza, staring at the blank computer screen. She finished the last mouthful of food and then rattled the mouse to wake the machine from standby.

In the bottom right of the screen an alert blinked: *MAIL*

Despite spending most of her waking hours at a computer, she couldn't remember the last time she'd received an email. Forum messages, tweets and pokes, yes, but email had fallen by the wayside long ago. She clicked on the alert to bring up her inbox.

The subject line read, *IM request userunknown*. She sighed. Spam. Still, perhaps this might be another distraction to keep her mind busy. She could dedicate the rest of the day to ramping up her filters and virus protection. She hovered the cursor over the delete button as she scanned the body of the text.

Protocol breach alert. User intervention may be required.

Below this was another phrase in a blockier font.

Click to launch instant messenger client.

A button glowed blue, changing from pale to dark and then pale again.

She was about to delete the message when something in the footer of the email caught her eye. It was a light grey logo, hardly visible. A letter Q surrounded by stars.

She clicked the blue button before even considering what might happen. Immediately, the email client disappeared to be replaced by a black screen with a green, flashing arrowhead prompt. She waited.

The screen remained unchanged for more than thirty seconds. Finally, words appeared.

Is that you Lex?

Her hands trembled as she placed them on the keyboard.

Yes.

James?

The arrowhead prompt blinked.

No. Sorry. It's Ethan.

ETHAN! Where are you? You OK?

I'm in prison. A virtual world.

Lex collected herself. Her hands stopped shaking.

I know. Been doing detective work. But are you OK?

Fine for now.

But

The green prompt blinked again for a few seconds.

But things are getting bad. We need help.

Bad is my middle name. Tell me everything.

And he did. Impatient to learn the facts, Lex prompted Ethan for more and more precise details. He struggled to keep up with supplying the answers. His typing speed was a snail's pace. It took more than twenty minutes to establish the information she needed. After mentioning glitches in the skybox of the sim, he announced that he was handing the keyboard over to somebody else, a boy named Kit. Clearly, he was the brains of the operation, and his typing speed was better too, although his spelling was awful. Lex demanded to know all the evidence about the skybox rip and Kit supplied them readily.

This is Ethan again. I thought of something else.

About the rip?

Yes. The pirate ship was wet with salt water.

Lex pondered this new information.

Got it. So it didn't come into the skybox direct from the repository, right? It came from another sim instead?

Don't know. That's what I wondered.

Have you found out anything about my dad?

She paused. How much of the truth should she reveal at this stage? She didn't dare distract him. But an image of Ethan with blood on his cheek appeared in her mind's eye. She had let him down before.

Yes. It's not good. He's deep in the centre of all this. One of the Mercy bosses. He knows everything.

There was a long pause before any more words appeared.

Have to go now. Libby's back. She had to act as bait to trigger the email alert. No idea what crime she's committed. The bots are on her tail.

OK.

You know I don't know how to get you out of there, right?

Right. But

Don't interrupt. I was about to say: but I will. I'll get you out, all of you. Nice work, Ethan and Kit.

Leave it with me, but stay in touch. Log on here this time tomorrow?

Lex stared at the blinking arrowhead. Nothing.

Good luck in there.

CHAPTER EIGHTEEN

Behind the Barricades

"Give me a hand, will you?" Ethan grunted.

Libby rushed to help him overturn a desk. Together, they reinforced the line of filing cabinets that barricaded the corridor.

"That should do it." He wiped sweat from his forehead. "Are the others secured?"

"Yep. Two corridors blocked off entirely, another with a way through if you know how and don't mind getting your knees grazed. We're safe from the bots if we stick to the computer suite, the canteen and the sports hall."

"Any luck finding food?"

She nodded. "Nothing in the cupboards, but Mal and Kit prized open an oven and found lunch in there waiting. Don't get excited, though. It looks utterly rank. What's Miss Earnshaw been getting up to?"

They rounded the corner. The door that led to the classrooms was jammed shut, a chair wedged under its handle and a taut web of skipping ropes holding it closed. Through a glass panel they could see Miss Earnshaw. Her face was expressionless though her mouth was fixed wide open. Every few seconds she retreated a couple of steps, then crashed into the door, rattling it in its frame.

"She's been doing that the whole time," Ethan said. "It's the same with the pupils at the canteen windows. We're lucky the bots don't have much imagination. Even so, I bet it was terrifying having her chase you."

"It worked, though. It raised the alarm and you got through to the outside world. But yeah. She can really move when she wants to."

Ethan gestured towards the canteen but Libby put a hand on his arm. "Hey, I wanted to talk to you. About your friend Lex—what she said about your dad and Mercy. I wanted to check that you're okay."

Something constricted within his throat. Since the IM conversation with Lex he had thrown himself into the physical work needed to secure the area. He had been trying to avoid considering Lex's news directly.

"I don't want to talk about that."

Libby nodded and let go of his arm. Ethan stared blankly at the barricade. His words rang in his ears: *I don't want to talk about that.* They were the exact words that his dad had used when Ethan asked him questions about his job at Mercy. And now Ethan understood why.

Mal and Kit welcomed them into the unlit canteen. They had set a table for four. The tray in the centre contained pale-brown shepherd's pie, flat yellow quiche and floury baked beans.

"It all came out of the oven hot, even though it wasn't switched on," Kit said. "Weird, but handy."

Ethan found it difficult to concentrate on eating. Earlier, only a couple of teachers had stood at the glass wall at the far end of the canteen, but now they had been joined by three of the bot pupils. They stood with their hands raised to shield their eyes as they peered into the darkened hall. Their mouths hung open as if they were envious of the food.

"Don't worry about them," Kit said. "They only get riled up if they identify a target. As long as we stay at this end and keep the lights off, they won't spot us."

Ethan, Libby and Kit ate slowly. In contrast, Mal was ravenous and scooped more and more food onto her plate. After a while she noticed the others watching her.

"Sorry," she said with her mouth full, "I haven't eaten for a while."

Ethan pushed his tray away. "Well, you're welcome to it as far as I'm concerned. If I never had to eat this slop again, it'd be too soon."

"I wonder if it's better or worse than real prison food," Libby said.

"We'll find out sooner or later," Kit said gloomily. "Once they're finished with us in the sim."

"Don't bet on it," Ethan said. "Lex will get us out. Out of Touchstone, and out of prison entirely. I know she will." He wondered if he sounded as optimistic as he intended. He certainly didn't feel it.

"Yeah. Of course." Kit stared at his plate. He obviously didn't believe it either. Or was there something Ethan hadn't yet considered? He thought of the odd way that Kit moved, stumbling and gliding in the same manner as Mrs. Benedict. What if Kit was not what he seemed?

Libby coughed in an obvious signal that she wanted to change the subject. "Anyway. Someone obviously thought all this stuff was great. The food, the school, everything in the sim."

"What makes you say that?"

"Look at this place," she said, gesturing at their surroundings with her knife. "It's dreary, but the attention to detail gives it away. It's no rush job. Don't forget that once upon a time Touchstone, or a bigger version of it, was built for holidays. The whole sim is pure nostalgia."

Ethan looked at the grimy tables and mock-wooden panelling of the walls. "You really think so?"

"I know so." She laid down her cutlery. "What the hell. I might as well tell you. My mom was a software architect, one of the developers who built this place. I don't mean the prison, before you get all antsy. I'm talking about the holiday sim, followed by the educational version that failed. Everything you see here is based on her childhood memories. Or, at least, her memories mixed up with the memories of the other developers on the team."

"Why didn't you tell us this earlier?" Ethan said. "We could have got in touch with her—she'd be the perfect person to help us!"

Libby's face fell. "She died. A year ago."

"Libby, I— I'm so sorry."

Mal reached out to hold Libby's hand. Libby managed a weak smile. "Yeah, I'm sorry too. It came totally out of the blue. The official line was that—" She cleared her throat noisily. "Anyway, she'd been acting weird before then. Distracted by some big work project. In phone conversations I only ever heard her refer to it as a 'rollout,' whatever that means."

"That doesn't seem odd in itself," Ethan said cautiously. He had no idea what a "rollout" might be either.

"There was more than that. She had this map of Great Britain pinned up in her study—not on the wall, but on the inside of a cupboard. I'd hear that door open whenever she went into her study—I suppose the hinge needed oiling. Of course, I snuck in to look—I was snooping all over by that point. She'd pinned labels onto the map, dozens of them. Just numbers. Took me a while to work out what they were. They were population sizes of cities. A million in the Capital, half a million in Midland, and so on. Every day, I'd hear that cupboard door opening and then Mom muttering to herself."

"Saying what?"

"All sorts. But sometimes the same phrase, which sounded scary even though I didn't understand it then and I still don't now. She said, 'We'd never stand against them.'"

"She must have been talking about Mercy," Kit said.

Libby smiled ruefully. "I wish I'd considered that at the time. After she died, I guess I asked too many questions. Every day I showed up where she worked, the company that runs the holiday sims. They tried to fob me off, then got more and more threatening. Then the cops arrived and I ended up in court. And I woke up in Touchstone."

"And now we know that Mercy adapted the holiday sims as a sort of prison." Ethan tried to process the implications. "So this 'rollout' your mom talked about, that might have involved Mercy too. You don't think—"

"I do now. I think that Mercy are planning to use the sims to imprison anyone from the Innards who gets sentenced."

Ethan thought of Lex's crusade. There was more to it than Libby suspected. From what Lex had told him, Mercy wouldn't even bother with the sentencing. Anyone who got themselves arrested would be plugged directly into Touchstone, or some other sim like it, without trial.

"And that was your only crime? Asking questions about your mom? I thought I had a raw deal. At least I was guilty of trespassing."

Kit snorted with laughter. "Trespassing? Ethan, you seriously think that should get you locked up for good?"

"There's no need to take the mickey. I haven't had much experience breaking the law." When Kit laughed again, Ethan said sharply, "All right then, tell us—what did you do to end up in here? Armed robbery? Murder?"

"Nothing so interesting, but I suppose I am a seasoned criminal, technically speaking. I thought you might have guessed already. I'm a hacker."

Ethan shrugged. "Makes sense. You and Lex would get along. You could talk to her about, I don't know, motherboards or whatever, until the cows came home. So it was your hacking that got you sent to prison?"

"Yep. Just like this Lex of yours, I was interested in Mercy. Except not for ethical reasons. You should *see* the security setup around their online systems. It was a red rag to a bull. I had to have a crack at it."

"And you got in? Into their systems?"

"Sort of. I broke the first level, but didn't find anything of interest. And then the police smashed down the door of my house before I could get any further."

"So you did it just out of curiosity? A challenge, like doing a crossword? You really should get out more, Kit."

Libby shot Ethan a look. "Hey, go easy on him. How about you, Mal? What did you do?"

Mal had finished eating but continued playing with the scraps on her plate. "Same as Kit, more or less."

"Hey, look." Libby pointed at the window. "Those bots are leaving."

They all crept along the length of the canteen. The group of bots—six of them now—were gazing in the opposite direction.

"They're not leaving," Mal said. "They're distracted."

Something sparkled in the sky beyond the village centre.

"Are they fireworks?" Ethan said.

The sky glowed a fierce orange. Now Ethan could hear sharp, echoing pops, and the canteen window began to rattle. Soon the sky above the hillside was filled with colour.

"Not fireworks," Kit said. "Look closer."

Ethan shielded his eyes. He saw three hills instead of one. The tree-topped one on which the pirate ship had landed now sat between two dullish brown peaks. Suddenly, intense red streaks burst from each of the outer ones.

"You've got to be kidding," he murmured.

They were volcanoes. The streaks were plumes of lava making enormous fountain sprays of red above the new mountains.

Libby groaned. "Talk about keeping a low profile."

"Miller's getting more powerful all the time," Kit said. "If he carries on this way, he'll be able to mould the entire sim however he wants. He'll even be able to . . ." He trailed off and stared out of the window.

The lava faded, but the eruptions had left cloudy streaks that lingered in the sky. It took Ethan a couple of seconds to realize that the shapes were letters.

The message read, *MILLER KING OF TOUCHSTONE.*

1010100   01100101   01111000   01110100   00100000   01000010   01110010   01100101   01100001   0

Ethan grumbled as he was shaken awake. "Just five more minutes, Mom."

"Wake *up!*"

His eyes snapped open. It was dark. Libby shook him again. His back ached terribly from lying on a floor softened only with thin seat cushions. He sat up, surprised to find himself in the canteen rather than his bedroom in the Ilkley Grove house.

"Kit's gone," Libby said.

"Have you checked the computer suite?"

"He's *gone* gone."

Ethan looked from Libby to Mal. Both of their faces were tight with concern. "Did the bots get in somehow?"

Mal replied, "The barricades are all fine, I checked them."

With a start, Ethan remembered his bot brother, Greg, walking straight through the kitchen door. "But this whole place is digital, isn't it? Maybe walls and barricades don't keep them out. We didn't think of that. Maybe they got to him."

Libby placed both hands on his shoulders and looked into his eyes. "I'm pretty sure that's not what's happened. Kit left because he wanted to join Miller. I'm sure of it."

"But why? Miller's insane."

"I know that. Kit knows that too. But Miller's plan, for what it's worth, is to reshape Touchstone into a world that suits him better. He has no intention of leaving, because if he did he'd be put in a high-security prison. I suppose Kit sees the appeal of staying too."

"Why would Kit prefer being in Touchstone to being free, out in the real world? Because he appreciates the developers' handiwork?"

"I guess he might have a professional interest. But haven't you noticed anything odd about him?"

"He moves in kind of a strange way. But I don't see why he'd want to stay locked up in prison."

"Sometimes you seem pretty smart, Ethan, and other times . . ." Libby shook her head sadly. "He didn't want to tell me either, but I guess I have the kind of face that makes people want to talk. I like to think I'd have spotted it anyway. He's sick. Out there, I mean. He's weak, and I'm pretty sure he's more or less confined to his house. He listed all the medication he has to take. It went on and on."

Ethan slapped his forehead. "Which is why he spends so much time at his computer."

"Right. Here in Touchstone he's fit and strong. You can see the appeal in staying. He's more trapped in his real-world house than he is in this *actual* prison."

Ethan remembered Kit's ungainly sprint on sports day, as though he were a baby animal taking its first tentative steps. His real body, and therefore the mind controlling his avatar, must be unused to rapid movement.

He touched his cheek. His scar hadn't been reproduced in the sim either. Their avatars were only approximate versions of their real selves. And Kit's avatar happened to be a dramatic improvement upon his flesh-and-blood body.

They ate breakfast in gloomy silence punctuated by the tapping of the bots at the canteen window. There were more than a dozen of them now. Earlier, a quick check had revealed that bots had gathered at the other blockaded entrances too.

Nobody said it out loud, but Ethan was sure they were thinking the same thing. Without Kit, they had no technical knowledge. Even worse, Kit was the only person who understood how to hack the computers to contact Lex in the outside world.

After finishing her meal Libby slipped away. Ethan rose to follow.

"Let her go," Mal said. "She needs some time alone."

He sat down again and surveyed the dingy canteen and serving kitchen. If the school really was based on the memories of Libby's mom, it would be a painful reminder of her death.

"What about you?" he said.

"I've had plenty of time on my own already."

Ethan wished he had the confidence to reach over and part Mal's hair to look into her eyes.

"I feel such an idiot, Mal. I was starting to suspect Kit of all sorts of things. I thought he might be a Mercy employee, a prison warden, a— I don't know what I thought, really. Maybe he could tell I didn't totally trust him."

"You had no idea what was going on in his mind. I've been here the whole time, and I've seen the two of you together. You've been a good friend to him." Mal placed her hand on his arm. It felt warm.

"Thanks. You're a good friend too. To me."

Her hair fell away to reveal eyes that shone in the half-dark.

"Mal . . . I've never met anyone like you. I wish—"

Her hand went rigid. She shook her head. "Don't."

Ethan had no idea what to do or say. They sat opposite each other in silence. Mal's head lowered again. Her hand was still resting on his arm; he didn't dare move a muscle. It was only when Libby returned that he pulled his arm away.

Libby's face was pink. Ethan guessed she had been crying. "I've been having a good think," she said, "and I've concluded that I have no idea what the hell we're going to do next."

"We're going to escape," Ethan said, though he knew how unconvinced he sounded.

"How?"

"Lex is on the case. She'll have an idea. Maybe she can get us something from the repository Kit talked about that might help us get away. A plane or, I don't know, a rocket."

"Ethan, I don't want to sound mean, but you must see that doesn't make sense. Touchstone isn't a real place we can escape from, like a desert island. Anywhere we go will still be part of the sim. Anyway, Miller has Mr. Jeffers in a *cage*, for goodness sake. He's—quite literally—holding all the cards."

"She's right," Mal said. "Without perks, we have no advantage."

Ethan frowned. Something jogged his memory. "Remember what Kit said about the perks? Didn't he say they might be controlled from somewhere within Touchstone itself? It'd kind of make sense to have them in here, so that the wardens and inspectors could access them during their visit. Remember, Mrs. Benedict gave me a merit badge."

Libby rubbed her eyes. "Even if that was true, it could be anywhere."

"Maybe. But if the perks are stored somewhere, maybe there are other controls too."

"You mean control the bots?" Mal's voice was hoarse, but she sounded interested.

"And maybe prisoners too. I was thinking about it when Russell was put on auto. It seemed weird that they didn't do it right here at school."

"I figured they wanted him to stew for a bit," Libby said, "or to scare the rest of us with a big song-and-dance ceremony."

"Maybe. Or maybe it's because they *couldn't* do it here at school. Maybe Mrs. Benedict needed to access the control centre. Which means it has to be—"

Mal burst from her chair. "The church!"

Libby nodded vigorously. "It makes perfect sense! She marched us all down there because Russell had to be near the tower. So when she came out of the church before the ceremony, she'd been changing the settings on Russell's profile, right?"

"Right. That has to be it."

"What should we do? Go there right now?"

"No. We're missing something," Ethan said thoughtfully. "It couldn't be as easy as that—there's no way we'd be able to just walk into the church."

Mal said, "If there's a lock, there must be a key."

Ethan leapt up. "No, not a key, but you're close! It's been staring us in the face the whole time!"

Libby folded her arms indignantly. "Would you mind not talking in riddles?"

"Think about it. . . . There's something we've seen everywhere there are bots in charge. In our houses, in every classroom and at the church."

"Look, I already said—"

Mal interrupted her, jumping up and down in her excitement. "Clocks!" She darted around the table to hug Ethan. He had no idea how to react.

Over Mal's shoulder he saw Libby's look of amusement. "Have you guys quite finished?"

Ethan pushed Mal away gently, coughing to hide his embarrassment.

"Sorry to interrupt your little moment," Libby said with a grin, "but what are we actually going to *do* with this information?"

Ethan thought of the clocks in his house counting backwards or freezing whenever the sim glitched. And what about the punishment ceremony? When Mrs. Benedict had exited the church, the door had opened smoothly, as if controlled remotely, then she had looked up at the clock tower, waiting for the minute hand to reach twelve. She had consulted something in her hand.

"The fob watches," he said with a sigh of relief. "They're the keys. Getting one of them is the only way we'll get into the clock tower."

Libby nodded slowly. "But Mrs. Benedict's gone. So who else has one?"

They all exchanged looks.

Ethan groaned. "The head teacher."

1010100   01100101   01111000   01110100   00100000   01000010   01110010   01100101   01100001   01

Ethan hefted aside one of the blockade desks. "Can you see what's going on outside?"

Mal stood on a stool to peer out of the grimy skylight at the top of the corridor wall. "Libby's coming back. The bots are huddled around the fire as if they're hypnotized."

Swirling orange patterns appeared on the corridor wall, produced by the flames on the all-weather pitch. Ethan had discovered the box of matches in a pile of items in the sports hall—leftovers from the perks that Mr. Jeffers had summoned. They had constructed the bonfire mainly from the mats used in the high jump event. Ethan had worked tirelessly for most of the morning while Mal and Libby had remained at the canteen window, distracting the bots. If everything worked as planned, Libby's fire would now command the attention of the growing group of teachers and pupils.

Libby joined them. Panting from exertion, she raised the rounders bat she held in her right hand. She had fastened a thick belt over the top of her coat; from behind her back she produced a cricket bat, which she gave to Ethan, and a hockey stick, which she passed to Mal.

They crept along the corridor with their weapons raised.

Libby pointed with her bat. "Take the next left. We can skip the science labs that way. I don't want to think what the bots might do with a Bunsen burner."

They passed the row of lockers where Ethan had first met Kit, and soon reached the glass doors of the assembly hall. The curtains along the right-hand side were drawn and the interior of the large room was almost totally black, but Ethan could make out dark shapes moving within.

"You're sure this is the only way to Mr. Tooley's office?"

"As far as I know," Libby replied.

"In that case, there's no other option. Are you both ready?"

Both girls nodded. Mal looked terrified. She was gripping the handle of her hockey stick so tightly that the bones of her fingers showed through her skin.

Ethan pushed open the door as quietly as possible.

The figures hovered at the left-hand side of the hall. Ethan gestured with his cricket bat, hoping that Mal and Libby could see him in the darkness. They moved in silence along the curtained edge of the room.

At first Ethan had the impression that the figures were growing in size, until he realized that it was because they were moving towards him. His hesitation lasted for only a second or two, but it was long enough to put him at a disadvantage. The figures knocked over chairs as they closed in.

"Run!" he shouted.

He swiped with the cricket bat, uncertain how far away the things were. At the periphery of his vision he saw Mal and Libby sprint to the far end of the hall. Ethan held his ground, swinging wildly with the bat. It made contact with the first of the shapes, sending a reverberating shock along the bat and through his arm. Something flailed towards him, grazing against his shoulder. He wriggled free, but after a couple of fumbles something jabbed at his stomach, hard. He dropped to the ground with a grunt.

The cricket bat had fallen from his hand during the fall. He reached out to grasp it, but even as his fingers closed around the handle he felt himself being hauled back. Both of his ankles were being lifted; he upended and his face crunched against the slick floor. Despite his panic, an odd thought passed through his mind: he wondered whether teeth could be broken in a simulated world.

He tried to cry out but once again his feet were yanked, and his face smacked against the ground.

He heard a click. Yellow light streamed into the hall.

"We're through!" he heard Mal shout. "Ethan! Oh—"

He grimaced, but not due to the pain in his legs and head. He knew what would happen next. His friends would run to help him. And there was every chance that they would get caught too. Whoever had him by the legs wasn't the only bot in the assembly hall.

He threw his arms forward, clawing for purchase on the slippery floor. He dragged himself forward a few inches, enough to make a lunge for the handle of the cricket bat; his fingertips scraped against its rough surface before he was pulled backwards.

The light now allowed him to see his attacker. The bot was a teenage boy whose cold eyes and wide-open mouth made him appear monstrous. He appeared taller and stronger than most of the teachers. Indignance at the unfairness gave Ethan access to new reserves of energy. With a roar he flailed again, then whooped with triumph as he grasped the handle of the cricket bat. In a single motion he lifted it and swung it in a wide arc. He heard a crack as the weapon made contact with the bot's shoulder.

The bot's grip loosened momentarily, and Ethan kicked both his feet against his attacker's torso. To his surprise, he managed to free one of his feet. He used it to prize the thick fingers from his other ankle. His leg came free, but felt strangely light. At first he was stricken with the peculiar fear that the bot had ripped off his foot.

As he staggered away he choked with laughter. The thing had only kept his shoe.

"Stay back!" he shouted as he sprinted towards the double doors. As soon as he entered, Libby and Mal each slammed one of the doors shut. Immediately, two bots appeared—a teenage girl and the boy who had attacked Ethan—lit from above by the corridor lights so that their own features cast strange, pointed shadows upon their faces.

The bots hammered upon the glass: the girl with both fists, the boy with Ethan's shoe. Even though the doors were locked tight, Libby and Ethan continued leaning against them with the full weight of their bodies until Mal dragged a wooden bench over and wedged it under the handles. They all slumped down against the wall in relief.

00   01100101   01111000   01110100   00100000   01000010   01110010   01100101   01100001   0110101

Outside Mr. Tooley's office was a small waiting area. Ethan guessed it was designed specifically for pupils awaiting punishment. In his own school within the Gates he had only visited the head teacher's office once. It had been a misunderstanding, really, after he and another boy had cracked their skulls together in the schoolyard while playing a game. The boy, Neil, who Ethan knew only vaguely, had assumed he'd been picking a fight and lashed out. They'd been scooped up by the on-duty teacher, their parents had been called in and the whole thing had been quickly smoothed out by the head teacher. But when his dad had first showed up at the school, Ethan had been terribly upset at the expression on his face—it had been pure disappointment. Now Ethan bristled at the memory. His disappointment in his dad—not only a Mercy boss, but an outright liar to his family—was surely far greater.

Above the blocky red sofa in the waiting area were shelves laden with sports trophies. All of the plaques were blank. A ragged poster pinned to the wall showed a schoolgirl whispering to a boy above the message, *Want to be trusted? Don't tell tall tales.*

"How can we know for sure that Mr. Tooley will be in there?" Mal sounded as though she hoped he wouldn't be.

"We can't be certain," Ethan said, "but every time there's been a reason for Mr. Tooley to show up, like when Miller started being an idiot in the canteen, he always appears from the direction of his office—even when he should be all the way over at the other side of the school. My guess is that he resets here whenever he starts a new routine."

Libby held up two skipping ropes. "Shall we?"

They set to work tying the ropes around the legs of the sofa and to the handle of a heavy filing cabinet. When they finished, the door to the office was tightly cordoned off.

Libby unlocked a nearby window and propped it open. "If we need it, that's our escape route." Then she laughed bitterly. "Who am I kidding? Not 'if'—'when.' Be careful, Ethan."

"So I'll be the one doing this, will I?" he replied, trying to sound lighthearted. He leaned through the lattice of rope and rested his hand on the doorknob. "Ready?"

"Ready."

He twisted the handle and pushed hard. At first the office was too dim to make out anything. He squinted into the darkness.

"Pupils!" the head teacher's voice boomed from within. "What is the meaning of this?"

Ethan reached for his cricket bat.

Mr. Tooley stumbled into the light. His mouth was twitching spasmodically and one cheek flickered with constellations of pixels. His movements were jerkier than before, his body tilting constantly. His arms twitched as he encountered the rope barrier, but he didn't look down at the obstruction; instead he stared out at the three prisoners. Now he was close enough for Ethan to see the spinning outer edges, the oscillating pixels, of the pupil of each eye. The cogs were more regular and less jagged than Mrs. Benedict's, which Ethan supposed represented processed data as opposed to the commands from a human operator.

Mr. Tooley fumbled impotently against the ropes. "Return to your classrooms at once!"

"Look." Ethan pointed at a golden chain that looped from a buttonhole of the head teacher's tweed waistcoat and into a pocket. He said to Mal, "You're smallest and quickest. We'll keep him distracted while you get the watch."

"Hey, Mr. T!" Libby shouted. "Look at me, I'm playing sports indoors!"

Mr. Tooley wrestled with the rope net. "This warrants the severest of punishments." His voice was becoming more monotonous and grating with each utterance.

Mal approached from the side. Mr. Tooley swerved towards her. In desperation, Ethan reached out to pull a drawer from the filing cabinet, spilling its contents noisily onto the floor. Mr. Tooley stared at the debris, his mouth hanging open and his face turning purple.

Carefully, Mal reached for Mr. Tooley's waistcoat pocket. Her fingers touched the golden chain, then worked along to manipulate the small bar that attached it to the buttonhole.

"Look at me!" Ethan yelled as he stamped on the documents and stationery that had fallen from the filing cabinet. "I don't respect school property!"

Libby joined him, leaping on the objects with undisguised relish. Mr. Tooley's entire body trembled as he watched on with a look of total disbelief.

Ethan saw Mal slip the golden bar from the buttonhole. She grimaced with concentration as she lifted the fob watch carefully from the head teacher's pocket.

Suddenly, Mr. Tooley's neck cricked and then he was staring down at Mal. He swung his arm wildly at her.

Libby leapt forward with her rounders bat raised. She swept books off a shelf as she passed, then took advantage of the distraction to swing the bat directly at the head teacher. It made contact with his neck with a sickening thud. Mal dropped to the floor and kicked against the door frame to push herself backwards; in her right hand she held the fob watch with its trailing gold chain.

"She's got it, Libby!" Ethan yelled. "Get him back into the office!"

Libby launched herself again at the head teacher, this time barrelling into his chest. Rather than pushing Mr. Tooley back, the force knocked him off his feet. His arms went stiff and his entire body pivoted on the tightened ropes as though he were performing an acrobatic routine. His outstretched arm knocked Ethan to the ground.

Ethan lay still, winded. He watched as Mr. Tooley toppled as if in slow motion, scrabbling for purchase on the ropes. Slowly but surely, the head teacher began to drag himself out of the cordoned office and into the corridor towards Ethan.

Libby recovered quickly and retreated.

"Over here, Ethan!" Mal shouted. "We can trap him in the waiting room."

But Ethan was paralyzed, staring into the whirling clockwork of the head teacher's eyes. Mr. Tooley continued to drag himself free of the ropes. His fingers fidgeted like spiders' legs.

"Pupils," Mr. Tooley said in an eerily calm voice as he slithered towards Ethan. "My only remaining option is complete expulsion."

Ethan felt certain that in Touchstone, expulsion didn't simply mean being banned from school.

"Prepare to be punished," Mr. Tooley said. "Prepare to—" He stopped in mid-sentence.

An array of expressions crossed the head teacher's face—first he appeared livid with anger, then beaming with happiness, then shocked. A wave of green pixels fluttered across his features. When they settled, Mr. Tooley now looked bewildered.

"Ethan?" he said in a quiet voice.

Ethan, on his feet now, backed into the corner of the waiting room. What had happened?

"Ethan? It's me! It's Kit." The head teacher's voice was as deep as usual, but its timbre had become entirely different.

Ethan shook all over. This was one bizarre development too far. The head teacher tried to roll over, pressing his nose to the floor, then stumbled to his feet and gazed about as if he was trying to find his bearings. Mal and Libby looked as shocked as Ethan felt. He saw Mal slip the fob watch into her coat pocket.

"Kit? Is it really you in there?" Ethan came as close to the head teacher as he dared. The pixelated, clockwork circles in his eyes had disappeared and the irises were now bright blue.

The body of Mr. Tooley nodded. "I'm so sorry I left last night."

The voice didn't sound at all like Kit, but Ethan reminded himself that he was speaking through Mr. Tooley's voice box, or whatever programming represented his voice box. "Where are you?"

After a pause, the Kit–head teacher replied, "I'm with Miller. I'm using equipment he's set up in the pirate ship." The head teacher's body swung to face the wall of trophies, his eyes narrowing. Something about the action suggested that, rather than the trophies, he was looking at something that Ethan couldn't see.

"We have to hurry. Miller doesn't know I'm using the gizmo to patch into this bot," the Kit–head teacher continued. "Who am I now, anyway? I picked the one that was nearest to you." His neck bent and his eyes widened. "Wow. Am I Mr. T? Weird." He frowned. "Miller's powerful, Ethan. I don't know what I can do about it."

Libby signalled to catch Ethan's attention. What was she trying to say?

"It's all right," Ethan said to the Kit–head teacher. "We've got a plan."

"Are you going to attack Miller?" The voice faltered again. Kit sounded terrified.

"We wouldn't stand a chance."

"Then what? What's this plan of yours?"

Ethan ignored Libby's shake of the head. "We know where the control centre is, the one you were talking about."

The Kit–head teacher nodded eagerly. "Where is it?"

"It's the—" Ethan glared at Libby as she tried to grab his arm to interrupt him. "It's the clock tower at the church. We're certain that's where the avatar profiles are stored."

The Kit–head teacher froze.

"Kit? Hey—perhaps you could sneak away again? We could meet—"

Then the head teacher's body began to shake. Gradually, Ethan realized that it was laughter. Soon he was doubled over with mirth.

"I can't *believe* you fell for that!" The tone of voice was entirely different now, sounding far more nasal. The body of the head teacher swung again towards the trophy shelves as if addressing somebody there. "Kit, you may be an irredeemable nerd, but I have to hand it you. This setup was nifty work. Although you have to give me some credit for my performance too." He snickered and repeated, in an exaggeratedly timid voice, *'I'm so sorry I left last night.'*

The head teacher—or rather, Miller—beamed at Mal, Libby and Ethan. He parted his arms and made a deep bow. Like an actor addressing somebody offstage, he said, "All right Russell, you can pull the plug on old Tooley now."

Then, with a wink at Ethan, he whispered, "Race you to the church, noob."

As Ethan, Mal and Libby watched, the head teacher's face became a shuddering mass of unconnected pixels, then a featureless beige smudge. The heavy body crumpled face-first to the floor.

CHAPTER NINETEEN

The Truth

Lex refreshed the instant messenger client. Nothing. Where was Ethan? He should have been online two hours ago.

She could barely imagine what he and the other prisoners might be up against. The brief mentions of bots and a rip in the sky conjured up a terrifying, twisted world, but despite the fear, she couldn't help but wish that she could see it all for herself.

One more try. F5. Refresh.

Nothing.

She had to stop staring at the screen. She had to eat something.

She closed the IM client to reveal the original email. She bent close to the screen to examine the light-grey letter Q of the Quicksilvr logo. Something struck her as familiar about the arrangement of the stars that surrounded it, and she gasped as pieces of the puzzle started to fit together in her mind like the cogs that barricaded Mercy's server.

A sharp skittering noise from behind her stopped as abruptly as it had begun, leaving only the faint hum of computer cooling fans. She held her breath. There it was again! The noise, though faint, reverberated throughout the flat. Her family had had a dog when she was a kid, and he used to make similar scrabbling sounds at the door when he wanted to be let in.

She tiptoed to the control panel and its small video screen. A few punched commands brought up the feed from the hidden camera that James had installed in the alley. The picture was grainy and speckled with digital noise, but she could make out the silver oblong of the reinforced door of the flat. Before it stood a lone figure wearing a long, dark coat. A black hat with a wide brim obscured the face.

That same person again. How many times had she seen him before? In the street near her flat, certainly, but hadn't she also stumbled into him outside Mercy's HQ on her second visit?

The man seemed about to leave. Something about his lumbering movement rang a bell. And was he wearing glasses under that hat?

She fumbled with the locks and flung open the door.

"Hey!" she called.

The figure froze.

She lowered her voice. "It's all right. Come in, Cecil. I'll make you a cup of tea."

His shoulders slumped. Finally, he turned and removed his hat, holding it before him in both hands. The grubby lenses of his glasses shone with moonlight refracted through raindrops. He nodded and followed Lex inside.

She took Cecil's hat and coat, but once he had entered she simply dropped them onto the floor. She directed him to the sagging sofa, then rolled her swivel chair to the low coffee table. Cecil looked about the flat, seeming surprised to be there. He was tense. Afraid.

"I was lying." Lex smiled at Cecil's suspicious reaction, then added, "I don't have any tea."

Cecil laughed. Lex was relieved to see the glimmer of humanity. He offered a cautious smile.

"But you came to talk to me, right? That's why you've been following me?" She saw him prickle in response. "I saw you, Cecil, and I'm guessing there were plenty of times I *didn't* spot you. How long have you been staking out my flat?"

He sighed. "I'm not . . . It's not what you—"

"Relax. I know what you're going to say, or at least some of it. As it happens, I figured it out a couple of minutes ago."

Cecil nodded vigorously. "I'm not—"

Lex interrupted, refusing to have him spoil her deductive triumph. "I know you're not a high-up employee of Mercy. If you *were* the big cheese there, you could have raised an army of police to bring me in."

Cecil's eyebrows raised in surprise. For a second Lex saw within his expression a familiar, quizzical look. Ethan must have inherited that from him.

"It was the logo that gave me the clue," she continued. "Quicksilvr."

"You know?"

"I know."

She brought up the Touchstone alert email on her terminal. She scrolled to the footer and zoomed in on the Quicksilvr company logo, the large letter Q surrounded by stars. She traced the outline of the stars with an index finger. "That's Orion, isn't it? The same constellation I saw pasted to the window in Ethan's bedroom."

"We've both always been stargazers, my son and I."

She nodded. "I was being blind. When I was snooping at Quicksilvr I discovered that you were high-ranking, a boss. But I didn't stop to consider what you were the boss *of*. So when did you set up Quicksilvr?"

"Ten years ago, give or take."

"And it was purely a VR holiday company when you founded it?"

Slowly, Cecil said, "Holidays, yes. But it was more than that. We had a real vision. We wanted to give everyone, no matter their background, access to the same experiences. Positive experiences. We wanted to level the field, socially speaking. No matter how poor you might be, you too could see the wonders of the world, or at least our VR representations of them. Even if you were confined to a wheelchair, you could walk the Inca Trail to Machu Picchu within one of our sims. It was a grand idea. But I do concede that it wasn't terribly commercial. The educational trips came a little later. They were Patricia's idea—Patricia de Witt, my business partner—after we started losing money."

"But what I don't understand is this. Why is there no record of all that, the beginnings of the company? I looked everywhere. Your name isn't associated with Quicksilvr anywhere."

Cecil's face fell. "That was part of the conditions of the buyout. When Mercy made us the offer, we were all but bankrupt. We would have agreed to anything. We *did* agree to anything. But I was shocked that they went so far. They removed all reference to Patricia and I from the accounts. It felt like a decade of our work had been wiped out. But that's pure vanity, of course. Our work was still there, intact. It was only that it didn't have our names on it anymore."

"And Mercy kept you both on as employees?"

"Yes. At first it was only for show, I suspect, with generous salaries to keep us sweet. But eventually they insisted that I show up at the office each day—the Mercy HQ, that is, rather than Quicksilvr. I wasn't even allowed onto the Quicksilvr premises. That was after—" His voice cracked.

"After what?" Lex's chair squeaked as she leant forward. "Cecil, it's okay. It's safe to talk to me."

"After Patricia was found dead. Suicide, they said. She'd been asking awkward questions for months. She was always more insightful, more curious, than me. I was too immersed in the code. She was the more practical member of the partnership." He rubbed his forehead and exhaled noisily. "Mercy made it clear that if I asked any difficult questions, I'd end up 'committing suicide' too."

His body began to shake with suppressed sobs. "I'm sorry," he said between gasps. "I mean, for everything. I didn't know! I swear I didn't. I'm sorry about you too, for following you after you showed up at our house. I had to know about . . . Oh, God, Ethan! On top of everything else, I let him get mixed up in all this!"

Lex had no idea how to react to his outpouring of emotion. She fetched a roll of toilet paper from the bathroom and handed it to Cecil, who took it gratefully and blew his nose. She waited for him to gather himself.

"Did Mercy threaten Ethan too? Even before his arrest?"

"They made veiled threats about him, and Caroline, and everyone else I love. I had no choice but to stay silent. When my son was arrested, I knew what they'd do with him. I'd imagine they couldn't believe their luck. Now he's a constant reminder that I can't expose Project Q. They've made him a hostage. Or I have. I don't know which."

"Cecil . . . I've spoken to him. To Ethan."

"What? How?" He almost bounced off the sofa in his excitement. "Have they hurt him?"

"He's safe in a sim called Touchstone. He's with someone who managed to tap into the mainframe and set up a means of communication. They—"

"—changed the emergency contact!" Cecil interrupted. "That's it, isn't it? Of course! What a superb idea! But that means . . ." His eyes darted rapidly. "Touchstone, you say? But what exactly is going on in there?"

"The sim's fragile. Sounds as if it's on its last legs. The bots are malfunctioning. And there are rips in the skybox."

Cecil's face turned white.

"Let's rewind a little," she said. "I've been digging, and I've found out plenty about the sims and about Mercy. I know they're planning to roll Project Q out to more and more offenders. And I've been gathering info about the fast-tracked sentences without any defence for the accused. But is it really just about cutting corners to save money?"

"I've no idea. All I know is that they'd go as far as killing to protect Project Q. I'd been trying to gather evidence myself from the Mercy offices. Memos, that sort of thing."

"The lilac folder! I've seen it!"

"I know you have. It was confiscated after Ethan was arrested."

Lex felt her cheeks glow. She remembered where she had found it, in the hidden compartment within Cecil's filing cabinet. "I hope I didn't get you in too much trouble. I was in a hurry. It got left behind."

Cecil waved a hand. Lex understood the gesture perfectly. It meant, "What more trouble could I be in?"

"Was there anything incriminating in the folder anyway? It was mostly blanked out with black pen."

"Almost everything I could get my hands on was redacted in that way. I didn't have anything, really."

Lex slumped into her seat. "Then we're no further forward."

Cecil clasped and unclasped his hands.

"Cecil . . . talk to me. There's something else, isn't there?"

In his eyes she saw hints of his years of grief and regret. "That folder . . . it wasn't much, but it was all the more frustrating because I'd already had the information once before. The real evidence, without any black marks. They were documents that I could never hope to find in the Mercy offices, from years ago, from soon after the takeover. Back when I was allowed into the Quicksilvr compound I had full access to the servers. I could get at almost anything. And so I did. I suspected something was wrong with Mercy, even then. I suppose I thought of the evidence I was accumulating as a sort of insurance policy."

"But what happened to it?"

"Oh, it's safe. Probably."

Lex leapt to her feet. "Where? Tell me, Cecil, where? We can do this. We'll need more than your evidence—Mercy will almost certainly go public with Project Q anyway, once they've spun it out of all recognition. But with evidence showing what they're really up to, and then Ethan's witness statement, when we break him out . . ."

Cecil appeared totally dejected. "It's no use. I can't get to it. I've been a fool, and I've compounded my mistakes again and again. The evidence is in the only place I felt safe in those days. It's in Quicksilvr."

"Where exactly? In some office on the Quicksilvr premises? Not in that barbed-wire compound?"

He rubbed the bridge of his nose. "Not exactly. I buried it. X marks the spot, sort of."

"You're talking in riddles! Spit it out."

"Sorry. It's buried deep within the computer code. The evidence against Mercy is right there, hard-coded into the holiday sims. All of them."

"In the sims? Then we need to get in there!"

"I'd never even get through the door."

Lex towered over Cecil. "Then it'll have to be me."

The new, faint glimmer of hopefulness in Cecil's eyes made her heart ache. She chewed her nails. "But I can't just walk in there either. . . . Wait—do you have the client list?"

"I can remember plenty of them. We mainly dealt with regular customers. Stinking rich, all of them. I'm certain plenty of the same people continue to use Quicksilvr for holidays."

Lex swept fast-food cartons and mugs off the coffee table and onto the floor, then rifled among the clutter on her desk. She dropped a notepad onto the table and tossed a couple of pens on top.

"Then here's the plan. You're going rack your brain and write down every single name and contact detail you can remember. And I'm going to go and steal us some teabags."

CHAPTER TWENTY

The Battle

"Hurry!" Libby yelled as she tore along the school field.

"We'll never get there before them," Ethan panted. Even in his hurry he was surprised to notice that Mal was able to keep pace easily, despite the fact that her legs were much shorter than his.

"We have a chance," Mal said without a trace of breathlessness. "Miller doesn't know about the fob watch. Even if they're already at the church, there's a chance we can catch them off guard and sneak into the building."

Ethan tried to clear his mind to concentrate on running, but his whirling thoughts distracted him. Even if they could use the fob watch to get into the church, what would they find inside? He imagined banks of computers like the ones at school. Without Kit's technical knowledge, what could they hope to achieve? But he had to concede that the alternative didn't bear thinking about either. If Miller gained control of their avatar profiles, he could do to them whatever he wanted.

The cricket bat felt solid and real in his hands. He hoped that he wouldn't need to use it. Hitting the teenage boy who had attacked him in the assembly hall had made him feel physically sick, even though the boy was virtual, not human. He couldn't imagine fighting Miller or any of the other prisoners, knowing there were real people behind the avatars.

He and Mal followed Libby into the graveyard behind the church. It was as empty as the school fields had been. Where were all the bots?

It wasn't long before he had an answer to his question.

They came skidding to a halt at the corner of the church. Miller, Russell and Anita stood in the public square before the huge building, looking up at the clock tower. Kit and Mr. Jeffers were with them, both with their hands tied behind their backs and their feet bound tightly. A purple bruise covered one of Kit's cheeks. Somehow, Miller must have tweaked the settings of Kit's avatar, allowing his body to show injury.

In a line before the church were fifty or more bots, including both teachers and pupils. Ethan gasped as he recognized the father and mother from his own bot family. All of the bots were motionless, standing evenly spaced with barely any room between them.

"I was hoping you might come and join us!" Miller's voice carried clearly across the square. None of the bots made the slightest noise.

"Miller, you have to let Kit go!" Ethan shouted.

Miller cupped a hand to his ear. "I'm sorry, what was that? I only heard a mousey little squeak."

"Let him go!"

Miller clutched his belly in a pantomime laugh. "Oh, so you're bargaining with me, is that right? Hi-lar-ious. And what do you have to offer in return?"

The fob watch tucked in Mal's pocket was their only advantage, but letting Miller know of its existence was unthinkable. Ethan glanced at the line of bots guarding the church doors, then at Miller, judging the distance. He had used his cricket bat to beat his way past bots before, so there was a faint chance he could do it again, and then Mal could use the fob watch to open the doors. But even if they could, Miller would reach the church before them.

Kit raised his head and his eyes met Ethan's. He looked desperately weak and barely conscious. He nodded slowly. Ethan frowned. What did that mean?

Suddenly, Kit toppled over, hitting the concrete base of the monument with the full weight of his body, which shimmered with pixels for several moments. He gurgled as if he were having some kind of fit. Miller, Russell and Anita turned sharply.

"Sort him out!" Miller barked. "We still need him! For now."

From his position on the ground Kit gave Ethan a wide-eyed stare. Then he began moaning in agony as his captors crowded around him.

Ethan finally understood. Kit was providing a distraction. He whispered, "Mal! Libby! Run for it!"

Without another word they dashed left, directly towards the church doors. Ethan ducked down and raised the cricket bat in both hands as a battering ram. He winced as he struck the first body and sent a teenage bot girl reeling. He heard the thuds of Mal's and Libby's weapons impacting against others. None of the bots made any attempt to protect themselves. They scattered like bowling pins.

"Capture them!" Miller screamed.

The bots sprung into life. Hands grasped from all directions and Ethan weaved as he ran in a desperate attempt to evade them. He was now only a few feet from the doors to the church.

"Hold up the fob watch!" he shouted.

He ducked from outstretched limbs. Mal fumbled to retrieve the watch and then brandished it high above her head.

The church doors swung open smoothly. Ethan glimpsed the lowest steps of a staircase that must lead all the way up to the clock tower.

He cried out in pain as something struck his right ear. He staggered and pushed against the ground to right himself. Fingers clutched at his clothes and nipped at his skin. Within seconds he found himself pinned between two young girls in school uniform. Their grip was absurdly strong and their fingers dug painfully into his flesh.

Libby and Mal had also come to a standstill, struggling in vain against their own captors. One of Libby's arms was held by Mr. Cooper, the biology teacher. She was writhing in agony.

The church doors were wide open. Ethan was so close that he could have reached out to touch them, if only his hands were free.

Miller strolled to stand directly before him. "You really are hopeless. I feel almost fond of you all. Perhaps I'll even miss you when you're gone. I'll take that, thank you very much." He plucked the fob watch from Mal's grasp and examined it. "Of course. A key—I should have guessed. Thanks an awful lot for doing the detective work to save me any exertion." He patted Ethan roughly on the head. Ethan wrenched free and snarled.

"Russell! Bring the geek with you. And you—" Miller was addressing the bots now "—keep hold of these three idiots until I return. Those are Mr. Jeffers' explicit instructions." He tossed a playing card onto the pavement and sauntered into the church. Anita and Russell followed him inside, carrying Kit effortlessly between them.

Ethan struggled again but the bot children held him tight.

"Mr. Jeffers says that you have to release us!" he shouted. None of the bots reacted.

"What's he going to do in there, do you think?" Mal had stopped trying to free herself but she was shaking violently.

Libby answered through grunts of pain. "He wants us out of the way. He'll access our profiles like Mrs. Benedict did. And he'll punish us. That is, he'll put us on auto so we won't bother him anymore. Then he can set to work remaking the sim in his own image. In summary, he's a lunatic."

Ethan wished he could offer some reassurance, but he felt certain that Libby was right on every count.

A sound came from the clock tower. Ethan looked up to see the hands on the clock face move, slowly at first, then faster and faster. But he was distracted by something above the tower. At the tip of its greenish, copper-plated spire he saw a strange shimmer, and around the ripples fizzed a golden braid of light.

The hands of the clock reached one minute to twelve and then stopped. Now the second hand worked its way slowly around the clock face. Ethan, Mal and Libby exchanged looks but there seemed nothing more to say. Ethan only wished that he'd had more time to get to know Mal.

A dull clunk signalled twelve o'clock. Ethan's hands made fists, but it was from tension rather than any expectation of a fight. How would it feel to be put on auto? Would he feel pain? Or would he stop feeling anything at all?

But instead he felt something entirely unexpected.

He felt freedom. Physical, actual freedom. The bodies of the two bot schoolgirls spasmed and then they released their grip. Ethan saw Mal and Libby's captors let them go too.

"The clock! It's overridden Miller's commands!" Ethan gasped. "Run for it!"

They pelted across the square, stumbling uncontrollably in their hurry. Mal pushed Libby aside in her hurry to escape.

A deep, rumbling hum came from somewhere behind them, high up. The clock tower.

Ethan checked over his shoulder as he ran. Libby was further behind him and Mal. She was limping. Her trouser leg was torn where Mr. Cooper had grabbed her.

"Faster, Libby! The punishment's started!"

Libby nodded frantically but she didn't pick up her pace. In fact, she was slowing down. She slowed to a jog, then a walking pace; she was limping badly.

Both Ethan and Mal skidded to a halt.

Libby stopped walking only metres from where Ethan and Mal stood. Her mouth opened but she didn't speak. Her eyes watered and she gave Ethan a pleading look, but then it faded and was replaced by a calm, neutral expression.

"Libby?" Ethan murmured, though he knew it was too late.

Now Libby stared at Ethan and Mal without any hint of recognition. Slowly, a vacant smile appeared.

Then she turned and strolled towards the church, her limp forgotten. She waved happily at one of the bot pupils as she crossed the square.

From the corner of his eye Ethan saw Mal begin to set off again to the church. He pulled her back. Her arm felt impossibly thin and fragile.

"Leave her," he said. "Libby's gone. We've lost her."

00   01100101   01111000   01110100   00100000   01000010   01110010   01100101   01100001   0110101

They ran through the village until Ethan felt he couldn't go another step. He waved a hand to signal for Mal to stop. She wasn't even slightly out of breath.

"Quick, in here," Ethan managed to say.

The alley ran alongside a bookshop that he had never seen open for business. Bulky, overflowing rubbish bins lined the passage; it occurred to Ethan how odd it was that somebody had actually designed them for use in the sim. He dragged two of the bins to block the entrance, then he and Mal crouched behind them. It was far from an ideal hiding place. If Miller or any of the bots tracked them down, they would be cornered.

Mal was shaking all over. Ethan pulled her towards him awkwardly, far from certain that she would find the action reassuring. They huddled together as Mal sobbed quietly.

"Poor Libby . . . poor Libby," she whispered. "It was my fault. I pushed past her. . . . I slowed her down. I was so frightened."

"No you didn't. We were all panicking. You didn't do anything wrong."

"I couldn't let it happen to me. The punishment. Not again. Promise me you won't let them do that?"

"I won't. I promise." Ethan chewed his cheek, absorbed in his own thoughts. "Mal . . . I thought you said that you blended in the whole time, before you found us all. So why would you have been punished?"

"I wasn't, not in the way you mean." Abruptly, she struck her head on the brick wall behind her and groaned. "Okay. I give in. I can't carry on this way. I'm so, so sorry."

"It's okay. . . . Hold on. Sorry for what?"

"For lying to you. This whole time."

Ethan suddenly felt very cold. He thought of the French textbook that Mal had been holding when she had appeared on the hillside, and the caption he had read in it: *J'ai le mal de mer*. After all that had happened since then, it hadn't crossed his mind again until now.

Summoning his courage, he reached up to push her fringe away from her eyes.

"No . . ." he whispered. "Don't let it be that."

Sunlight funnelled by the narrow alley made a spotlight upon her face. Ethan looked into her dark eyes. At first the dancing shadows seemed only a trick of the light. But then he saw that surrounding each dark pupil were the jagged teeth of slowly spinning cogs.

He pushed her away, more roughly than he intended. Mal pulled her legs up sharply and pressed her face into her knees.

"That's why you didn't spot us sooner!" Ethan cried, forgetting to keep his voice down. "And that's why you lied about your name! How long have you been . . . Are you just like them? All the other bots?"

Mal barely looked up. Her face had become crumpled and red. "I don't know. It happened right there on the hillside. I was running with the rest of them. I was part of the herd. I wasn't thinking, not in any way that you'd understand. Then—there was a crash of thunder, that's the first thing I remember. And I heard the school bell. I remember being surprised that I didn't reset to the school when the others did. And then I realized something so strange. I realized that I'd *never felt surprise* before."

She shuffled to sit directly before him. "I'm *real*, Ethan. I mean . . . I *feel* real. I don't understand this any more than you do."

Ethan curled up against the opposite wall, keeping his distance.

"But I'll say it again. I'm so sorry for lying. I hated it."

She took a breath and then tucked her hair behind her ears so that her eyes were no longer hidden. The spinning, jagged circles became dizzying. Ethan screwed his own eyes shut. What did this all mean? Did he even know this girl, really?

Then, slowly at first but then with an accumulating sense of certainty, he felt calmness return.

"I'm sorry too," he said finally.

He opened his eyes. Mal was watching him with a hopeful expression.

"I do know you," he said. "I know who you really are. Even if it's a made-up name, you're Maldemaire. You're my friend, Mal. And I trust you."

She exhaled in relief. "But what about the fact that I'm programmed? That I was created by someone else?"

"It's hard for me to understand. But do you remember what Kit said about the AI? That they—that *you*—are far more complex than he'd thought. There are supposed to be limitations on your programming so that you can't access all that complexity, but you've broken all the rules. I'm sure of it."

"I'm still just made of code, though."

"I can't believe that. Some computer programmer might have been responsible for the way you acted at first, but he or she didn't count on whatever happened during that storm, whatever it was that set you free from all those restrictions. Besides, from what I know about DNA, I'm made of code too, sort of. My parents' genes gave me a template that I can either stick to or not. You're alive, Mal. And not only that. You've changed, even during the time I've known you. You've learned new things, you're . . ." He waved his hands in the air, struggling to express himself. "You're just you."

Mal wiped at her eyes, making a sodden streak on the sleeve of her jumper. Her hair was a mess. How could she not be real?

"Anyway," Ethan continued, his voice growing hoarse, "who's to say what's *really* real, here in the sim? When you look at me you're only seeing an avatar. Sure, I exist out in the real world, but in here we're all the same."

Mal bent forward and hugged him. Her hair smelled sweet. Real.

"But what are we going to do?" she said quietly. "We've lost Kit and now Libby. Miller will find us too, eventually."

"I have absolutely no idea. We need a miracle."

01010100   01100101   01111000   01110100   00100000   01000010   01110010   01100101   01100001   0

And a miracle occurred, more or less.

They sat in the alley without any plan or any hope of survival. They were together, and that was enough.

It was Mal who noticed it first. "Do you hear something?"

Ethan listened carefully. A faint splintering noise came from further along the alley, in the opposite direction to the high street.

"Keep quiet. It could be the bots." Perhaps they had found a way around the barricade, through the bookshop. Perhaps, after having located the pair of them, the bots were taking the most direct route. The noise continued, a steady tap-tapping.

"No, it isn't them." Mal moved along the alley cautiously, staying low to the ground.

Ethan followed. The alley opened out into a yard situated behind the bookshop and a neighbouring hardware shop. It was paved with large, square slabs—and it was from these slabs that the sound was coming. Ethan stared as flecks of concrete burst up in tiny showers of dust. The dust clouds moved across the slabs, leaving behind a spidery trail of indentations.

He shifted around to get a better view. "They're letters!" Spinning on his heel, he pointed to a storage unit fixed to the fence at the rear of the yard. "Here, climb up onto this."

From their new vantage point they could read the words that had already formed on the concrete.

ETHAN

Mal gripped his arm. "What's going on?"

"Wait. It hasn't finished."

Where were you? Worried.

The words appeared with greater and greater frequency. Each line of letters became visible only once the dust had settled.

Only option to broadcast one-way. Found the answer! We're breaking you out.

You were right about ship. Holiday sims border Touchstone skybox.

ONE of you gets out => you can ALL leave.

There's a catch. You have to get through the skybox rip. Can't help you there.

Mal hopped up and down, making the storage unit rattle beneath her. "You can escape, Ethan!"

Ethan's mind reeled. "Yeah. But . . ."

But the broadcast wasn't quite finished.

Another catch. Mercy project over. They don't care about you guinea pigs.

Glitches show Touchstone failing fast. Won't last long.

Get out, Ethan. Get out as soon as you can.

After another pause, three final letters appeared.

LEX

When he climbed down, Ethan found that his arms and legs were shaking uncontrollably.

"She must really care about you, this Lex, to do all this," Mal said.

"She's only a friend." Ethan's mouth was dry. "Mal . . . I'm not going to—"

"Shut up. Yes, you are." She reached down to trace the chipped letters on the ground with a finger. "The only thing we need to figure out is how you're going to reach the rip above the pirate ship."

Ethan racked his brain. "There's no way to do it. But it isn't our only chance. The rips appear when something happens to force the sim out of its routines."

"What do you mean? There's another one?"

"It isn't going to be much easier to reach."

"Where is it?"

He took her by the hand and led her along the alley and out to the high street. The sky had become violet and blocks of pixels shuddered across it like murmurations of starlings. He pointed along the street to where the steeple of the church tower was visible over the rooftops of the shops. The new rip in the sky looked as ugly as a wound, blue and raw at its edges and black in the centre.

CHAPTER TWENTY-ONE
Sweet Dreams and Bon Voyage

"More champagne, Alexandra?"

Lex murmured a refusal. She needed to keep her mind clear. The first glass had gone straight to her head, to the extent that she was getting worried about shooting her mouth off, revealing her plan and all the other incriminating thoughts bouncing around in her head.

Her main concern was Ethan. Since he had failed to show up for the IM chat the day before, she had thought of little else. But even if he hadn't read her one-way message, or if something worse had occurred, she couldn't afford a change of plans. She had to get into one of the holiday sims to dig up Cecil's buried evidence. If Ethan was able to make it out of Touchstone at the same time, all the better.

The interior of the limousine was huge. On the leatherette couch opposite Lex sat Florian Bastain, Chief Executive Officer of numerous fashion houses, wealthier than everyone Lex had ever met put together and, most importantly, a regular Quicksilvr patron. Yesterday he'd fallen into her trap—hook, line and sinker. They had exchanged a flurry of emails, though Florian hadn't known he had been talking to Lex. Instead, he had been under the impression that he'd been chatting to Gertrude Lamma, the proprietor of Glamma Couture. "Gertrude" had made profuse apologies for pulling out of their holiday plans at the last minute, but was delighted to announce that her niece, Alexandra Raymond, would take her place.

Florian returned the bottle of champagne to its silver bucket. He made a show of being offended. "I suppose you're used to rather better refreshment than we can provide."

Lex gave a thin-lipped smile and fought the urge to scratch at her scalp. Her hair was pinned tight beneath her jet-black bobbed wig. Maybe she ought to have chosen a beehive hairstyle, which would at least have given her space to breathe. The limousine jolted on a pothole and her hand shot up to steady the wig.

Florian twisted in his seat. "I say, driver, do be a little more careful!"

The driver's black cap bobbed in response. The limousine slowed. Lex cursed silently. It felt as though they'd never get there at this rate. Since she had been picked up from the lobby of the Glamma Couture offices, where she had rushed out to meet the car to avoid the doormen intervening, the journey had already taken more than an hour.

Florian was younger than she had expected, although his crimped and lacquered black hair made him look more like a waxwork than a real person. During her research she had learned that the original source of his wealth was a construction firm that specialized in creating more Gates. He was just another ruthless entrepreneur, using other people's misfortune to his own advantage. She hoped she had managed to disguise her contempt.

Sitting beside Florian was a woman who had introduced herself as Lady Yasmine Hargreaves. She was slender, but her upper body was made bulky by a thick fox fur wound around her shoulders. Lex supposed that Lady Yasmine might be considered attractive, though in a way so bland that she would struggle to describe any of her features in any detail. From their limited conversation it appeared that Lady Yasmine's main functions in life were to organize and attend parties.

Lady Yasmine tugged the fur stole from her face to murmur, "Oh, will Noel be there?"

"I believe so." Florian didn't take his eyes from Lex. "You'll like Noel. He's the razor-sharp wit of our group." He turned to view the road. "The cars ferrying the remainder of our party will be winging their way now, if that isn't a mixed metaphor. I'm told that there will be a dozen of us this year, including yourself."

"What about Emma Finely?" Lady Yasmine said. "I do hope she won't be there. Her comments at my latest fundraiser were off-colour, to say the least. Absolutely no manners, that woman."

Florian didn't answer. His attention was fixed on Lex. "It's such a dreadful shame that your aunt couldn't join us."

Internally, Lex recited facts she had prepared about her "aunt" Gertrude. Before leaving the flat she had rehearsed in the mirror for more than an hour.

"However," Florian continued, "we ought to celebrate having you in her place! Of course, I mean no offence to your aunt, but it's wonderful to have new blood. The average age of our little group is, I fear, creeping inexorably upwards." He gave a tinkling laugh. "Not that such things matter at our holiday destination, of course!"

He seemed to be waiting for Lex to say something. She couldn't think of a lie to tell, so she spoke from the heart. "I've never been in a simulation. Is it strange, the first time?"

"Ah, an innocent!"

Lady Yasmine played with the tail of her fur stole. "It's peculiar at first. In fact, it's rotten. I wouldn't be surprised if you felt nauseous the entire time."

Florian tutted. "Oh, nonsense. It's nothing as bad as that. You see, Alexandra, you would only really become disoriented if you were to select a simulated body—or avatar, I should say—that is unfamiliar to you. There are those of us who find the temptation of adding *improvements* too great to resist."

Lady Yasmine scowled and watched the high hedgerows slip past the window.

"Your aunt, too, is often guilty of that," Florian continued. "As one grows older, the appeal of spending time as a younger person can become tremendous. She pays the price, of course. Although she spends weeks at a time in a fresh young body, she is frequently plagued by dizziness. Forgive my presumption in saying this, Alexandra, but you should not consider changing a hair on your head when we enter the simulation."

Lex fidgeted in her seat and willed the limousine to travel faster. "You haven't told me what kind of simulation you've chosen?"

"Ah! This year it's my turn to choose. And, being the creature of habit that I am, I have chosen a tried-and-tested favourite. By this afternoon we shall all be passengers on the *Titanic*."

Lady Yasmine shot Lex a sidelong glance. "I do believe she flinched, Florry. Don't worry, dear. There'll be no iceberg."

"The sinking aspect was offered as an option," Florian said, "but I was careful to state that we won't require it. Rather than the icy waters, we will enjoy the luxury and finery of the ship itself. It's modelled at half-scale, so we will be together in close quarters. Nice and cosy."

Lex was relieved when the car pulled to a stop. Through the tinted windscreen she could see the Greek columns of the Quicksilvr entrance. The driver exited and, moments later, the door slid open. Three other cars, all identical with black-tinted windows, had already parked before the entrance. Florian offered his arm to Lex and they entered the building together, to the disgust of Lady Yasmine, who scowled as she noticed the battered boots protruding from the hem of Lex's long skirt.

The interior of the building was as grand as the façade. Decorating the curved wall of the large chamber were red velvet chaise longues and murals of saplings, interspersed with real plants in enormous, ornate tubs. The white tiled floor gleamed and reflected the candlelight from the chandeliers overhead, making Lex dizzy as though she were falling through starry space. The chamber echoed with laughter.

A well-dressed group of men and women stood in the centre of the room, chattering excitedly. Florian led Lex from person to person, introducing her, but he was clearly more interested in showing her off than allowing her to speak to anybody. Lex was familiar with most of their names from the email chains she had read in order to infiltrate the group, but she simply smiled politely and didn't attempt to match names to faces. She would never see these people again, after all.

A man dressed as a hotel porter, with a round brocaded cap and matching red jacket, barred the only internal door. The butt of his gun was visible, tucked into a holster under his jacket. Lex looked around to see that the exit was flanked by thuggish men wearing tuxedos.

As the guests began to move, Lex secured herself in the centre of the group in the hope of blending in. She tried to ignore the sinking feeling in her stomach.

The porter held out a hand as the first of the guests approached. A tall woman wearing a cloak deposited a slip of card onto his palm. The porter scrutinized it carefully and then nodded, stepping aside to allow her to pass.

Florian was next in line. He released his card high above the porter's hand so that it fluttered down and the porter had to scramble to catch it.

Other guests entered and then the porter shifted his attention to Lex. His expression was polite but firm. She smiled and made a show of patting the pockets of her mum's jacket. "I'm so clumsy! I think I've forgotten my invitation."

"I'm sorry, miss," he said in a neutral tone. "In that case I'll have to ask you to stand aside."

"But if you ask anyone else in my group, they'll—"

"No invitation, no entry."

Lex wavered. It was inconceivable that the plan might fail before she even got started. There was no way she could return home. She thought of Cecil, busy drawing together the complicated web to ensure that the rest of their scheme panned out as it should. All for nothing.

She glanced at the porter's gun. Perhaps if she appeared as though she was going to leave, then lunged at the weapon, she might take him off guard. . . . But then what about the apes in tuxedos standing behind her?

She continued to stare stupidly at the porter, paralyzed with indecision.

Somebody approached the porter from behind. It was Florian. He pulled a face at the porter's back; Lex gave a helpless shrug in response.

Florian sauntered to the porter's post. "May I have a brief word?"

The porter hesitated, then pressed a button. Immediately, a shutter dropped down to block the doorway, hiding the two men. Lex shifted from foot to foot, uncomfortably aware of the guests queuing behind her, muttering in their impatience.

The shutter slid open smoothly. Florian patted the porter's shoulder in a friendly manner and slipped his wallet back into his waistcoat pocket. The porter, to his credit, gave no hint about the bribe he had received. He stood aside and nodded cordially at Lex as she entered.

1010100   01100101   01111000   01110100   00100000   01000010   01110010   01100101   01100001   01

Lex allowed herself to be led by Florian along the corridor and through a door marked *Launch Booth Alpha*. The circular room echoed with the chatter of the guests, who lay reclined on sloping, padded black seats. A curved top supported each of their heads, like chairs in a dental surgery, and the seats were arranged in a tight circle so that the occupants' feet all pointed to a central column. A fat cable ran from the base of each seat and into the column. Outside the ring of chairs, a narrow walkway allowed four porters to move from person to person to ensure that each headrest was positioned correctly. A serious-looking woman wearing a white lab coat sat at a computer terminal, peering intently at the screen.

Florian hadn't said a word about bribing the porter. He took one of the remaining seats and patted the seat next to his. Lex gave a gracious smile as she settled herself into the chair. More guests took their places, until all the seats were occupied.

The porters retreated and the serious-looking woman moved to stand by the central column. The lab coat was unnecessary, Lex thought. Perhaps it inspired confidence in the guests to see somebody looking overtly scientific.

"Let me welcome you to Quicksilvr." The woman's voice was clear and confident. "My name is Gillian Mayhew. I will be your dedicated technician during your stay on the *Titanic*. Before you begin your vacation, I'd like to explain a few details. Firstly, I want to reassure you that you will be completely safe within the simulation. There will be no threat of falling overboard, for instance. Any accidents will result in your resetting safely to your own cabin. If you have any concerns, please speak to the captain or any of the onboard staff, who are all non-player characters, or bots."

Someone to Lex's right gave an exaggerated moan of disappointment. "Bother! I was hoping to be the captain!"

Gillian smiled. "You have all been assigned the identities of esteemed guests on the *Titanic*'s maiden voyage. None of you will be expected to lift a finger, unless that is your wont. I assure you that you will have a far more rewarding time as a passenger than as an active member of the crew."

Lex rolled her eyes. So these millionaire socialites had chosen to take a fantasy holiday, role-playing as *other* millionaire socialites. How typically unimaginative.

"When you awake within the sim," Gillian continued, "you will find yourself within your cabin, either alone or with your allocated partner, as per your booking requests. Your wardrobes will be stocked with all the outfits that you are likely to need, although more can be summoned instantly by visiting the tailor's workshop. The precise form of your avatar will be customized as per your booking."

Lex noticed Lady Yasmine relax visibly. She was obviously very concerned about bodily improvements.

"I can tell that you're all eager to begin your holiday," Gillian said, "so I'll be brief. There is only one further piece of information, but I stress that none of you are at all likely to require it. If you decide that you would prefer to leave the simulation entirely and awake here in this room, perform this simple action." She placed her hand onto the back of her neck in a karate-chop gesture. "Simply tap three times with the edge of your hand like this—" she tapped three times, gently "—and your vacation will come to an end." She smiled again. Lex chose to imagine that her cool manner masked disdain for her rich clients.

Gillian spread her arms wide. "So then. Please settle in and relax while we initiate the launch pods. Sweet dreams and bon voyage!"

Her white lab coat fluttered like wings as she strode out of the room. The porters returned and resumed fussing with the headrests. A porter placed his hands on Lex's temples and pressed her gently but firmly to the surface of her seat. In the curve of the headrest on either side she saw a single blue dot of light.

The room fell silent. Lex saw the porters slip silently out of the room. *Hold on*, she told herself. *Don't move a moment too soon.*

The central column began to emit a soft hum. The blue lights of the headrests of the opposite seats changed from pale to intensely bright.

She flinched as the headrest made contact with her temples. It was bending inwards. She arched her back; the headrest nipped at the nape of her neck, but she pulled herself free before it closed to become a full circle. Her head felt lighter. She turned and then laughed; the headrest had clamped around her black wig, yanking it from her head. She swung her legs off the seat and rubbed at her neck.

Florian was watching her. Though he was now held in place by the circular headband, his eyes were wide in startled confusion. Lex hesitated, clueless how to explain herself.

The hum from the central column increased in volume and the cables that connected it to the pods writhed. The lights glowed with more intensity until the whole room was bathed in blue light, so bright that Lex could scarcely make out the faces of the reclining guests. She watched as a sharp, thin tube protruded from the armrest of Florian's seat and burrowed into his arm. His eyelids fluttered and closed, though beneath the lids his eyes continued to dart about. The other guests had also fallen into a contented half-sleep.

CHAPTER TWENTY-TWO

Escape

Ethan crouched as he followed Mal to the bushes that marked the boundary of the church graveyard. The heavy objects in his pockets made a clinking noise with each step.

Their journey to and from the school had been punctuated by long periods of hiding from the bots scouring Touchstone for any trace of them. Almost all of the bots were now under Miller's control, the only exceptions being a handful that had glitched, becoming lodged halfway through walls. Ethan and Mal had been in and out of the sports hall within minutes, salvaging the equipment they needed from the climbing wall.

They had seen no sign of Miller or the other prisoners, but Ethan reminded himself that it didn't mean that they had given up. There was no way Miller would leave the clock tower, having conquered it.

Through gaps in the bushes he could see Russell and Anita standing on the shallow roof of the main church building. He presumed that Miller was in the tower, guarding whatever hardware allowed him to access the avatar profiles and the punishment controls. Ethan hoped Kit was in there somewhere too, and that he was intact. He didn't want to imagine what kind of state he might be in.

He glanced up at the roiling sky at the tip of the spire. The rip was wider now. Its blue outline bled into the darkness at its centre, like water gushing into a ravine.

"They'll see you the second you come out of hiding," Mal whispered.

Ethan nodded. He had hoped that inspiration might strike, but his imagination had let him down.

"So there's no point hiding."

He frowned. "What do you mean?"

"I mean me. Even if you make it onto the roof of the church, the only way Russell and Anita won't notice you climbing the tower is if they're looking somewhere else. And the only way they'll look somewhere else is if they see someone else they're after. And the only other person they're hunting is me."

"No."

"It's the only way."

Ethan fell silent. He tried to visualize exactly what had happened during their last encounter at the church. "Hold on—you're right!"

Mal smiled weakly.

"Well, you're half right. Think about it. Remember when we escaped earlier? When Libby was punished, when she was put on auto, we were standing only a few feet from her, weren't we? And we were definitely visible from the clock tower. So why weren't we punished too?"

Mal shuddered at the thought of Libby's slow transformation. "Because . . . there must be a limit to the range of whatever machine is in the clock tower."

"Exactly. We know Mrs. Benedict had to bring Russell here to punish him. And we were just beyond the church square when Libby was caught. If we keep outside that radius, we'll be okay. Anywhere beyond the monument will be safe."

"But Libby started to change when we were *all* in the church square."

Ethan shrugged. "Whoever distracts Russell and Anita won't be within range anyway."

Mal seemed not to hear him. "The only explanation is that the punishment can only be targeted at one person at a time."

"It doesn't make any difference—we're not going to be targeted at all. One of us only has to make a distraction from beyond the radius, while the other climbs the tower."

He chewed his lip as he gazed up at the spire. It wasn't the climb that was bothering him.

Mal squeezed his arm. "It's okay. We both know it has to be you that escapes."

She was right, but that didn't make Ethan feel any better. He cleared his throat. "Lex said she needs only one of the prisoners to get out, then she can free the rest. And once we're out, we'll be able to help expose Mercy—the company that put us all in here in the first place. I think I might be able to tell her something that will help. It's something Libby said—or rather, her mom. Lex doesn't know the half of Mercy's plans yet."

"Sounds a worthy cause." Mal sounded uninterested. Ethan cursed himself for dwelling on events in the outside world. How could Mal possibly understand?

"It could be any of us that leaves, though," he said weakly. He knew exactly what she would say next.

"I'm not a prisoner, remember."

"I know." He rubbed his eyes, which were beginning to itch. "I won't leave you, Mal. I'll find a way . . ." With a surge of despair he realized that he had no idea what he wanted to say.

"There's nothing to be done. I'm an AI. I'm a bot with an overblown opinion of herself. We both know I can't escape. Whereas you and the others can get back to the real world. Where you belong." She paused. "Hey, do me a favour. Tell me something. What's it like out there?"

Ethan tried to control himself. Showing how upset he was wouldn't help Mal. He puffed out his cheeks. "Well, parts of it look the same as Touchstone. Except they're private, hidden behind walls and gates to keep other people out. And then there are cities—huge places, dirty and full of people. They're sad and they're dangerous."

Mal gave a wry smile. "And you're sure you'd rather be out there than in Touchstone?"

"It's like you said, Mal. It's where I belong. In here the rules are fixed. We're puppets. In the real world it can feel that way too, sometimes, except that's not how it is. Everybody has the power to control their own lives. Nobody's watching over us, not in the way they are here. And there are people out there that need me."

For the first time, it occurred to Ethan that he didn't care how embroiled his dad was with Mercy. He wanted to see him, and his mom. And he realized with a jolt that they almost certainly *did* need him too.

"Good answer. But it was only a joke question."

It didn't seem a joke to Ethan. Mal tucked her hair behind her ears to reveal flickering eyes that now seemed to represent a spark of humanity rather than the data processes of an artificial intelligence. When she smiled, his stomach lurched. For all that he missed his family, how could he believe that anyone in the outside world needed him—no, that wasn't the right word—*liked* him more than Mal?

"There's no time to get all dewy-eyed." Mal hoisted herself to her feet, careful to stay hidden behind the bushes. "So we're agreed. I'll be the distraction. Besides, I don't think I'd be any good at climbing that tower. Too much hard work."

Ethan's voice cracked as he said, "I promise, Mal. I'll find a way."

"In that case, let's make it 'see you later,' rather than 'goodbye.' Come here." She pulled him into an embrace. They were both shivering. Carefully, Mal wiped his eyes with the sleeve of her jumper.

"Okay?" she said.

"Okay."

She began making her way along the edge of the graveyard. She didn't look back.

1010100   01100101   01111000   01110100   00100000   01000010   01110010   01100101   01100001   0

Ethan kept Anita and Russell in sight as picked his way between the gravestones, treading lightly to avoid making noise. The pair on the rooftop were facing in the opposite direction, looking out onto the church square. When Ethan reached the rear of the church he pressed himself flat against the wall. He sighed with relief. Even if Russell and Anita did look around, he would be out of sight for now.

A porch protruded from the rear of the building—perhaps it was intended to be a separate entrance for the absent vicar. Ethan shimmied up one wooden prop and scrambled onto the porch roof, clenching his teeth each time the contents of his pockets jangled. He perched on its apex, gathering his strength and courage. The roof of the main church building was only a few feet above him.

He raised himself above the guttering for a second. Anita and Russell were still overlooking the square. He was close enough now to hear their voices.

"The school, then?" Russell said.

Anita replied, "Miller says the school's his. 'A king needs a palace,' he says."

"But I thought the pirate ship was his palace."

"Maybe that's his holiday home. You could ask him to make you a new place over in the housing estates instead? Shove a dozen houses together to make a mansion."

Russell grunted in response.

"He's got big plans, you know," Anita continued. "Soon enough, you won't recognize this place at all. I want a palace too, but a proper one, a castle with turrets and a drawbridge and knights. And I'll make Kit program Libby to be my maid-in-waiting and call me 'ma'am,' and Ethan can be a medieval butler or something. Did they have butlers in those days?"

Ethan resisted the urge to make his move. Just because they weren't looking in his direction, it didn't mean it would be safe for him to come any closer yet.

The wait was becoming almost unbearable, but then he heard Anita say, "Hey, what's that?"

"What?"

"Over there, by that row of shops. Could have sworn I saw something move."

This was it. Ethan kept a close eye on Anita and Russell as he crawled onto the church roof. He tried not to dwell on the fact that if they turned he would have nowhere to hide.

"There! That was someone's foot, I swear! And it's not as though there are any bots on the loose anymore." Anita raced along the shallow roof to pound on the door to the clock tower. "Miller—come out here! Something's up!"

The door swung open to reveal Miller, who shielded his eyes as Russell pointed out over the square. He seemed unsurprised. "Go and make sure the geek's ready to trigger the punishment."

Russell disappeared into the tower. After making sure that Miller remained occupied watching the church square, Ethan rolled right, coming to rest against the wall of the tower. He crouched behind the open door. Through the gap between the hinges he saw Russell reappear, giving Miller a thumbs-up sign.

"Over there—it's the girl!" Miller shouted. "Target her!"

Sure enough, Ethan could now see Mal at the far side of the square, leaning against the wall of the nearest shop. Russell ducked into the tower.

Ethan pressed his body flat behind the door. The bricks above him were weathered and at several points the cement had flaked away. He shuffled to the very edge of the roof, then fished in his pocket to retrieve one of the metal climbing pins stolen from the sports hall. Reaching up as far as his arm would stretch, he dug the pin into the cement between bricks, and within a minute he had a second pin in place, and two more for footholds. He made his way upwards, wincing at the effort of remaining silent rather than the physical exertion.

"Kit says she's out of range!" Russell cried as he stumbled out of the doorway beside Ethan.

"She knows what she's doing," Miller said thoughtfully.

Ethan pulled two more pins from his pockets. He swung himself around the rear of the tower to continue his climb. He gulped with relief; he was now out of sight of the group on the church roof.

He heard Miller say, "Something's up. Where's the noob, Ethan?"

A shuffling noise suggested that Miller was pacing up and down on the church roof. Ethan hoped against hope that he didn't notice the pins embedded in the tower wall.

"Keep your eyes on the girl," Miller said, "and be ready to punish her if she takes a single step closer."

Ethan released the breath he had been holding and began making his way further up the tower. Now that he was clear of the roof of the main building, he was suspended high above the graveyard. He told himself not to look down. Instead, he fixed his gaze on the greenish copper spire above him. At its tip the sky fizzled and crackled. The air around the rip was laced with blue veins, and within the golden outline of the rip there was only a void.

After placing and climbing four more pins he managed to haul himself onto the top of the brick section of the tower. The structure swayed as he raised himself to cling onto the spire. Green copper oxide stained his palms. The spire seemed terribly narrow, as if a gust of wind might bring it toppling to the ground, and him along with it.

Below him, Mal was edging towards the monument that marked the perimeter of the punishment machine's range. Nearer to the church he could see Libby standing shoulder to shoulder with the line of static bots.

He felt a movement at his thigh. He looked down as something dropped from his pocket. He floundered to catch the metal pin, but it slipped between his fingers. It fell with a clang onto the roof of the church. He jerked from the edge of the tower, hugging the spire to stop himself from falling.

"What was that?" Miller cried from below.

Ethan clung to the spire, motionless. He stared down at Mal. Even from this distance he could see the terror on her face. She stared at the roof where Russell, Miller and Anita stood. Ethan knew that it meant that they were on the verge of discovering him.

Mal took her hand from the stone monument and took a step forward. Now she was dangerously close to the perimeter. Ethan willed her to stop.

Abruptly, she broke into a run. She bellowed a shout without words. Ethan almost shouted too.

"Switch it on!" Miller yelled. "Punish her!"

With a jolt of horror, Ethan realized that Mal's actions would be for nothing if he didn't continue his climb. He wrapped his legs around the spire and began to shimmy upwards. His hands ached and slipped on the rusted copper. The tower began to rumble beneath him. He couldn't look away from Mal, who continued her race across the square. He wished she would look up again. Perhaps he could gesture to her somehow, make her turn back. But deep down he knew that this had been her plan all along, once she had worked out that only one person could be punished at a time. Her eyes were locked on the doors of the church. Her shout grew louder.

Violent motion rocked the tower as the punishment machine powered up. Ethan gritted his teeth and continued his painful ascent.

Below him, Mal swerved. Perhaps she was turning back after all? But no—her left leg appeared to be moving at a different pace than her right. It swung out from her body. Ethan saw her panic. Her voice cracked, but then she shouted again. Patches of sickening green flicked across her face and neck, and sections of her flesh disappeared and then reappeared.

Her shout became a scream.

She stopped, frozen with a foot raised above the pavement. Then her body blinked out of existence, only to appear back where she had been standing a moment before. She oscillated between positions as though she were a video image caught between frames.

Just as Ethan was beginning to wonder if she was trapped permanently, she lunged forward. She had to yank at her left leg with each step as though it was no longer under her control.

The spire juddered. Ethan heard the sound of thunder and the sky flashed blue.

He blinked to dispel the blurry streaks on his retinas. He craned his neck to look down into the church square.

He groaned.

Mal was now moving at a walking pace. When the thunder abated, Ethan realized that she was no longer shouting, though her mouth remained wide open.

Slowly, her head tilted up. She looked directly at Ethan.

Her mouth stopped its contortions. She smiled. Ethan saw warmth there, along with pleading. Then she blinked and her expression became neutral. She changed direction and walked casually in the other direction as if she had all the time in the world.

Ethan had never hated himself more.

"He's up there!" Miller must have noticed Mal's final glance. A clang of metal signalled that he had discovered Ethan's climbing pins. "Bots! Climb the tower and bring Ethan to me!"

A skittering sound from below grew louder and louder. It sounded like animals scratching wildly from within a cage. Ethan tried to push what had happened to Mal out of his mind as he clambered his way up the spire.

A head appeared over the edge of the brickwork below him. It was a wide-eyed bot girl. Her eyes were fixed on Ethan. A young boy and then several adults joined her, all jostling for position to grasp hold of the spire.

Ethan redoubled his efforts, pulling his way up painfully. The loose copper plating tore into his palms. Blue lightning from the skybox rip stung his eyes. Each flicker was accompanied by a crack of thunder that came from within the dark hole. The burning blue light around the rip was sucked into it in torrents.

His foot was trapped. He struggled to shake himself free and then looked down to see a familiar face. It was the bot who insisted that he was his father. His eyes were wild, the swirling cogs now bigger than the pupils, and his face was distorted into a silent howl. His fingers dug into Ethan's calf so that he couldn't climb any higher.

"Miller! Call him off!" Ethan shouted.

He saw Miller on the church roof, watching him struggle. He was grinning. "And why would I do that?"

"You don't understand! The sim's falling apart. If you stay, you'll all die!"

"Liar! You just can't stand the power I have here. I'm more than king of Touchstone, don't you see? I'm a god! I'm a god! Seize him! Bring him to me!"

Ethan flailed against the bot's grip on his leg. His father's tweed suit had torn at the shoulder where it had snagged against the plating of the spire.

"I have to escape," he said, more to himself than to Miller.

In place of the bot's face he pictured the features of his real dad. The fingers dug deeper into his calf. The illusion didn't last; his father's ordinarily pleasant expression twisted into a snarl. All those memories of his dad, all those happiest moments from his childhood, were false. His dad wasn't who he claimed to be. But he had a hold over Ethan, all the same. He wouldn't release his grip.

"I don't want to die here, Dad. I'm scared."

The bot's face twitched. For an instant his cruel expression disappeared, to be replaced by anguish. His grip slackened.

It took Ethan a moment to realize he was free.

Frantically, he threw himself upwards with both arms outstretched.

It felt as though the top of his head was burning. The blue light enveloped him and he struggled to see.

Far below him he could make out Mal, strolling towards the high street.

Then something pulled him from above. He was yanked from the church spire and he was falling upwards.

CHAPTER TWENTY-THREE

Launch

Lex slipped through a door labelled *Launch Booth Mu.*
The interior of the room appeared exactly the same as
the one she had left, except that it was empty of people.
She cracked her knuckles and sat before the computer
terminal. A prompt flickered in the top-left-hand corner.

The information that appeared onscreen was exactly
as Cecil had described. She hoped that indicated that he
would prove as reliable in carrying out the rest of their
plan. After only ten minutes, the headrests of the ring
of seats around her glowed blue. The central column
hummed, pulsing in time with Lex's taps on the keyboard.

Launch pods initiated.

Number of guests?

Lex entered "1."

Enter duration of stay in days.

Her hand wavered over the keyboard. It didn't really
matter, did it? She pressed "1."

Enter simulation code or user reference code.

This was the real test. She typed "cwright dev." The prompt stopped blinking. She gritted her teeth.

Development console active.

At the prompt she typed "Identify ProjectQ."

ProjectQ / ref Q889b

> State location

ProjectQ / loc 3191

ProjectQ unavailable / restricted

She shrugged. Of course it was restricted. What kind of prison would allow someone to walk in the front entrance? But the location reference—what might that mean? Cecil hadn't mentioned this. She felt a growing sense of panic, made all the worse by her nagging, guilty thought that any of the sims would allow her to access Cecil's cache of evidence—it didn't have to be Touchstone that she entered. It was only the fate of Ethan and the other prisoners that were at stake at this moment. Only.

> Identify loc 3192

No simulation located.

Okay, try the other side.

> Identify loc 3190

No simulation located.

What if there was no sim adjacent to the prison skybox? She shuddered. There was no backup plan. But Ethan had mentioned a pirate ship falling from the sky, hadn't he? So there had to be at least one sim close enough for something that big to slip through.

She stared at the numbers. Perhaps they represented an array, with the skyboxes arranged in rows and columns.

Upwards.

> Identify loc 3291

Simulation located.

Initiate simulation?

It was the best she could do, and there would likely be no second chances. She wondered what it would be like to be a swashbuckling pirate. She typed "Y" and hit the return key.

Immediately, the central column thrummed into life. She dashed over to the nearest pod and pressed her head into place, moments before the curved headrest snapped closed.

Blue light filled her vision. Something cold pricked against her forearm. She felt, rather than saw, a sparkling golden glow. Her eyelids fluttered and she slipped away, into the machine.

CHAPTER TWENTY-FOUR

Reunited

He was falling upwards

pue

then

he was falling downwards.

Ethan hit the ground hard, his shoulder wrenching as he tumbled forwards. He lay with his eyes screwed shut, panting heavily. He felt his limbs for breaks or sprains. The insides of his eyelids were golden. The air was hot and damp.

He opened his eyes. The sky above him was a rich, cloudless blue. The rip in the skybox appeared far less ragged now. It suddenly occurred to him that he hadn't considered whether the bots might be able to follow. He rolled to one side and scurried away. The last thing he wanted was to have someone land on top of him.

An ache in his right leg forced him to limp. Roots like thick cables threatened to trip him up and trees with narrow, curling trunks towered above him. He reached out to trace the curve of a creeper that wound around a tree, then touched one of the enormous leaves that hung down.

Where was he? And more importantly, where was Lex? The phrase "out of the frying pan, into the fire" sprang to mind. What was the use of escaping one sim prison only to become lost in another? But then he remembered the vision of his bot father clambering up the church spire and he shuddered. Perhaps he should look on the bright side.

His sense of optimism didn't last long.

The nearby foliage rustled. At first Ethan thought the warm wind was blowing the leaves, until the tree trunks themselves began to shake. The ground beneath his feet trembled.

Something burst from the undergrowth. It was grey-green and far bigger than Ethan. He glimpsed white streaks of curved teeth. As he darted into the foliage, the teeth snapped shut inches from where his head had been.

He ducked beneath branches as he hurtled through the forest. Daring to look behind him for a second, he saw a scaly muzzle swinging from left to right, head-butting trees to clear a path.

Some part of his mind worked independently of his body. Bipedal. Tall, but perhaps only twice as big as himself. Late Cretaceous period. Albertosaurus.

As a child, Ethan had been fascinated by dinosaurs. Now, face-to-face with as real a specimen as he could ever encounter, he reminded himself that this wasn't an academic exercise or a treat. This Albertosaurus wouldn't thank him for being correctly identified. He stumbled through the jungle, grabbing trees to haul himself forward. The twisted bark bit at his skin and his injured leg shouted with pain.

It was no use. The Albertosaurus roared and Ethan felt its hot breath on the nape of his neck. His legs trembled with each bellow, making him stagger as he ran. The clack of the dinosaur's teeth seemed so close that he touched the back of his head to prove to himself that he hadn't been bitten.

He saw the tree root protruding from the ground a fraction of a second too late. His foot hooked into its loop and he stumbled with his arms windmilling. For a couple of seconds his momentum kept him sailing forward, before he lost his footing entirely. He burst through the foliage and into a clearing and slammed into the ground, winded. Behind him, the Albertosaurus bellowed in triumph.

Then Ethan heard a different, far shriller noise. He looked up and groaned in dismay.

Another beast stood directly before him.

The huge copper-furred cat reared up onto its hind legs. Some remote part of Ethan's mind identified it as a sabretooth tiger, but he felt no sense of satisfaction when his identification was confirmed; the beast's jaws opened to reveal long, razor-sharp teeth.

He lay there, exhausted and unable to move. The sabretooth squatted onto its haunches.

And then it leapt.

Ethan closed his eyes and waited to die.

Shrieks and roars accompanied the sounds of heavy bodies thumping on the ground.

He rolled onto his belly to watch.

The sabretooth had bounded directly over him. Its forelegs were locked around the neck of the Albertosaurus and its claws tore into its scaly hide. The dinosaur snarled, trying to orient its muzzle to lunge at its attacker, but the tiger was too nimble. It scrambled up onto the neck of the Albertosaurus, all the while continuing its frenzied attack. The dinosaur tossed to and fro in agony and frustration. Eventually, it changed tactics. Rather than trying to snap at the sabretooth it shook its body madly. The tiger clung on for ten seconds but then skidded off. It crouched in the dust, ready to pounce again at the dinosaur.

But the Albertosaurus didn't attack. It regarded the sabretooth, clacking its teeth together. Then it lumbered into the depths of the jungle.

Ethan scurried back on his hands and feet, unwilling to take his eyes off the tiger.

The beast's heavy head swung to face him.

"Don't worry," it purred. "He won't be coming back any time soon."

0 01100101 01111000 01110100 00100000 01000010 01110010 01100101 01100001 0110101

Ethan blinked up at the tiger.

"Close your mouth," it said. "You look an idiot, gawping like that. Aren't you at least going to say hi?"

He struggled to form words. "Lex? Is that you?"

To his surprise the tiger actually smiled, revealing its long fangs. It settled gracefully into a sitting position, as perfectly poised as a statue.

"I was as surprised as you, when I arrived." The low voice seemed to come from somewhere deep within the tiger's body, but now Ethan recognized a hint of Lex's sarcastic tone. "I'd expected to find myself on a boat. I would've enjoyed being a pirate captain."

"You'd have enjoyed it less if you'd ended up as a crewman mopping the deck."

The tiger smirked. "I'm glad you've developed a sense of humour. Tough luck that you kept your normal weedy body instead of a more jungle-appropriate avatar. Are you okay? I was worried you wouldn't make it."

"I almost didn't. It was a close thing. But I'm all right—unlike the others, back there." He gestured upwards. The skybox rip now appeared as faint and pale as an airplane contrail.

Lex rubbed her huge front paws together. "I'm sorry. But are they all in one piece, the prisoners?"

"Some of them have been put on auto—a sort of mind control. But they're alive and safe, as far as I know."

"Good. In that case, we can get them out of there."

"Some of them won't come quietly." Initially, Ethan was thinking of Miller and Russell, but he realized the same objection might apply to Kit too. Even so, it was Mal who loomed largest in his thoughts. Of all of them, she was the one who deserved to escape. But she was the only person who never could.

"They won't have a choice. We're going to break them out whether they want to or not."

"A couple of them are seriously mental, Lex. Just . . . bad people." He hesitated. "And there's someone else. A girl."

The tiger raised a furry brow.

Ethan blushed. "She was a bot, but she broke free of her programming. I hoped . . . There's no way to help her, is there?"

Lex tugged at her whiskers. "What's her name?"

"Mal. Maldemaire. She's about my age. She's warm, kind. She has this fringe that gets in her eyes. . . ." Why was he saying all this out loud? It was hopeless to think that he might ever see her again. "It's all right, Lex. I know what your answer will be."

"I'm sorry."

"Forget about it." He shivered, despite the heat and humidity. "So, what happens next?"

"Leave it to me."

"Lex—you have to tell me what's going on."

Lex pulled a face. Ethan almost laughed at the odd spectacle of a tiger looking ashamed. "Sorry. I'm so used to keeping everything to myself. Come over here."

Ethan followed the huge beast as she plodded to the centre of the dusty clearing. Lex pointed with a paw. He peered at the ground but saw nothing there.

"You're a bit of a stargazer, isn't that right?"

Ethan looked up at the bright blue sky.

"Not up there. Down here. Do you know the shape of constellations off by heart?"

"Probably. Yes."

The tiger sighed with relief. "It's the only part of the plan I didn't consider. These things—" she held up a heavy paw "—are superb for fighting, but not so great in terms of fine motor skills."

"You're not making any sense."

She pointed again at the forest floor. "Do me a favour and draw the constellation of Gemini, right there in the dust. Nice and big."

Ethan stared at her, trying to judge whether she was making a fool of him. Lex's feline face was impassive. He found a long stick and stooped to begin drawing the long vertical stripes of the twin figures of Gemini, then the joined horizontal line that represented their arms.

He looked up. From the expression on Lex's feline face, he guessed that she was expecting something to happen.

"Castor and Pollux," he murmured.

"Same to you."

Ethan shook his head and gestured with the stick. "The stars. They give the twins their names." At the top of each figure he scraped a circle in the dust to represent the two largest stars, the heads of the twins.

The air before him shimmered. It reminded him of the skybox rip.

"It's all right," the tiger purred. "This is what we've been searching for all this time."

Ethan watched open-mouthed as an object materialized upon the network of lines. It was a small cabinet carved from dark mahogany. It looked comically out of place, but somehow familiar.

"If you hadn't guessed, this is your dad's work."

Ethan stared at her stupidly.

"He was the one who told me to draw Gemini to make it appear."

"He told you? But—" He suddenly remembered where he had seen the cabinet before. An identical version sat on the desk in his dad's study at home.

"He's innocent, Ethan."

Instantly, tears stung the corners of Ethan's eyes. "But . . . you said—"

"I was wrong. He was the boss of Quicksilvr, the company that built the sims before Mercy got their hands on them. I've met him. In fact, I'm only here because of him. He's a good guy, Ethan, just like you said."

Ethan's legs buckled. Along with a wave of relief he felt something unexpected: anger. Without realising it, he had been slowly working out of his system any sympathy for his dad. Now his love for him returned in an overwhelming rush.

Lex misunderstood his expression. "Don't get carried away. We're not finished here. Do me a favour, would you?" She pointed at the mahogany cabinet with a paw. "Open the top drawer and take out what you find. I'd only knock the thing over."

He did as he was asked. The drawer contained a sheaf of documents, all in pristine condition. He leafed through them, his eyes growing wider with every page.

"It covers everything! Memos, emails, you name it. They go back more than a year. All with Mercy logos and watermarks. There are references to the decision to start fast-tracking sentences. Let's see . . . cost-cutting . . . trials without representation . . . This is it—you did it, Lex!"

"No. Your dad did it, long ago. This was his insurance policy when Mercy bought out his company. All I'm doing is help him get it back."

"But if he had all this evidence all that time ago, why didn't he use it? Expose Mercy's plans?"

"He might be a good man, but he was scared. Don't take this the wrong way, but he was a coward. It doesn't matter now. What matters is that he came through, finally. History will call him a hero, kid."

Ethan nodded, but he felt far less certain. When he was younger he had considered his dad the bravest person in the world. But it had been Ethan who had survived the prison sim and outwitted Miller and the bots to escape. And what had his dad been doing this whole time? Sitting at home drinking tea and biting his nails?

The tiger stretched out lazily, sending up clouds of dust from the forest floor. "Anyway. I've got a subroutine all set. Once I trigger it, those documents will be sent to a dozen key people: media, government, RealWorld. Once the truth is out, Mercy won't have a leg to stand on. Keep reading, would you? I'm hoping for juicier evidence than the fast-tracking."

Ethan rifled through the sheaf of papers. A pile had been separated from the upper documents, bound together with string. Everything beyond that point referred not to the fast-tracked sentences, but something named "Project Q."

He looked up in awe. "This is all about Touchstone, what they call the 'test project.'"

Lex yawned. Ethan had a feeling that she was trying to act more casual than she really felt—or perhaps her feline form was beginning to affect her responses.

He tried to grasp at a train of thought. "No . . . Lex, you can't send these ones."

"Why not? This'll bring Mercy down once and for all. The fast-tracking, the sims, everything."

"You're wrong. It isn't enough."

"Not enough? We can release all those innocent prisoners. We can stop Mercy cutting corners with the justice system. Are you crazy?"

"Don't you see? Exposing the trials without defence, that's fair enough. But that isn't everything. We'll get the prisoners released, only to send them straight to the cities. They'll end up looting in gangs and fighting with police. They'll still be trapped."

Lex watched him carefully. "You've changed since I last saw you, you know that? All right, I accept what you're saying. But it's a step in the right direction. And we don't want anyone else thrown into prison sims the way you were, do we?"

"You don't understand. This 'Project Q' isn't just about creating cheaper prisons." Ethan began to feel more certain. "They're only the tip of the iceberg. There's a far bigger plan going on."

"How do you know that?"

"A girl told me, or at least she gave me the clue by accident. One of the other prisoners, Libby de Witt."

Lex sprung onto all fours. "De Witt? I know that name. Patricia de Witt was your dad's business partner—one of the sim architects! What did she say?"

Despite the relief of pieces of the puzzle coming together, Ethan felt a stab of annoyance that Lex had recognized the name and that he wasn't breaking entirely new ground. "I think Libby's mom knew more about Mercy than they could allow. I think she was killed. She discovered the *real* purpose of the sims. They're not only about saving space, or money, or reducing numbers of prison staff, Lex. Patricia de Witt was involved in a plan to roll out the project to every city in the country."

The feline eyes darted. "So that the crime rate would fall in every city?"

"It's gone far beyond preventing crime. They want to use the prison sims to train people, just like they were trying to do with us. They want to break their spirits and brainwash them. Starting with prisoners, but only because they're a captive audience, so to speak. They won't stop there. Mercy will brainwash anyone they can get their hands on."

He almost relished Lex's confusion. He slowed down, thinking it through as he spoke. "Libby's mom said, 'We'd never stand against them.' But she didn't mean Mercy! She meant the people living in the cities, once they'd been made into obedient drones, no better than bots in a sim! Don't you understand what Mercy's capable of? Not only do they have all this sim technology, they can also arrest whoever they want, whenever they want."

Lex appeared stunned.

Ethan was sure he had found the answer. "They want to build an army! Whole cities full of brainwashed drones, all obedient and ready to do whatever Mercy command. This isn't about reducing crime. It's about Mercy taking over the country!"

Lex swiped at a nearby bush, ripping it to shreds with her claws. When she spoke, her voice was little more than a growl. "You're right. Exposing the evidence about the sims would reveal our hand. And now that Project Q is finished, Mercy will bury the whole thing. They'll have learned lessons and they'll move on to the next stage. Bigger plans."

"What about my dad's company? Could he hold things up?"

"Mercy have the tech now. But it's the infrastructure that's more valuable. Any new sims will operate on the Quicksilvr network your dad and Patricia de Witt built. There's a chance that might be our way in. But that'll all come later. We're playing a long game." She glanced at the mahogany cabinet. "Come on then. Better kick this thing off."

Ethan separated the sheaf of documents that referred to the fast-tracked sentences and handed them over to Lex. She pinned them to the ground with a paw and stared at them in concentration. Ethan rubbed his eyes. The papers had disappeared.

"It's done," she purred. She gazed at the other documents that Ethan held. He looked at his hand to see that those papers, too, were gone.

"Don't worry," Lex said. "I've put everything relating to Project Q somewhere safe and secret. Now to the next matter in hand. Let's get you the hell out of here."

00011   00100000 01 10011 01100001 01 11011   01
10010 01101001 01110100 01110100 01100101 01101110 001   011
11001 00100000 01010100 01101001 01101101 00100000 01001101 011
01010 01101111   00101110 00100000 01001100 01100001 011
01111 01110101 01110100 00100000 01100001 01101110 01100100 001
00100 01100101 01110011 01101001 01100111 01101110 00100000 011
1001   01001010 01100001 01110010 01100101   0010

010011 01101000 01100001 01110000 01101001 011

01111 00101110 01000010 01101001 01101110 01100001 01110010 01111100

01100110
C11APTEO

10001   # CHAPTER TWENTY-FIVE
1101000   The Real World

1 00101110 For a horrible few seconds Ethan felt as though he had   01
0 01010100 detached from his body.   01
1 01110010   After tapping his neck three times with the edge of
0   110 his hand, as Lex instructed, the jungle had melted away.   01
0 01101000 The last thing he had seen was Lex's feline face, which   01
00101100 remained after everything else disappeared, like the smile   0C
0 01100101 of the Cheshire Cat.   01
0 01101111   Darkness enveloped him, though he felt certain he   1
01100001 wasn't looking at it. He had no eyes and no head, and he   01
1 01100110 existed outside of time and space.   0C
0   111   Then, with a wrench, he was solid once again. He was   01
1 01110101 lying on his back. His limbs felt unbearably heavy and   01
01101001 clumsy, possessed of a weight that he hadn't experienced   0
0 00100000 for . . . how long? With some difficulty, he reached up to   01
1 01100001 touch his right cheek. His fingers grazed a deep, though   01
0   011 healed, scar that ran from below his eye to his jawline.   1
01101000   Reality.   01
                1

It was cold. His body ached from the chill and from lack of use. He winced as he swung his legs off a hard bench. He felt a surge of disgust that not even padded seats had been provided for the prisoners' unconscious bodies—but at least he hadn't been strapped down. He supposed that it reflected Mercy's opinions of the benefits of virtual prisons: the prisoners' bodies were trapped because their minds were trapped. There was no need for chains or bars.

A gagging sensation rose in his throat. He doubled up, coughing. His movement produced grey plumes from the folds of his clothes. He had been gathering dust.

At the foot of the bench was a column with cabling wound around it. It reminded him of the creepers around the tree trunks of the jungle. Radiating from the column were other benches, each occupied by a sleeping body. Libby, Kit, Anita, Russell, Miller. Everyone except Mal. Each of their heads was circled by a metal brace with pinprick lights that cast a blue glow on their faces. They looked serene in their sleep. Their eyes moved constantly under their closed eyelids.

On the wall behind each prisoner was a screen. Constantly updating charts indicated heart rate and brain activity. The screens emitted steady beeps.

Ethan jumped at another, sharper sound. It was a siren, coming from somewhere outside the small chamber. He forced himself to remain calm. Lex's plan was working. They had agreed that as soon as he had exited the jungle sim she would hack the Quicksilvr system to raise the alarm. Any guards within the prison compound would be drawn away by the siren.

He had to move fast. Reciting Lex's instructions under his breath, he moved from bench to bench, tapping commands into the keyboard beneath each screen.

Fifteen minutes. That was how long Lex estimated he would have from the moment he left the sim to the moment the defences would go up. Now that he was free, a lockdown sequence would be initiated and Lex could do nothing to hold it off. A firewall would be triggered, blocking anyone from entering or exiting the sim. Anyone still in there would be trapped for good.

He wasn't going to leave anyone behind.

In his haste his fingers slipped on the keys. He told himself to slow down. There was no telling what repercussions any mistakes might have.

He heard a cough from somewhere behind him. Kit was now sitting up, leaning heavily on an elbow. Was he well enough to survive out in the real world? The other prisoners began to stir too.

The final console was above Miller's head. For a brief moment Ethan considered leaving him. He could let him remain a king, or even a god, in Touchstone—that was what he wanted, wasn't it?

No. If Ethan took it upon himself to decide that Miller was guilty and deserving of punishment, that would make him the same as Mercy. He tapped out the commands to wake Miller.

"Ethan?" Kit's voice shook. "What's going on? Are we—is this . . ." He gazed around the room. "You did it! I don't know how, but you did it!" His face clouded and his voice became fainter. He spoke through rattling wheezes. "I'm so sorry. About switching sides. I was scared. You kept talking about escape and all I could think was . . . I don't know. In the moment, siding with Miller seemed the best way to let me stay in the sim in safety. I didn't realize how mental he was."

Ethan helped him sit up. "I know. It doesn't matter now."

Libby and Anita had awoken too. Libby hung over her bench, retching. Perhaps waking was even worse for her, having spent the last day on auto, unable to control her avatar. Anita blinked sleepily without seeming to comprehend what was happening.

Russell and Miller were still lying on their benches, but they became restless as if they were in the grip of vivid dreams.

"Listen," Ethan said hurriedly, "we don't have long. We're all getting out of here. Right now."

"We're escaping? For real?" Libby managed to say between dry heaves.

"For real. Whatever happens next, we have no choice but to leave it to the authorities. But I mean the real authorities, not Mercy. There's nothing to worry about anymore, I promise. We'll be treated fairly."

Libby glanced at Russell and Miller, both still asleep. "They won't go quietly."

"Leave it to me." Ethan thumped a control panel. The door of the chamber slid open and the full volume of the siren filled the air. Kit clapped his hands over his ears.

Miller and Russell woke and stumbled groggily to their feet. Miller appeared horrified to find himself no longer in Touchstone.

"There's no time to explain!" Ethan bellowed over the siren. "We have to get out—the whole machine's about to blow!"

Miller rubbed his eyes and spun to look at the central column and the data screens. "Why should I trust you?"

Ethan considered saying the same thing in return. Miller was the one who had tried to kill Ethan and his friends, rather than the other way around. Instead, he shouted, "Can't you hear the alarm? And don't you want to escape? The base is abandoned. We're free, if we can get out quickly!"

Miller scanned the apparatus for signs of danger. Kit and Libby shared worried glances.

"He's right, Miller!" Libby screamed. "Look! There's smoke coming from the machines—it could explode any second!"

Russell leapt towards the door, but Miller pulled him back roughly.

"It's a trap," he snarled. Then, to Ethan, "Isn't it, noob?"

"Maybe," Ethan said quietly, standing his ground even as Miller came up close. "Maybe not. But we're all going to leave together, all the same."

Miller's sneer faltered. Ethan could guess what he was thinking. He was remembering that this was the real world. He had no perks and no special powers here.

Miller scowled and raised his fist.

Ethan ducked the punch and lashed out blindly with his own right hand. It made contact with Miller's jaw with a sickening crunch. The boy's body whipped sharply to the left.

Miller nursed his cheek, his eyes wide with shock. He prodded Russell in the ribs, but the other boy barely registered his presence. Russell looked terribly anxious, glancing about in search of smoking machinery.

"Get out," Ethan said firmly. "We're free and we're alive. Get out while that's still the case."

The deadlock lasted a few seconds more. Then Miller turned and fled from the room, pushing Russell aside in his sudden frenzy.

The other prisoners followed him along the empty corridor. Ethan supported Kit, who was unsteady on his feet. The corridor led them past offices and other bare chambers filled with launch pods.

At the end of the passage, light streamed from a narrow vertical panel in a reinforced door. Beyond it was the outside world. The real world. Miller rattled the handle to no effect.

Libby raised an eyebrow at Ethan.

"Hold on," he said, with more assurance than he really felt. "Give it a minute."

They waited in agitated silence. Ethan's heart thumped in time with the siren.

Any minute now.

The corridor strip light blinked off for a second before sparking again with a pinging noise.

"Now," he said. "Hit the wall panel."

The outer door swung open. Another victory for Lex.

Cool air wafted into the corridor. Real, breathable air.

They pushed outside in a huddle. Ethan held Kit tight as the boy's legs gave way beneath him.

"Hold it!" a voice shouted.

"Hands up!" said another.

Ethan's eyes took a second to adjust to the daylight. Figures framed the exit. Two gun barrels were pointing directly at them. Ethan heard the growl of a dog. He saw other guards raised on platforms, giving them a vantage point over the prisoners. They could kill any of them in an instant.

He and the other prisoners froze, unwilling to move forward and unable to retreat into the building. Kit, wheezing heavily, blocked their way.

After all of Ethan's struggles within the sim, and Lex's adventures in the real world, this was how it would end.

Ethan raised his hands slowly. He looked up at the sky. It was far less blue than the sky in Touchstone, more of a mottled grey dotted with scrubby clouds. But it was beautiful because it was real.

The guards peered down the sights of their rifles. Ethan heard the click of safety catches being released.

"Lay down your weapons!"

It wasn't the guards shouting. The voice came from a building Ethan could just make out in the distance.

Somebody appeared at the corner of the building. The megaphone raised to his lips obscured most of his face, but Ethan recognized him immediately.

His dad put a hand flat against his brow to shield the sun. Their eyes met. Ethan saw a slow, grateful smile appear on his face.

01101001

0110

01000011
010

01000101 01010010 01000011

CHAPTER TWENTY-SIX
A Ghost in the Machine

Lex scrambled through the front entrance, then grabbed at one of the Greek columns, using it as a pivot to swing herself around ninety degrees. At the same moment, a black van burst out from behind the overgrown hedgerows of the lane, its brakes screeching as it skidded into the parking area. People in armoured uniforms began piling out even before the van stopped, followed by two men and two women all wearing dark suits. They paid Lex no attention as they strode along the edge of the Quicksilvr building.

She raced after them. Shouts came from somewhere ahead. She rounded the corner to see Cecil holding a megaphone to his lips. His hands were shaking uncontrollably. Further away, through the barbed wire fence, she saw a group of teenagers standing at the entrance to the prison compound, flanked by Quicksilvr guards and Copernicus the attack dog.

Cecil lowered the megaphone as the newcomers arrived. The armoured troops arranged themselves into lines either side of him, joined by the men and women in business suits.

"About bloody time!" Cecil hissed at them. "I thought you'd left me to handle this on my own."

When he saw Lex he gave a grin of relief. He raised the megaphone again. "Quicksilvr security staff! You all remember me! My name is Cecil Wright. I have with me representatives of every level of government. Mercy is currently under investigation. We're shutting this project down, as of right now. I repeat, right now! Lay down your weapons."

The guards hesitated and exchanged uncertain looks. The only sound now was Copernicus' continued barking as the dog strained at its leash.

The guards placed their guns on the ground.

"Come forward, all of you back there," Cecil said, addressing the prisoners. "You have nothing to fear anymore."

Two teen girls stepped forward immediately. A burly, shaven-headed boy looked from side to side as if contemplating escape, but then shrugged and followed them. Another boy, smaller and wiry, darted to the left. Government officers raced to apprehend him.

"Let me go!" the boy screamed. "I'll kill you! I'll kill you!" He flailed frantically against the officers but was soon pinned down.

Officers escorted the other prisoners out of the compound and onto the area of flattened grass. The rearmost member of the group was a thin, pale boy wearing glasses. He leant heavily against the wall, panting. The door behind him was shut tight.

Lex moved to stand beside Cecil. "You got my email, then?"

"And not a moment too soon. I forwarded the evidence to everyone on our list. My contacts in the government only stretch so far—most of them they assumed I was telling tall tales. We're lucky that enough of them want to see Mercy brought down." He lowered his voice. "But where was the rest of the evidence? There was nothing in there at all about Quicksilvr."

"It's funny you mention tall tales," Lex replied. "But all of that is probably something we should talk about later. Your son's been doing some decent detective work himself, and you're not going to be happy about what he's discovered."

Cecil's face creased in concern. He shielded his eyes again. "Speaking of Ethan," he said, "where did he go?"

01100101 01111000 01110100 00100000 01000010 01110010 01100101 01100001 011010

"No. No, please no," Cecil moaned behind Lex.

The voices of the government officials and guards faded as Lex led the way along the corridor of the prison building. A bench had been pushed up against the outer door to block it, slowing them down. In here the siren was almost deafening. Lex sprinted along the hallway, checking each room she passed.

"He wouldn't be so stupid," she gasped. "Would he?"

Cecil only grunted behind her. His bulky physique wasn't made for running.

There was only one room left. She tried the handle but it was jammed. She looked at Cecil. The colour had drained from his face.

"You told him about the firewall?" Cecil panted. "He knows there's no way out once it's deployed?"

She nodded. She had told Ethan too much.

Cecil gritted his teeth and pressed his weight against the door. It edged open, inch by inch. The interior of the chamber was dim and it took several seconds for Lex to be able to see. The only light came from the wall-mounted screens. Each contained a single word in flashing blue text. *Lockdown.*

A couple of the benches were hidden behind the central column. Lex and Cecil walked around the ring of benches in opposite directions. Cecil's hands grazed each seat as he passed, as if he didn't trust his legs to keep him upright. He arrived before she did. When she reached him, his gaunt face was illuminated blue as he looked at the figure lying below him.

The lights glowed softly on Ethan's temples. He looked peacefully asleep, other than the movement of his eyes beneath their lids. Cecil placed both of his hands on his son's chest so that they rose and fell in time with his breathing.

"Don't move him," Lex whispered. "If you break the connection, he's a goner."

Cecil nodded but didn't look up. A tear made a blotch on Ethan's T-shirt.

"Cecil . . . look at this."

They both stared at the screen on the wall behind Ethan. It carried the same *Lockdown* message as the others, but there was more text beneath.

Dad and Lex,

I'm sorry I had to trick you. I wish I could see you both.

But there's somebody else that I need to see again too.

And we all know this is the only way we have a chance of getting evidence about Mercy's real plans.

I can be a ghost in the machine.

I'm going to need your help.

E x

Cecil's body slackened. Cautiously, Lex threaded her arms around his waist from behind.

"He's right," she said quietly. "We were being blind. This is the only way we can bring Mercy down."

Cecil nodded sorrowfully. He knelt down, laid his head on his son's chest, and wept.

00011
10010 01110100 01110100 01100101 01101110 011
11001 00100000 01010100 01101001 01101101 00100000 01001101 011
01010 01101111   00101110 00100000 01001100 01100001 011
01111 01110101 01110100 00100000 01100001 **01101110** 01100100 001
00100 01100101 01110011 01101001 01100111 01101110 00100000 011
11001   01001010 01100001 01110010 01100101   001

010011 01101000 01100001 01110000 01101001 011
01111 00101110 01000010 01101001 01101110 01100001 01110010 0111100

01100110
C11APTEO

CHAPTER TWENTY-SEVEN

Awakening

1 00101110
0 01010100
1 01110010
0   110
0 01101000
  00101100
0 01100101
0 01101111
  01100001
1 01100110
0   111
1 01110101
  01101001
0 00100000
1 01100001
0   011
  01101000
0 01100001

This wasn't right.

The air was warm against Ethan's skin. He heard the screech of gulls. He tasted salt on his lips.

When he pushed himself up into a sitting position his hands dug into soft sand. He was wearing a crumpled white shirt, open at the neck, and shorts. A golden beach stretched before him, melting into the crests of lapping waves.

What had happened?

He had reversed all of Lex's instructions to operate the sim computers. Why hadn't he arrived in Touchstone? He shuddered at the thought that he had locked himself behind the firewall for nothing, without being able to see Mal and without having achieved a thing.

Gradually, he became aware of another sound. Underpinning the swell of the waves was a repeating tone, muffled but insistent. It was close by. He looked to either side. It seemed to be coming from beneath the sand.

He homed in on the sound and began to dig. His fingers encountered something just below the surface and he brushed sand away to free it. As soon as the object was exposed, the beeping sound stopped.

It was a television set, partially buried and facing upwards. It was bulky and looked exactly the same as the one in his sim house on Ilkley Grove. But it wasn't the television itself that most surprised Ethan. Rather, it was the green text that shimmered on the screen.

You're an idiot, you know that? A brave idiot, but an idiot all the same. Touchstone burst like a bubble as soon as you and the other prisoners left.

His stomach lurched. If Touchstone was gone, so was Mal. Disappeared, deleted. His promises and his stupid sacrifice had been worthless.

He blinked away tears to read on.

You've been floating in the digital ether for weeks. Pretty scary. But we had your body safe and sound and I knew we'd find you eventually. I had a hell of a time pushing you to another sim—somewhere safe—but I love a challenge. You'll be all right where you are, for now.

So. Welcome to your temporary home. Give me a day or two, and I'll set up two-way comms somehow, then we can really get this show on the road. You and me against Mercy.

I know you have lots of questions. But for now, take a breather. I'll speak to you tomorrow.

Explore the island. Try heading to the centre.

Lex

The thought that he had been missing for weeks was terrifying. It was only now that he realized how much faith he'd had in Lex. He'd been certain that she would watch out for him.

He clambered to his feet and turned from the glittering sea. He felt exhausted, as if he had been on the move the entire time he'd been missing. Or maybe it was the realization of what had happened to Mal that filled his body with a dull ache.

For lack of any other plan, he followed Lex's instructions and set off inland. A short distance from where he had awoken, the beach ended at a line of palm trees. The trees provided shelter from the sun even though they were sparsely distributed. Before long he glimpsed between their trunks a building. Its walls were constructed from bamboo poles, with palms woven together as a roof. It was two storeys high, complete with balconies and ladders, and its upper storey protruded above the treetops, presumably giving a view over the island. The pale bamboo blinds that covered each of the upper windows wafted in the warm breeze.

Lex had done well. Except—

"What took you so long?" a voice said. "I've been waiting for you for hours."

Against the glare of the sunlight Ethan could only make out a silhouette in the entrance to the house, but he knew instantly who it was.

00   01100101   01111000   01110100   00100000   01000010   01110010   01100101   01100001   0110101

"Lex! Come on, it's almost time."

Lex took a deep breath but remained sitting at the desk. Idly, she reached out and pushed at the telescope so that it pivoted loosely on its tripod, coming to rest pointing at the window plastered with pictures of constellations.

There was still time. Just one last check.

Her hands darted over the computer keyboard. Charts representing Ethan's life signs flicked up in separate windows. All fine, all normal. She rotated on her chair. Beside a box that contained Ethan's astronaut figurines was a second screen. It showed a livestream of the desert island sim, patched in from the Quicksilvr servers. In the foreground, palm fronds swayed lazily, occasionally obscuring Ethan and Mal, who sat side by side on the beach with their backs to the camera.

Lex knew she would have to work hard to establish the two-way communications she'd promised. It ought to be something in keeping with the desert island theme, rather than a TV screen. A coconut telephone, perhaps? She realized that she was looking forward to the coding challenge. The audio would be tough, though. She would swallow her pride and ask for help if she needed it.

Muffled voices came from the front of the house. Though they were attempting to keep their volume down, it was clear that Caroline and Cecil were excited. They had been awkward with her, on and off, still getting used to her being here. Lex had turned down the offer of staying in their house three times before she had finally relented. She had to admit that Ethan's bedroom was more comfortable than her old room in the flat.

Cecil's head poked around the edge of the door frame.

"Did everything go okay at the site?" Lex said.

"Ethan's fine. There's a four-man guard on Quicksilvr, round the clock. People I trust. You look after him in there—" Cecil pointed at the monitor displaying the livestream "—and I'll make sure he's safe in the real world."

"And no trouble from Mercy yet?"

"They're leaving well enough alone, for now. I'm a PR disaster waiting to happen." He beamed, ducked away then returned a moment later. "By the way, they're running a repeat of the PM's statement on Channel Four if you feel like gloating."

Lex flicked on the TV. The sound was muted but rather than turn it up, she focused on the Prime Minister's body language. Throughout the press conference her mannerisms were the usual positive, confident reinforcers—hands clasped, then spread wide, then a pointing-without-using-the-index-finger gesture. But her face told another story. It told of her realization of the government's complicity in Mercy's plans. It told of the government's paralysis when the extent of the injustice hit home, how many thousands of people had been locked up needlessly without being allowed to defend themselves. And, more selfishly, it told of the Prime Minister's understanding that she could never hope to retain her position for long, after such righteous public outrage.

The image blurred. Lex was about to bash the TV when she realized that it was her own vision that was at fault. She was exhausted. Over the last few weeks she had been totally immersed in technical work, keeping Ethan safe while ensuring he remained snuck in between the layers of Mercy's servers. Now she was satisfied that he was untraceable and she could finally relax.

Cecil had been hard at work too, of course. He'd been the one wrangling with the politicians. The few government officials willing to hear him out had eventually taken the evidence of fast-tracking seriously, and had used their influence to spread the news further. It had taken a week for the cabinet to become involved, and even then, it was only grudgingly. Perhaps it was RealWorld's involvement, amplified by the mainstream media, that had forced the story into the public domain. After that, the government couldn't ignore the truth.

She turned up the TV volume.

"—outrageous situation, and one that has quite rightly caught the attention of the entire nation." A bead of sweat glinted on the Prime Minister's forehead. "These so-called 'fast-tracked' sentences are entirely unacceptable. And to respond to this unique situation I can only echo the nation's bewilderment and grief for the lost months of these many innocent citizens. As of today, I pledge that this injustice will be remedied. No half-measures, no compromises. I am pleased to announce that *every* arrest and *every* sentence during the last two-year period will be retrialled, overseen by a committee selected by myself personally. No stone will be left unturned. And let us not be complacent. The oversight that resulted in this catastrophe may have been simple, unwitting human error, but it still—"

Lex flicked off the set in disgust. Sure, she'd got what she wanted. She'd won. But the fact that no blame had been attributed to Mercy rankled. But what had she expected? Mercy's claws were dug too deep into the government, their crimes too closely associated with the Prime Minister's own neglect, for them to receive any meaningful punishment. At first Lex had been paranoid that nothing at all would happen until, only days after the press conference, the first prisoners were released following their retrials. Politicians could work fast when they wanted to. And Mercy had chosen to lose a battle in order to continue fighting a war.

Knowing that Ethan would ask after them, she had kept track of the kids that had been imprisoned in Touchstone alongside him. It had taken Cecil some fancy footwork to secure their retrials without revealing details about Project Q and the sims. But he'd managed it, and justice had been done. Libby de Witt and Kit Carruthers were free and had received the government's profuse apologies. Anita Thorne had been released too, though stealing TVs during an early riot had been a genuine crime, she had more than served her time already. Russell Reynolds had a history of violent crime linked to the riots, so he'd gone to one of the new juvenile detention centres. It was all above board, as far as Lex could tell.

Miller Williamson had come off worst. Before being caught, he'd spent years orchestrating the earliest riots from the safety of his own bedroom, riling people with false information on online forums, just for the kick of being in control. The number of crimes, and perhaps even deaths, for which he was responsible were impossible to calculate. As far as Lex was concerned, a maximum-security redbrick would have been the ideal home for him, rather than the standard prison he'd eventually landed himself in.

And then there was Mercy.

Mercy had retreated into the woodwork. A brief public statement had referred only to "discrepancies" and "unfortunate occurrences." Watching Matthew Solomon deliver the statement on TV, Lex had shouted at the screen, "Yeah, and what about the drone cities, what about the brainwashed armies?"

Mercy would lick their wounds and return, having learned their lessons from Project Q. They had the knowledge and they could rebuild the technology. Even the government wouldn't be able to hold out against Mercy, if its plan came to fruition.

But at least Ethan would be there for the ride, within Mercy's servers. An inside man, a ghost in the machine.

"Lex!" Caroline called again from the front of the house.

"Just a minute!"

She checked the screens again for good measure. The image of the desert island had begun to dim as night fell in the sim. Ethan and Mal were still sitting on the beach, gazing upwards. Ethan's arm was raised to the sky, no doubt pointing out some constellation or other. His face bobbed towards Mal and their lips drew close together.

"Soppy idiots," Lex muttered. She flicked the monitor onto standby and stood up.

The sound of the doorbell echoed through the house.

"Lex, come on!" Caroline called. "The government car's here. Oh, I can see him! There's James!"

Lex took several deep breaths before she left the room. There was no way she was going to let her brother see her cry.

01110100 01101000 01100101 00100000 01100101 01101110 01100100

Acknowledgements

An early draft of this novel was written several years ago, when I was trying my hand at writing for the first time. I'd like to thank my wife, Rose, for her patience and support, particularly in those early days when any lack of confidence might easily have scuppered the whole thing.

Thanks to Caitlin Lonning and Chris Boor, who read an early version of the manuscript and offered excellent suggestions.

Thanks to Sandra Kasturi at ChiZine for taking on the book, and for Leigh Teetzel for her terrific editorial work.

100
01101111
011011101
11 01100101 0
01110110
0010000
111001

About the Author

Tim Major lives in York in the UK. His love of speculative fiction is the product of a childhood diet of classic *Doctor Who* episodes and an early encounter with *Triffids*.

Tim's novels and novellas include *You Don't Belong Here*, *Blighters*, and *Carus & Mitch*. He has also published a non-fiction book about the 1915 silent crime film, *Les Vampires*. His short stories have appeared in *Interzone*, *Not One of Us* and numerous anthologies, including *Best of British Science Fiction 2017* and *The Best Horror of the Year Volume Ten*, edited by Ellen Datlow.

Tim's SF novel, *Snakeskins*, will be published by Titan Books in spring 2019 and his first short story collection, *And the House Lights Dim*, will follow in summer 2019.

```
01001010 01100001 01110010 01100101 01100100 00100000 0101001
01101000 01100001 01110000 01101001 01110010 01101111 0010000
01101001 01110011 00100000 01110100 01101000 01100101 0010000
01100100 01100101 01110011 01101001 01100111 01101110 0110010
01110010 00100000 01101111 01100110 00100000 01110100 0110100
01101001 01110011 00100000 01100010 01101111 01101111 0110101
00101110 00100000 01001000 01100101 00100000 01100011 0110000
01101101 01100101 00100000 01110101 01110000 00100000 0111011
01101001 01110100 01101000 00100000 01110100 01101000 0110010
00100000 01101001 01100100 01100101 01100001 00100000 0111010
01101111 00100000 01110101 01110011 01100101 00100000 0110001
01101001 01101110 01100001 01110010 01111001 00100000 0110100
01101110 00100000 01110100 01101000 01100101 00100000 0110110
01100001 01111001 01101111 01110101 01110100 00101100 0010000
01100001 01101110 01100100 00100000 01110100 01101111 0010000
01100001 01100100 01100100 00100000 01101000 01101001 0110010
01100100 01100101 01101110 00100000 01101101 01100101 0111001
01110011 01100001 01100111 01100101 01110011 00100000 0110110
01101001 01101011 01100101 00100000 01110100 01101000 0110100
01110011 00100000 01101111 01101110 01100101 00101110 0010000
01000011 01101000 01100101 01100011 01101011 00100000 0110111
01110101 01110100 00100000 01001010 01100001 01110010 0110010
01100100 01010011 01101000 01100001 01110000 01101001 0111001
01101111 00101110 01100011 01100001 00100000 01100110 0110111
01110010 00100000 01101101 01101111 01110010 01100101 0010000
01101111 01100110 00100000 01101000 01101001 01110011 0010000
01110111 01101111 01110010 01101011 00101110 00100000 0100010
01100001 01110010 01100101 01100100 00100000 01101000 0110000
01110011 00100000 01100010 01100101 01100101 01101110 0010000
01110111 01101111 01110010 01101011 01101001 01101110 0110011
00100000 01100110 01101111 01110010 00100000 01000011 0110100
01101001 01111010 01101001 01101110 01100101 00100000 0111001
01101001 01101110 01100011 01100101 00100000 00110010 0011000
00110001 00110100 00101100 00100000 01100011 01110010 0110010
01100001 01110100 01101001 01101110 01100111 00100000 0110100
01101110 01110100 01100101 01110010 01100101 01110011 0111010
01101001 01101110 01100111 00100000 01101100 01100001 0111100
01101111 01110101 01110100 01110011 00100000 01100110 0110111
01110010 00100000 01110100 01101000 01100101 00100000 0110100
00100000 01100010 01101111 01101111 01101011 01110011 0010001
00100000 01000011 01101000 01100101 01100011 01101011 0010000
01101111 01110101 01110100 00100000 01110111 01110111 0111101
00101110 01100011 01101111 01110010 01110111 01111001 0110111
01100011 01101000 01110010 01101111 01101110 01101001 0110001
01101100 01100101 01110011 00101110 01100011 01100001 0010000
01100110 01101111 01110010 00100000 01110011 01101111 0110111
01100101 00100000 01100111 01101111 01101111 01100100 0010000
01100110 01100001 01101110 01110100 01100001 01110011 0111100
00100000 01110010 01100101 01100001 01100100 01101001 0110111
01100111 00100001 00100000 00100000 00100000 00100000 0010000
```